THE BLACK WIDOW CLUB

Mary Powell

ISBN: 1497583489
ISBN 13: 9781497583481
Library of Congress Control Number: 2014907058
CreateSpace Independent Publishing Platform
North Charleston, South Carolina

To the Foolish Hearts
and all that we have shared

$\mathcal{P}$ R O L O G U E

We once were girls.

In Houston in the '50s, we pedaled bicycles along MacGregor Boulevard, winding our way past rows of stately homes set well back from the pavement on huge expanses of immaculately trimmed St. Augustine grass, past the columned Sakowitz mansion, and beyond that to a sheltered, private spot we called Hilly Park. Once there, we rolled down the grassy slopes until our hair lay in tangles and our sides ached with laughter. It was beyond us to imagine the future—or to reckon the sweet innocence of those shared moments.

Today, I face an unforgiving mirror and try to summon energy for whatever lies ahead. I wonder if it's possible to slip out of this lovely world with a shred of dignity—or maybe just a touch of style.

I

Our midsize plane hit the runway with a hard bang, then bumped twice more before settling into a smooth taxi to the gate. I took a deep breath, certain now there would be no flight mishaps, and looked over at Lynn, who rolled her brown eyes at me as if to say she wasn't overly impressed. Maybe it hadn't been the most comfortable of trips, but we were safe and on time.

From the loudspeaker, a welcome to Mexico came first in Spanish and then in heavily accented English. Across the aisle, Kitty was busily repacking her carryall while Totie impatiently waved a bright scarf at the closest flight attendant. She had asked for a wheelchair and wanted to be certain it was forthcoming.

In the two hours since we had left Houston, I had more than sufficient time to revisit concerns about this trip. As the one in charge of planning, I had a special investment. But it was more complicated than that. It had all been my idea—this thought that we might live out our remaining time together in a beautiful, stimulating spot rather than slowly deteriorating in a nursing facility or at home with a caregiver, not necessarily of our own choosing.

It had started six months earlier when I introduced the subject following the death of one of our friends. We were having lunch at a favorite teahouse that day, and I was burdened by the awareness that only four of us remained. Only four, from a vibrant group who had bonded in junior high school and had continued to enjoy one another's company over the years.

"Have any of you made firm plans for the future?" I asked.

They looked blank for a moment, as if measuring "the future."

"I'm on a waiting list at that new retirement place out off Westheimer, if that's what you mean," Lynn said. "But I'm not too excited about it. Since I don't have a dance partner these days and I don't play golf, a lot of their niceties are lost on me."

"You could hang out there with the other old gals and hope to catch a single man, or one with a wife about to check out," Totie suggested wryly.

"I could," Lynn said, refusing to take the bait for a familiar dissertation on the relative unimportance of men or marriage.

Totie, alone by choice after a colorful history of relationships, had an attitude. "Men our age are looking for a nurse with a purse," she liked to drawl in her throaty Mae West voice, "and, sugar, that sure don't sound like me."

Kitty spread her hands in an uncharacteristic show of helplessness and shrugged. "What are the options? I bit the bullet for long-term health insurance, but I don't intend to give up my house and garden until they drag me out. And I don't want to live with my kids, even if they'd have me."

We laughed, well aware that Kitty and her kids got along best in small doses.

"What I'm wondering," I said, "is couldn't we do something together and help each other to the end?"

I looked around at blank faces.

"You mean, like a commune?" Lynn asked.

Kitty's cell phone rang at that moment. She fished it from her purse and began a conversation with someone interested in buying something she had for sale. Kitty, who had accumulated a variety of properties, houses, antiques, and collectibles over the years, always had something for sale.

"I think this is important," Lynn said, lowering her voice, "but I'd rather not talk about it today. After all, we just put a dear friend in the ground."

"Seems like a perfect time to me," Totie said, reaching for the warm breadbasket. "Without something to remind me that the end is near, I refuse to think about it."

"Since Allie brought it up, and obviously has some ideas, I think she should give us an overview." Kitty, famous for multitasking and running the show, had jumped back into the conversation.

"I have no answers, only questions," I said.

"Then give us your questions," Kitty said.

"But please not today," Lynn insisted, and the issue was tabled for the time being.

A wheelchair and an attendant were waiting on the tarmac for Totie when we descended from the plane into the Mexican sun.

"I'm likin' this personal attention." She grinned up at us. "I bet we could all get a chair if we wanted."

We shook our heads and started the long march into the airport. Totie was recovering from a knee replacement, and some of us thought she was stretching it out a bit.

"I don't know about this," Lynn said, slightly out of breath and wiping perspiration from her forehead with a tissue. "It's been a while since I've walked on an airstrip, and where's that perfect climate you promised?"

"We're in the city, and it's late afternoon, and this pavement soaks up the heat. It'll get better." I grasped for reasonable responses, but I had never been to our planned destination myself. I had heard about it from a travel agent who promised beauty, comfort, modern amenities, and a community of retirees living the best of all possible worlds. What if that guy had just seen me coming and sold me a bill of goods? It happens to old people all the time.

If this trip turned out to be a disaster, I would have to take full responsibility. I had talked them into a monthlong commitment so we could get a good taste of the place. We had never spent that prolonged a period of time together, and much as we cared for one another, there was distinct reluctance. The weather had been a big selling point. To leave Houston, which had the climate of Calcutta, and spend July in a lakeside paradise had indeed sounded too good to be true. But if it was true, why weren't people flocking there? Why were we the only ones making our way to the terminal, looking confused and out of sorts?

"It'll be okay," Kitty announced cheerily. "We've signed up for an adventure, and this is only the beginning."

Lynn looked skeptical.

When we were younger, and there were ten of us, we had named ourselves the Foolish Hearts, after a love song popular in the '50s. The designation had pleased us then, a tribute to the romanticism of our youth. As we aged, the name hung on with a slightly different flavor. It became a piece of nostalgia, a reminder that romance was sometimes unproductive and dangerous. A Foolish Heart became one who clung to lost loves, dreams of greatness, and expectations of perfection. We had come to know better. But still there were times we wanted— needed—to dream.

The questionnaire I had concocted at Kitty's request looked like this:

Hello you Foolish Hearts,

Please indulge me and fill this out as carefully as you can. Get it back to me when you're through and we'll meet to go over the results. I'll find a B and B around Austin so we can enjoy the wildflowers while we talk about more serious matters.

WHAT'S YOUR PLEASURE?

* Describe your ideal living location at this stage of life.
* List your three most favorite activities.
* List your three least favorite things to do.
* What do you need help with in your everyday life?
* What do you like to take care of by yourself?
* How much privacy do you require?
* What are your favorite luxuries?
* What are your greatest concerns?
* What constitutes for you an ideal day?

I put it in the mail with trepidation. What if I didn't get a response? Surely they wouldn't ignore it.

Kitty called first.

"Why don't we just move to Oregon?" she suggested. "I've looked it up, and Oregon, Utah, and Delaware are the best states to die in. Washington, DC, is the worst."

"Better and worst on what basis?" I asked.

"Whether you're in the hospital or at home. And if you're in pain, whether you can have plenty of painkillers. Whether the doctors can administer a lethal dosage should things drag on. These states have the best options."

A word is in order here about Kitty's intuition. Although I hadn't said anything specific about an easy death, it was part of my thinking. However, I wasn't ready to get into that just yet with her, or any of the others.

"I wasn't thinking about dying as much as about living well," I told her, which was only partially true. "Oregon and Utah and even Delaware are too far north for my taste. Being cold is not part of my game plan."

"You'd like the Garden of Eden?"

"Just fill out your paper, Kitty."

"I'm trying. But it's hard."

"Nothing important is easy. These are end-of-life choices."

"You think we have a choice?"

"It depends on what we're willing to consider and how much we're willing to spend."

Totie called suggesting a cruise ship or a residential hotel. I commented she could do either without us.

"Just trying to think outside the box," she said.

The questionnaire wasn't as clear as it had seemed when I was creating it. I spent a while on my own answers and still hit some blanks. But my favorite spot had to have a view of hills and at least be in sight of water. Ideally, it would be near a river or a lake, but close enough to a city to have the advantages of good medicine and first-class entertainment. And the climate had to be conducive to growing things and being in touch with the natural world. I wanted to have windows open and hear birds singing. I wanted an occasional rainstorm or cloudy day, but no tornadoes, floods, or ice storms. Not too much traffic so I could drive without taking my life in my hands. Not so full of predators I couldn't take a walk alone. But I wanted reliable services—phone, electricity, water, and television. Every choice was limiting, which was the point. I struggled on.

My three favorite things to do changed from day to day. What I didn't like was easier. Listening to the daily news—filled with warnings, horror stories, and often manufactured reports—is discouraging. I no longer wish to process information about the world as if time were measured in seconds rather than days or years. Neither do I like being involved with three meals a day. Two are plenty. And I don't like a lot of social obligations just by way of keeping busy.

Totie was with me on that last issue, as was Lynn, but Kitty loved having places to go and things to do. Totie liked the beach; Kitty, the woods; and Lynn, the mountains. Totie didn't like housework. Lynn wanted to avoid the computer and the telephone. Totie wanted to be cooked for and driven around. Kitty wanted a big, well-appointed kitchen.

Yes, everyone filled out their questionnaires as best they could and then called me with changes, as if, once written, they would be held to their decisions. Even Lynn sent in her ideas, though she made it clear she was not committing to join us. But of course she'd visit if we really got this off the ground. Totie wasn't sure she could hold up her end financially, but we said we'd cross that bridge when we came to it. We needed a one-story structure with a place for overnight guests, something spacious enough that we could escape each other should we choose. Adjoining town houses were a consideration, but Kitty pointed out the expense of individual overhead.

"What if we have an emergency?" Kitty asked.

"Which we will," I stated the obvious.

"Then we need to be thirty minutes from a really good hospital."

That went on the MUST list. There were other things that went on the SHOULD list. We should have, we decided, someone to do the grocery shopping. And we should have fresh flowers on a regular basis. We should have a massage therapist available, and a private swimming pool with a hot tub, because it was the easiest exercise you could do. We had fond memories of swimming pools, beginning with the Shamrock Hotel, but now it must be private, because bathing suits were notably unkind to old bodies.

I had laid out my notes, along with the questionnaire responses and a map of Texas. I figured we had but a single move left in us, and it better be good. The area around San Antonio looked best to me. It was close to the heartland of the state, the Hill Country, and still had good medical facilities. But it didn't have that extra zing I thought would sell my friends. It was later that day when I picked up a newspaper and the headlines of the Travel section hit me. RETIRE IN MEXICO, it suggested boldly. Did we dare?

Back at the airport, we managed to locate and claim our bags, though it took a little doing to figure out the system—if there was such. Totie's wheelchair attendant was smilingly helpful, herding us in the right direction, clarifying with hand gestures or simple English words.

"Taxi?" he asked.

We nodded and followed him single file, carefully maneuvering our luggage wheels across the large gathering room. I was smiling to myself at our strange little parade when a uniformed guard solemnly stepped out, held up his hand, and indicated with an official jerk of his head that we must push a button before progressing.

"Customs," Kitty announced knowingly. "Hope for green."

Each of us pushed, and each got a green light, with Totie emitting a brief cheer at every success.

"I like this place already," she announced. "Going through customs is a little casino game."

"Only one out of ten gets a red, I'd say," Kitty told her.

"Well, I'm interpreting four greens in a row as a clear welcome sign," Totie answered, unwilling to bend to the facts.

We climbed into a sunny-yellow taxi, and while our luggage was being loaded atop the cab, I took the passenger seat up front. Self-consciously, I announced our destination to the driver.

"Ajijic?" I said, hoping he'd recognize it.

"Sounds like a hiccup," the travel agent had instructed as he slickly displayed pictures of beautiful Lake Chapala and surrounding mountains on his laptop.

Before long, we were traveling on a major highway in Guadalajara, a metropolitan area of about six million, at what appeared to be rush hour. Having spent our lives in Houston, we were well accustomed to traffic, but still not prepared for this. Cars and trucks, laden with cargo or passengers, sped around us on either side. From my seat next to the driver, I looked over to read the speedometer. It said one hundred. Damn!

"It's in kilometers," Kitty reassured me. "That's only sixty." From the backseat, she had checked as well.

"I'm not feeling too well," Lynn said.

"You haven't even eaten anything yet," Totie told her.

"Just nervous, I guess," Lynn said. "And I'm hot."

The cab windows were open, and their hair was blowing awry, that which wasn't stuck to their faces.

After about twenty minutes, the road narrowed, and the scenery began to change. We were now on a divided four-lane highway, not too crowded and bordered by what appeared to be simple farms and homes in varying stages of construction.

Soon we began to climb, and I could see a line of mountains. The sign on the road said *camino sinuoso*. I didn't know the meaning of *sinuoso*, but I could guess.

"Are we going to cross the mountains?" I asked the driver, using hand signals, and he nodded yes. I was glad it was still light. The driver used the left lane, passing lumbering trucks and old clunkers struggling in the right-hand lane. Later, someone would advise me it was safer to use the left-hand lane going up the hill, because if a vehicle broke down, you couldn't always see it until you were right upon it. The road was that *sinuoso*.

After the climb, we started our descent and soon came upon our first glimpse of Lake Chapala. It was huge, stretching out as far as we could see, and it glistened there in the late afternoon sunlight like a beacon of hope. The mountains were a lush green, and flowering trees and shrubs of all colors dotted the landscape like Christmas ornaments. I had been beset by doubts, but things were beginning to look up.

We came down the hill, our eyes pinned on the lovely lake spread before us, and soon found ourselves in a traditional Mexican town characterized by dilapidated buildings, street markets, a multitude of short dark-skinned people on foot, old cars and trucks weaving in and out, huge ficus trees with whitewashed trunks, bougainvillea spilling down brick walls, and of course, a cathedral.

"Are we here?" Lynn asked, her voice oozing apprehension.

"Ajijic?" I asked the driver.

He shook his head and, directed by a traffic cop who gestured as if his livelihood depended on it, took a right turn at a light so strangely positioned I hadn't noticed it. If we were to move here, I thought, driving would take some getting used to.

We moved along, the lake to our left, down what one in Texas would call an industrial highway. Businesses lined the road. They seemed to mostly offer food, car repairs, and home furnishings. I was beginning to feel apprehensive once again.

"Look." Lynn pointed as we came upon a Walmart.

"Shit," Totie said.

"I thought we were simplifying." Now even Kitty was sounding doubtful.

Just past the Walmart, we passed through a colonnade of massive trees, their broad bases painted white and upper branches aflame with large orange blossoms. The trees, like ancient warriors with crossed swords, rose and stretched to touch across the four-lane avenue.

"Mmmm," we registered approval in what seemed like unison.

"Estamos in Ajijic," the cabdriver announced our arrival.

II

O ur surroundings had changed subtly: homes and businesses were set back from the road, there was a walking-biking path, more of the faces we saw were of a light complexion, and there was less shabbiness and a sense of something more familiar.

"This reminds me a bit of San Miguel," Kitty ventured.

"They say Ajijic is the new San Miguel," I said, quoting someone's hype.

"That sounds like hype," Kitty said.

"Probably," I said. "But it caught my attention."

We passed a twenty-four-hour *farmacia* and a twenty-four-hour *clínica*, a resale shop, and a movie theater with first-run American movies, wondering aloud if they were in English. We passed coffee shops and donut shops and gyms and day spas and restaurants where people sat dining on the street, like Paris someone said.

The cabbie turned suddenly down a cobblestone street, and we began to jiggle along.

"Quaint," Kitty commented on the village as Lynn leaned forward, checking out the architecture, the paintings that decorated home entrances and even businesses, scabby horses cobbled at the curb, and pots of something simmering on the sidewalks that lined the narrow street.

"It's not quaint; it's authentic," she said.

"How do you know they're not just putting on a show for the tourists?" Kitty showed her suspicious side.

"It rings true to me," Lynn said, not about to take on Kitty on this point. "I'd think their horses would be better fed," she added.

"I'm likin' it," Totie said.

"I hope we can find a clean place to eat," Lynn said.

"I have reservations," I said.

"Me too," said Lynn.

"No. I mean reservations at a restaurant recommended by the travel agent."

"Well, bring it on," Totie said.

When we reached our destination, a quiet residential neighborhood, the driver first opened our doors, then gave a tap on his horn. Stiff from the ride, we climbed out slowly and stood on the cobblestones, stretching, admiring a thick growth of deep-blue flowers that cascaded from the stucco walls bordering the property. As the driver unloaded our luggage, an older gentleman with the air of a host opened the large metal entry door and invited us in. We followed, anxious to see what lay ahead. A few steps inside the property stood a lovely fountain surrounded by a well-tended garden featuring unmistakable blue agave cactus. Beyond that, down a path of stone pavers, a swimming pool and bubbling hot tub sparkled in the late-afternoon sun.

A single-story structure curved around the pool. There were four rooms with common walls. Each had a door and a window that opened onto the pool, and each unit was painted a different color, with a matching rocker positioned beside the door. Off to the side stood a thatched roof palapa with a grill, a couple of tables, and leather-like lounge chairs. As we approached, a tabby cat, studiously involved in licking itself, looked up with guarded eyes. On the lakeside, a chain link fence dripping with foliage offered security while allowing a view of the water and the mountains beyond. It was perfect—the outside, at least. My agent had sent information via the Internet, but I was wary of virtual tours.

Kitty had taken to helping the houseman, Raphael, decide which luggage went with which room. "Anyone have a preference about your room? Speak now, or forever hold your peace."

"They're all exactly alike except color and proximity to the pool," I said.

Lynn took the orange door nearest the pool. Totie wanted the purple door. I opted for yellow, and Kitty for green. We felt like kids in a candy shop. Inside, the rooms were simple but charming with tasteful Mexican decor. There was an overhead fan, a back window with a mountain view, a rustic table and chair, good lighting, a firm full bed with the softest of linens, a well-equipped bathroom, and plush towels.

"The driver's ready to go." Kitty had come to find me since I was in charge.

"*Cuanto cuesta?*" I had practiced how to ask what he charged.

"Five hundred," he said.

Trying not to gasp, I said, "*Momento,*" and pulled Kitty aside.

"That's outrageous," I told her. "I'm not going to pay five hundred dollars, even if he did take four of us, with luggage, about thirty miles. That's more than a hundred dollars apiece. I'm going to bargain. What do you think is fair?"

"I think he's asking for five hundred pesos, and that's less than ten dollars apiece, which is very fair. Besides, he's unloaded all our luggage."

Embarrassed, I went back. "Five hundred *pesos?*" I asked.

"*Sí.*" He nodded, smiling as if he knew exactly what had just transpired.

"American okay until I get pesos mañana?"

He nodded.

I gave him $60.

He handed me a card and broke into surprisingly good English. "If you need taxi while you in Ajijic, my cousin is very good driver and very responsible. He has van big enough for your people, and you call, he be here in ten minutes."

"Thanks," I said. "What about you?"

"I live Guadalajara," he said. "Work the airport." He gave me another card. "Call when you ready to go home."

"That'll be a while."

"*Que vaya bién*," he murmured softly, the Spanish equivalent of "Have a good day." We would hear it many times.

The cousin's name was Raul. When he greeted us that evening at the fountain with a subtle bow and an endearing smile, I felt that all was well with the world. He handed us each a card and watched patiently as we struggled to pronounce Raul Alejandro Carmona Ibarra.

"Raul is fine," he told us.

"Are you rolling that *r*"? Kitty asked.

He nodded.

"I thought you only rolled double *r*'s in Spanish," she said.

"Double *r*'s, yes, and single *r*'s at the start of a word," he told her.

"I never could learn how to roll my *r*'s," Totie said.

"Imagine my name to be spelled with a *t* before the *r*."

"Trowel," Lynn said.

Raul held up his hand in a gentle motion. "Now, think the *t*, but don't say it."

We all tried it, some softly, some louder. After a few tries, we had it—a soft, rolling *r* at the start. We beamed, feeling suddenly proficient.

Raul appeared to be in his late twenties, spoke excellent English, and was strikingly attractive—slender, wide shouldered, with soft eyes and dark-brown hair that curled around his collar. Totie rushed to establish that we'd be visiting for three weeks and would need him daily. He smiled again, revealing dimples, and something in our guts whispered that we were among the luckiest of women.

Raul drove us to dinner at an old hotel right on the water. It wasn't far from where we were staying, but none of us was up to walking at night in a strange town. We chose to sit outside, where we could enjoy the stars and watch the lights that twinkled across the lake, the herons and egrets at the water's edge, and an occasional fishing boat sliding through the quiet water. After the sun had set, the air cooled considerably, and we were glad to have brought sweaters.

"Can you imagine what it's like in Houston tonight?"

"Hot and humid, like it is every night from May to October," Totie said.

"They must do a lot of watering to keep everything so green here," Kitty observed.

"Not in the rainy season," I said.

"And when's that?"

"Now."

"So when does it rain?"

"Almost every night."

"Really?" Lynn raised an eyebrow. "So it's going to rain tonight, and tomorrow will be sunny?"

"That's what they tell me."

"Sounds like hype," Kitty said.

"Actually, they say it hardly ever rains till after sundown," I told them.

"*By eight, the morning fog must disappear,*" Totie broke into the *Camelot* song.

"We'll see," Kitty said.

The next morning, over coffee, we were talking about the night's rain, complete with thunder and lightning, and what we were going to do first that day, since the sun was out and everything looked beautiful. What should we do? Walk the beach, go into town for lunch, check out the shopping, take siestas, or try one of the recommended restaurants for dinner? With so many options, the day seemed too short.

After our initial excitement, it took a few days to get a pace established. Totie and Lynn liked to sleep in. Kitty and I liked to rise early and walk. There were those who took a nap, and those who didn't. There were those who wanted to stay out late in the evening, and those who were ready to put on nightgowns when the sun went down.

"This is getting complicated," I announced. "At this rate, we'll never get anything done."

"What do you want to get done?" Totie asked. "I thought we were on vacation."

"She makes a good point," Kitty said. "Why don't we make a list every night at dinner of possible things to do the next day, and then we can have a sign-up sheet?"

"You all have a good time," Lynn yawned. "I'm signed up for an art class."

"When did we get so picky?" I wondered aloud.

"When our energy and our curiosity began to wane and pleasing ourselves became more important than being popular." Though it had been a rhetorical question, Kitty seemed to feel it necessary to answer. "Be patient," she told me. "And remember, we're trying to accommodate four distinct individuals so that everyone has a good time and no one gets on anyone's nerves."

"And if we can do that, maybe we can all live together and take care of each other instead of going to the old folks' home," Lynn said with a tinge of sarcasm.

"Well, because I really like you all, I'll keep trying," I said, as if this whole thing hadn't been my idea in the first place. "Who's going to do the sign-up sheets?"

"Kitty, of course," Totie mumbled.

III

We "girls" had been together forever, it seemed. Our group first numbered ten, and Kitty was always the center. Bright and ambitious and craving family, she created one for herself and has kept us together through time and space. At first she planned to be a model, then she was called to be a missionary, and eventually she ended up in medical school, though she got sidetracked and never quite finished. She was the first to drive, the first to be married, to have sex, and to get divorced. It was at her house when her mother was away on "business trips" that we experimented with cigarettes and gin and boys.

Our adventures were tame, by today's standards. Most of us went to the altar as virgins, which was considered quite important back then. Kitty had ideas about that too. I recall a particularly rowdy sleepover when she appointed me, long before the days of designated drivers, as "monitor of the magic door" to the bedroom so no boys could enter. It was a fitting, if unplanned, metaphor for the preservation of our virginity. At least she didn't want it to happen on her watch. Kitty is our core, and despite her need to be in charge, she'd do anything for us. Anything.

The first time we made a pact, we were fourteen. Kitty had decided we should have a sorority. She had created and mailed exotic invitations, lettered in calligraphy and enhanced with silver glitter. We were directed to present ourselves at an unfamiliar address at 6:00 p.m. on a Friday evening, for swimming, food, and a secret initiation. Surprised to be included, I tried not to let my excitement show.

Twelve girls had been on the list, and all but two accepted. Sandy Lefkowitz and Lois Goldstein declined, because they already belonged to a Jewish sorority. Kitty had known that but included them because they were cool and probably because she wanted to build goodwill. That was her way.

Totie's father drove, and mine was to pick us up at 9:30 on that unforgettable Friday night. I remember being dropped off at an attractive house set well back from the curb in what my father would call a ritzy neighborhood. We followed a trail of balloons down a curving side path bordered by blooming jasmine, through a wrought iron gate, past which a large swimming pool beckoned. I can still recall the sense of importance I felt as I lay down my towel, stepped out of my shorts, and tried to slip into the water like Esther Williams.

It was Houston in mid-September, and the day had been brutally hot and humid. As a child of the Great Depression who had grown up in a world at war, a girl who lived in an apartment house with a single tree and window fans, this evening float in cool turquoise water was a first taste of personal luxury. Tall pine trees circled the pool and stretched high overhead. Through their line of stately trunks, a thumbnail moon beckoned just above the horizon. Music from a portable record player enveloped us.

"*The night is like a lovely tune,*" it sang. "*Be still, my foolish heart.*"

The house belonged to Kitty's older sister, newly married and still in college. And living in a house like this? I found it confusing, even as I heard the girls talking about her husband being a real catch—good-looking and rich, too. He came out and said hi to all of us, and there was a lot of giggling and flirting, like eighth grade girls flirt with twenty-three-year-olds. It seemed silly and pointless to me. And I didn't like her much, Kitty's sister, even though she was the hostess. She frowned and acted bossy, like she was our mother, not just a girl who got lucky. I, who had been told that girls should be sweet and soft-spoken, remember thinking he'd get tired of her pretty soon.

After about an hour, we left the pool, dried off, and were directed to the food table. There was an assortment of sandwiches—pimento cheese, tuna fish, and cucumber and cream cheese—on white and brown bread, with crusts trimmed and cut into diamond shapes. I had seen something like this in pool party photos in *Good Housekeeping* magazine. Wooden salad bowls were piled high with chips, Cokes and root beer lay on ice in a shiny red cooler, and a chocolate cake topped with cherry pie filling sat proudly on a glass serving pedestal. Kitty said she had made everything that day, and weighing my own talents in that department, I felt grossly inadequate. I helped Mother in the kitchen sometimes but would never set out to create a party all on my own, even if I had a place to host it and the money for all the trimmings. After we ate, Kitty brought us inside and issued instructions. We were to go to the powder room, one at a time, take off our suits, put on our underwear, and come out and sit in a circle in the living room.

"No way," one girl said, "not with that guy here."

"They've gone," Kitty assured her, "and they won't be back until nine."

So we did what she said. We had seen each other in underwear lots of times, dressing and undressing for gym class, but this was different, sitting in a circle, in our panties and bras. I was glad to be wearing my best—not my sister's hand-me-downs with the tiny holes and bad elastic. Two of the girls had their periods, so they got to keep on their shorts and just take off their blouses. They hadn't been swimming, anyway. Swimming when you had your period was frowned upon.

When everyone was out, Kitty spread towels across the two lamps so that the room took on a shadowy, somewhat spooky air, and she began in a low, clear voice.

"We are here tonight to create a society of girls who will be the future leaders of the world. We will help each other excel in junior high school, in high school, in college, and in life. We will support each other and never, never let each other down."

I looked around. I hardly knew some of these girls. Totie was beside me in the circle. She and I had lived in the same block for all of our school years, and she was always fun to be with, always making me laugh, though we occasionally didn't see eye to eye. She enjoyed breaking rules, and I was more serious about school and doing what was expected of me. Her real name was Janice, but she had renamed herself Totie after a favorite aunt. Upon learning that my middle name was Alice, she had started calling me Allie, and it stuck.

Lynn, who sat next to Kitty, looked completely self-assured. Her dark hair was cut in a pixie style, and her soft, oval eyes were like drops of milk chocolate. I knew her mostly by reputation. She was knockout cute, and a cheerleader, and everyone wanted to be her friend, including all the boys. She smiled whenever she saw me in the halls at school, but I felt far out of her league.

Kitty had come to my house once with her mother to see about buying the four-unit apartments we lived in and owned. Nothing ever came of the deal, but when we got to junior high, she remembered and acted friendly. She was a serious student too, and I suppose there was some competition going on with Kitty way back when.

I was having trouble with this pledge, or whatever it was. I liked the idea, but it sounded like a lifetime deal, and I wasn't sure I could carry that out. No one else seemed to be bothered. Then Kitty told us we were going to go around the circle and everyone had to tell something secret about herself so that we would be bound by our secrets. My mind was racing, searching for a suitable secret.

The first girl told about walking in on her parents when they were "doing it."

"That was my secret," someone else complained.

"Sorry," Kitty said, "but repeats aren't allowed."

Someone had seen her brother with a boner, and it was "huge and red." I wasn't quite sure what a boner was, but I got the general idea. I had no brothers and still found it hard to believe that my parents "did it" and was wondering if all the secrets had to be about sex. My turn was coming up. Totie showed that she could touch the tip of her nose with her tongue. It was more of a trick than a secret, but no one had known it before, so it was accepted and everyone ended up trying to do it, with no success.

"I don't believe in Heaven," I blurted out when my turn came.

There was silence in the circle until Kitty asked if I had ever told that to anyone before.

"No," I said. "I just decided it last Sunday."

"You're in good company," she said. "Mark Twain didn't either, or Bertrand Russell."

I was relieved to be off the hook, but embarrassed at the way my confession had been accepted in silence. Everyone I knew believed in Heaven. But we were all supposed to support each other, so I guessed it would be okay. In fact, it felt good to be able to say what I thought and know they couldn't think badly of me for it.

"Who's Bertrand Russell?" Totie whispered, but I didn't answer. I was making a mental note to look him up in the library encyclopedia.

Our sorority, which was briefly named Eta Beta Pi (Totie's suggestion) was short-lived, but I'm amazed to look back and see how we managed to keep together through high school and beyond. One of the girls had an undiscovered congenital abnormality and died of a heart attack in her early twenties. I still recall the shock. How difficult it was to cope with death at that time, considering how commonplace it has become.

One of our group married a Frenchman she met in college and moved to Europe, but we see her when she comes to visit family. One lives in Maine and has had Parkinson's for the past ten years. Another, in Georgia, has stopped corresponding. One died after a nasty car accident five years ago. One is in a memory unit now and only recognizes us on good days, and Elaine passed last spring after a long and tedious bout with cancer.

The losses come regularly now, with these friends and others, and I've come to regard them as natural as the movement of the seasons. Still, we four—Kitty, Lynn, Totie, and me—remain tightly connected. We've buried many of those who knew us best—parents, siblings, husbands, lovers, and even children. Because I see us as players in a process begun long ago, I have, perhaps unwisely, built a small altar to our connection. It feels quite special, almost sacred.

We did excel, and we did support each other, and I've tried to stay true to that pledge over the years, even though it was child's play. We ended up having to prick our fingers that night and mix our blood on a napkin, which we all passed around the circle and held to our mouths. And then Kitty said, "Repeat after me." And we repeated this, though I've often wondered both where she got it and how she had the nerve to present it. Here it is: "I swear that if I divulge any secret offered here tonight, I will allow my body to be burned and my ashes to be scattered to the four winds so that my memory will be lost to my fellow man forever."

We all said it, and I remember thinking at the time that I had to be careful not to tell anyone that Totie could touch her nose with her tongue. But now I'm telling, so let the chips fall where they may.

IV

We are in Ajijic, Mexico, five thousand feet above sea level, in July 2009, dressed to the nines, out for an evening on the town. My friends may be slightly stooped and wrinkled now, with sagging breasts and irritable bowels and trouble remembering their cell phone numbers, but when they get dressed for a night on the town, it's not all bad. Lynn was in purple and teal, with a gold shawl that picked up both colors. Totie was in black—her fallback position. Her hair was presently strawberry blond, freshly washed, and her eyes were shining, with a touch of blue shadow. Kitty wore white pants, a black top, and a serape-style overlay that might not work on someone else but looked impressive on her tall, slender figure. I had chosen white pants as well, with a lavender camisole and matching overblouse. We met at the pool, looked at each other, and beamed.

"*Take it to the limit one more time,*" Totie mouthed an Eagles line as Kitty poured wine.

Raul, our favorite taxi driver, was full of compliments and offered to take pictures of the group. Then we each got a picture with him.

"You could be in the movies." Lynn looked up, saluting him with her wine glass as she posed for the camera. It was good to see her smiling, even flirting.

We'd been there five days now—and every night, a different restaurant. Tonight's destination featured live music by locals. Before long, Totie had taken the microphone, and resting on a high stool, looking a bit like Peggy Lee, she was doing a Karaoke version of "I Will Always Love You."

We were in Ajijic and Totie was singing and attractive men of advanced age were approaching our table to get acquainted. We had already been advised there weren't a lot of available straight men there, but that's irrelevant. There were interesting people here, making us feel welcome.

We ordered—chicken and fish, and something for Totie, who hadn't yet let go of the mike. Now she was singing "The Rose" and beckoning me to come sing with her. I'm pretty bad, but good enough for Karaoke, so I made my way to her side and looked out at the audience. *Such fun,* I thought.

After our song, we returned to the table for dinner. Lynn had sent back her chicken because she was afraid it wasn't done. The last time she was in Mexico—many years back—she had gotten very sick on undercooked chicken and was understandably cautious. At her insistence, Kitty, Totie, and I started on our fish. As we ate, Lynn indulged in chips and the house salsa.

"This is safe," she told us. "I read that the vegetables in the restaurants here are treated with a natural disinfectant, so there's no problem. This salsa is made with nothing but fresh tomatoes, onion, peppers, and garlic. Mmm. And it's good, even though the chips are really tough."

It took a while for her revised meal to come, and when it did, she wasn't happy because it was dried out. She picked at it, eating the rice and more chips and salsa. And then Totie decided she wanted to dance.

She requested "Proud Mary" and pulled us all onto the dance floor, and just when it was getting good, she fell. Kitty was at her side immediately, asking if she felt dizzy, if she could get up, and if we should call for the Red Cross ambulance. The ambulance took her to a twenty-four-hour clinic where a lovely young woman treated the knee, and the person, and presented a business card. *Dr. Lara,* it said.

"You should go home with your friends," she told Totie after wrapping the knee and giving her some pain medication. "If you have continued pain, come see me tomorrow."

The next morning, Totie was still having problems, and Lynn had a seriously upset stomach. She didn't want to leave her room at first and then conceded that maybe she could sit by the pool, only a few feet from the bathroom.

Kitty dosed her with Kaopectate and promised to try and get something stronger from the doctor. Lynn groaned and looked out of sorts.

"I can't afford to be sick," she complained. "My class starts on Monday."

I offered to stay with her, but she refused, and I welcomed the chance to witness more Mexican medicine.

Dr. Lara, who had so charmed us last night, wasn't in the clinic when we arrived, but her office directed us to a Dr. Ferrano. Disappointed and not expecting to find another sweet and beautiful English speaker, Kitty and I pulled out our dictionaries, ready to translate if necessary. Our hope to bring back medicine for our languishing sister was also fading.

When we were listing requirements for a retirement spot in the states, doctors had been a big problem. Between the four of us, there were at least twenty doctors whom we saw a minimum of once a year. Some of us saw doctors once a week. We were all reluctant to lose the old medical relationships or try to establish new ones. Nevertheless, Kitty suggested we could begin by finding a new dentist who would take us all—same for an eye doctor and an ENT specialist. I could do without my chiropractor if I had regular massages, and no one was wed to their podiatrist, though we all had one on our list. With three years of medical training and a lifetime of scientific reading, Kitty could help us decide if we needed a specialist, but we definitely needed a cardiologist and someone who could prescribe medications and bone-density exams and blood work and whatever else came along. Oh yes, we needed a dermatologist too, to burn off those pesky little precancerous cells that keep popping up. And doctors in new places aren't always taking new patients, and some won't even talk to you if you're on Medicare.

"We need a GP who's just starting out, who makes house calls." Totie's suggestion had been met with knowing laughter.

⁓

Dr. Ferrano's office was small, but clean. There was a reception area with a high counter behind which sat an attractive receptionist. The room had a marble-topped table with a flower arrangement and a few empty chairs. A man wearing Crocs stood, chatting in Spanish with the receptionist.

"You must be the American ladies who called this morning," he said in perfect English.

We nodded. Three mutes caught unaware. Not what we had expected.

"Come on in." He waved us into his office.

"Is it okay if we all three come?" Kitty asked with uncharacteristic timidity.

"Whatever you prefer," he said, sitting at his desk and turning to the computer mounted on his left. He pulled up a form and hit the print button, and the machine began to spit out a paper.

"Obviously you're the patient," he said to Totie. "I'll need your name, your age, your medications, and a brief medical history."

"How long do you have?" she said with a laugh.

"As long as it takes," he answered quietly, sliding the printed form and a pen toward her. "Take your time and fill this out for me."

"Did you attend medical school in the states?" Kitty asked.

He nodded. "I'm a New Yorker—attended Johns Hopkins, did my internship at Philadelphia General." He hit a button on the computer, and a screen saver of photographs came up. "Then I met the love of my life, this beautiful Mexican woman." He pointed to one of the pictures. "And she gave me two beautiful daughters." He pointed again. "And now a granddaughter." He hit another button, and a multitude of baby pictures shot onto the screen. He beamed as he described one after another. "Grandparent pride isn't limited to women," he announced.

"It looks like you have a lot of time with your family," I said.

"What better way to spend your time?"

"Doctors in the states are always so busy. Their families often suffer."

"I'm busy, too, but in Mexico, we do a better job of prioritizing."

As we spoke, I watched through the glass wall of his office as three hummingbirds visited a bush full of red hibiscus blossoms.

"That's beautiful," I told him.

"Aren't they wonderful? And there are three hundred varieties of hummingbirds—not all around here, of course. They migrate, you know. Can fly five hundred miles without resting. Amazing, with those tiny bodies and huge hearts that beat ten times a second. When they stop to rest, they're starved and exhausted—at great risk of dying—but their metabolism slows down to accommodate it. They're my daily reminders," he said. "When things start going a little fast, I stop and ponder on the wonder of the natural world, and it keeps me in balance. That, and these Crocs." He stood up and walked around the desk, proudly showing us the ugly plastic shoes that I had observed, with some distaste, on my grandchildren.

"You can wear these all day, and your feet, your legs, never get tired."

Kitty and I exchanged glances. Totie was busy filling out her form.

"Doctor," Kitty changed the subject, "we have a friend back where we're staying who ate a lot of salsa last night and is having stomach cramps and diarrhea today. Is there something you recommend? We're here for a month, and it's likely to happen again."

"Stay away from the salsa," he said. "When the uneaten portions go back into the kitchen, it probably gets recycled, mixed with other half-eaten bowls, and there's a good chance of germ cultivation. Probably happens in the states, too. It's not just a Mexico thing. But even if it's fresh, sometimes the peppers just don't set well on tender stomachs." He turned to the computer and began to type. A few minutes later, a piece of paper shot out of the printer, and he signed it and slid it across the desk to Kitty.

It was a prescription form listing a diarrhea medication (Treda), another for Antiflu, and any one of four listed antibiotics selected for the 2009 season in the event of respiratory or urinary tract infections. Each was complete with instructions for dosage. At the top of the page were his name, address, and medical license number, as well as those for his office, fax, home, and another only for emergencies.

"You used to be able to get these meds across the counter, but they've begun tightening up," he said to Kitty, who was agape at the abundance of information he had just proffered.

"Well, now about me," Totie said, handing him her information sheet. "That's about the best I can do."

He studied it for a while and then turned back to his computer.

"My problem is in my knee," she said with a hint of impatience.

"He knows that," Kitty told her as Dr. Ferrano continued to enter information in the computer.

"There's a worldwide database on medication. I've been involved with it for the past ten years and have found it to be extremely helpful, especially preventing synergistic reactions when a patient is taking numerous meds for a variety of reasons. The pharmacies are supposed to follow this, as are the docs, but more and more patients see too many docs and take too many meds, and a lot falls through the cracks."

He pointed to a chart that had come up on the computer. "You are now officially in the database. Look here, this blood pressure medicine may be contributing to your asthma and attendant breathing problems. And the antidepressant is working against you, too. Don't let anyone give you new meds without checking this website."

He began typing again. "Anyone taking more than five medications has a prescription for trouble. No wonder you got dizzy, dear. I'm going to put you on a new regimen, and you'll feel a lot better in a week."

"How about my knee?"

"We'll get to that in a minute," he said.

I looked over at Kitty, who was shaking her head ever so slightly, but said nothing. I knew what she was thinking. Present yourself for treatment, and you will receive treatment. If you don't like it, you can ignore it. He seemed quite knowledgeable, but was quite forceful as well. I knew she'd check it out before she let Totie change all her medications. Fortunately, the problem today was in her knee, and we weren't about to insult him before he had taken a look at it.

After a few minutes of silence, during which time the doctor typed efficiently on the computer, another prescription-size paper shot out. He studied it for a minute, nodded, and set it aside.

"Now, my dear, let's look at that knee."

He walked around to where Totie was sitting and kneeled down to palpate the sore knee.

"When they replaced my first one, they told me I'd need the other one done sooner or later," she said.

"Not if you'd lose some weight and do some exercises," the doctor said.

"Well, I'm not into that," she said.

"Your choice," he said. "For now, I recommend you stay off it, keep it elevated, alternate heat and ice. In three days, get yourself a knee brace at the pharmacy."

"I brought one," she interrupted.

"Good. Then use it. Take Advil if you're uncomfortable, and be careful on the cobblestones. People here who are unsteady often fall on them."

As he talked, he lifted the stethoscope and began to listen to her heart. Then he looked in her mouth, inspected her hands and nails, and pressed the lymph glands in her neck. As he walked back to his desk, he began goose-stepping across the room.

"What does this remind you of?"

"Hitler's army?" I ventured.

"Hitler learned it from Mussolini, and Mussolini learned it from Alexander the Great. If an army is trained to march this way, they'll be in excellent condition, good enough to cross the Alps. This is aerobic, good for the thighs, good for the belly. When you get to feeling better"—he turned to Totie—"you can try it."

He walked back around to his desk and picked up the scrip. "Here's what I'm recommending. We're cutting out the Lasex completely and changing the blood pressure med to another that has a diuretic effect. Cut the Lipitor to one a week and see if it doesn't have the same effect on your cholesterol. Of course, the best way to handle cholesterol is through diet. Lots of good fruits and vegetables here in Mexico. Take advantage of them, and the fish, and the chicken. Just be sure it's completely cooked. I'm not sure how long you've been on this antidepressant, but you might try tapering off. Those things play havoc with other meds, and sometimes we outgrow the need for them." He sat back, folded his hands, and smiled.

Totie smiled. Kitty and I smiled.

"How much do we owe you, Doctor?"

He wrote *$700* on a small slip of paper and handed it to Kitty. "You can pay the girl outside, and if you need a receipt for insurance, she'll give you one. And if you have any problems or questions, call or e-mail me. I try to get back within two hours."

"Do you take credit cards?" Totie asked the girl at the desk.

"I'd prefer pesos," she said.

"Oh, pesos. Yes. Kitty, do you have seven hundred pesos?"

Kitty paid the girl, and we left the office in a state of wonder. We had been there for two hours. We had learned about Mexico, about a pharmacological database, Crocs, hummingbirds, and Alexander the Great. We had prescriptions for just about anything that could arise, we had a doctor on call within two hours, and it had cost us about $65 US.

"I think I'm in love," Totie said.

"So are you going to start practicing the goose step?"

"I might." She grinned.

V

*L*ynn was delighted to have the prescriptions and the assurance that came with them. She would feel better soon and could probably make her Monday class. Before long, Totie, too, seemed rejuvenated. It was Kitty who began to look tired after spending the better part of two days seeking out the freshest of vegetables, cooking chicken soup, and ministering.

On Sunday afternoon, while the others rested inside, I was stretched out by the pool with a book. "Hola," I heard a soft voice call across the courtyard, and looked up to see our property manager, Caroline, carrying a large pan between two colorful potholders.

"Raphael told me you had some problems the other night and had been eating in." She set down a large pan of lasagna. "There's a salad, too, in the car, and some bread. He'll bring it in."

"How thoughtful," I said. "We had planned to order out."

"I don't do this for all my guests, but you're rather special."

"Three hundred fourteen years between us." I made a slight grimace.

"I was referring to your prolonged stay," she corrected me. "Most of my guests stay a week or two. I'm curious if you're house-hunting."

"Possibly. Any tips?"

Caroline was a storehouse of information. She had moved to Ajijic with her husband ten years earlier, and they had started a small restaurant. It had been their dream—to live in paradise and support themselves doing something they loved.

"You know what makes God laugh?" she commented matter-of-factly. "Humans making plans."

Her husband had turned up with pancreatic cancer and lived only two years. Now a young widow, she was supporting herself with a variety of jobs. She sold and managed real estate, catered, and held monthly trunk shows. She was well-spoken and attractive, with auburn hair and a porcelain complexion.

"'If I were you, I'd head back to the States,' people told me after he died, and my mother in Chicago absolutely demanded that I come home, but I love this place," she told me. "I decided to give it six months before I made a final decision, and by that time, I knew I could live here alone. More than that, I wanted to."

"So what do you find most appealing?" I asked.

"I call it the magic of the lake," she said without hesitation.

"I had expected you to say the climate or the natural beauty."

"It's all connected. The lake helps create the climate; the climate provides for a long, lush growing season. This was a fishing village long before the Spanish conquest. The lake has always attracted people with connections to the land. It encourages a gentle life-style. You won't find much greed or violence here. The surroundings are supportive, and people usually respond in kind."

"Sounds idyllic."

She laughed. "Some will tell you otherwise. That's just my read on it. You find what you're looking for, I suppose."

I liked this girl and invited her to come back, eat with us, and get to know my friends. She smiled and said she had plans, but she'd be back for the pan in the morning and hoped to see everyone then.

We four ate later around the pool, with a soft breeze and romantic Mexican ballads playing in the background.

"I could get spoiled," Kitty said.

"Me too," I agreed.

Totie nodded, her mouth full of lasagna.

"You were born spoiled, Totie." Lynn laughed.

I hadn't allowed myself to imagine the place would be so appealing, but certainly, I had brought them here in hope. Were we too old to make such a major change? Or could we extend our love affair with life a little longer, find new friends and things to enjoy, find better health and sweet health care, a system that treated us more like we want to be treated? When we had said—maybe confessed—to Dr. Ferrano that we were checking out the area as a possible place to finish out our days, he had recommended that we buy a house.

"Don't go for the retirement/nursing homes," he had said. "Some of them are good, but the better arrangement, if you can afford it, is to buy a house with a casita. Hire a middle-aged couple to take care of things and to take care of you. If you choose carefully, and you treat them well, you will be beautifully cared for until the end. This is a country where the young are cherished, and the old are respected."

Good old Dr. F. You couldn't ignore his recommendations. You might question them, but they seemed to have a ring of truth.

"Maybe we should visit the best old folks' home here," Kitty suggested during our Italian dinner, "to get our own perspective."

It was put on the agenda as a possibility for the next day, but no one was promising they'd be up for it.

"Well, if we visit a home for old folks, I think we should also check out houses with casitas," I said, knowing that was in the back of her mind anyway.

"I had thought that, too," she said. "I'm also thinking I need to get my cell phone upgraded so I can call home. Raul said he'd take me by the store, and they're open until eight tonight."

I had just seen her relax. "How about tomorrow?" I suggested.

"Mañana?" Kitty said, shrugging her shoulders. "Why not?"

Hearing Kitty's mañana, I was thinking how quickly our priorities were changing. The sunset before us was a blend of purple and pink, with lightning dancing on the horizon. Probably soon, there would be another rain, and in the early-morning light, hummingbirds, pressed to break their evening fast, would flock to the hibiscus bushes outside our windows. A trip to the Walmart now would surely spoil this moment of beauty and anticipation. Mañana. It *is* catching.

I told the others about Caroline, how pleasant and self-possessed she seemed.

"I can't imagine myself at forty living alone, making my way in another country," Lynn voiced what I had been thinking.

"Lord, at forty, we were all up to our ears in husbands and children," Kitty said.

"And getting stuff," Totie added.

We laughed. Totie had always fought the attitude of our time to acquire goods. She took little pride in her possessions and some satisfaction in traveling light.

"When you move as often as I have," she said, "you can't get attached to your stuff."

Kitty, on the other hand, had so much stuff she could hardly keep track of it. Insurance, repairs, and climate-controlled rental units took a healthy bite from her budget.

Lynn and I liked nice things, too. But we had all come to a place in life where we were getting rid of things rather than getting more.

"If we lived here," I said, thinking aloud, "we'd need to sort through our stuff, get rid of a lot."

"And get more—like Mexican stuff," Kitty added.

About 10:00 the next morning, Caroline showed up, bringing four sticky buns and a pound of fresh-ground coffee.

"We just met, and I love you already," Totie said, serving herself.

"This is a promo for the new coffee shop on the square. I took them by some buns to see if they wanted to carry them regularly, and they paid me in coffee, which I don't drink."

"The lady wears many hats," I said, and she nodded agreement.

"It's amazing what you can do if you have to."

"We were talking about that last night, and we're impressed," Kitty said.

"I have a lot of good connections. If you need anything, just let me know."

"Right now, I need to know how to get to my art class," Lynn said, handing her a paper flyer with a difficult address.

"No problem. I'm heading that way," Caroline said.

"Do you know Raul?" Totie asked.

"The cute guy that drives the taxi van?"

"That's the one," Totie said. "He's been carting us around. So does everyone here know everyone?"

"After a while." Caroline smiled.

"That girl is a treasure," I said when she and Lynn had gone.

"So we've been here a week, and we have three really good connections," Totie said. "I think that's a sign."

"I think we need to slow down a little. If it seems too good to be true…" Kitty trailed off.

"Oh, Kitty, just relax," I told her. "We won't jump into anything."

VI

The first time I visited a nursing home was with Kitty. I had dropped by her house in Houston, and she invited me to come along on her regular visit to see her mother. I wasn't prepared for the scene. Before I could accustom myself to the piercing smell of urine, a woman with the saddest of eyes stopped me in the hall and asked for help. She sat in a wheelchair, holding a doll and pleading with me to help her get her baby out of there. I retreated as best I could and caught up with Kitty in a room where her mother lay, rambling in Czech.

"She remembers every family member from her childhood, but I'm not sure she recognizes me," she said.

Something difficult was going on there also—a passing of the torch. We all had feared and respected Kitty's mother. She never hesitated to tell us what we were doing wrong and was seldom affectionate, so one was always left to wonder if she liked you or not. When that kind of person loses her faculties, it's particularly troubling. Such people thrive on being in control, and when, one day, they can't remember what the car keys are for, they're usually quite unpleasant about it. Kitty did her best, but it was a painful and worrisome vigil, and it went on for years.

We all try to do our best. My sisters and I went to visit our dear Aunt Edna in a psychiatric ward after she had set fire to my mother's bed.

They were living together at the time in a retirement community chosen with great care. Edna was curled in a ball that day, looking so pitiful and childlike.

"I didn't mean to hurt your mother," she told us with tears in her eyes. She knew who we were, and she knew what she had done. "Those men on television told me to do it," she explained.

Eight months previously, when we were choosing a retirement space for the two to share, we were more worried about my mother than about Edna. In order to join this particular community, one had to be of good mental and physical capacity. Prospective residents had to walk in under their own steam and not display obvious confusion. Edna was ditzy, but she had always been ditzy. Cute, we called her. Mother couldn't walk more than a few steps without stopping to rest, but she had a will of iron, and on that particular day, her secret was well guarded.

We made an offer on a relatively expensive apartment and agreed to a handsome sum for monthly food, transportation services, and other amenities, and no one checked Mother's or Edna's limitations too carefully. When one of them would need nursing services or assisted living for a short or long term, there was a clinic on the fifth floor; when they needed total nursing care, that was available also, in an adjacent building, so as not to interfere with the residents' lives (or remind them what lay in store).

The setup was actually very appealing and, for the late 1980s, was a premier project in Houston. Mother liked it, and there were times I even thought I might want to be there. There were couples in their fifties signing up, and it was all so new and fresh and lively. There was a dress code in the dining room, and only canes, no metal walkers or wheelchairs, were allowed there. Fresh flowers decorated the lobby, and music and activities were scheduled for each evening. I approved of the place, and so did Mother, who made all the decisions.

Shortly after they moved in, Edna began acting strange. She was leaving food on her face in the dining room. Mother would remind her to "wipe her face," and still, it happened. When I called Mother to chat, Edna picked up the phone. I'd notice Mother's conversation was guarded, and then she'd say, "Edna's on the phone." She was listening in, not wanting to talk. She had become suspicious and was acting strange. Mother took her to visit with the head of the establishment, and Edna pulled it together and acted very sane. Mother worried and moved a card table, a jigsaw puzzle, and a chair out to the end of the hall to have a place where she could look out a window, be by herself, and feel comfortable.

We were working on getting Edna a psychological exam at a private clinic when she set fire to Mother's bed. After the scene that caused, complete with fire engines and evacuation of an entire floor, she was banned from returning to live with Mother. We found what appeared to be a very classy, expensive facility where Edna had to wear a bracelet that buzzed when she stepped outside the door. The last time I went to visit her, I ran into a woman in a wheelchair in the hall. She smelled of urine and carried a doll on her lap.

She grabbed my hand. "Help me get out of here," she begged.

They're not called old folks' homes now, of course. They're elder-care facilities, retirement homes, nursing homes, Alzheimer's units, and variations thereupon. Some are markedly better than others; some are quite promising. But eventually, as my mother experienced, you'll come to the end of the line. After Edna went to her fancy prison, Mother continued on at the retirement home. For a short while, she was very happy. She found a group of friends with whom she shared stories and did volunteer work at a nearby hospital and played Rummikub every night. That's when she told me, "It doesn't get much better than this," and then she had a stroke. She was eighty-four.

"What happened to me?" she asked when she came awake in the hospital and I was there, so happy to see her eyes focusing.

"You had a stroke," I said, and she turned her head. She didn't want to hear it, but she recognized it as the truth.

Over the next year and a half, I watched her fight back, to 95 percent, as her cardiologist characterized her recovery, and then she had another stroke. And never in between did she confide to me that life was good. She endured all the tests and procedures, the pain and effort, the loss of dignity, the interventions—to what end? There is a time and place when it would be oh so nice to check out.

When we set out the next afternoon to visit an elder facility in Ajijic, I feared what we would encounter, but what we found was a pleasant environment, with a number of people of various limitations. It was okay, but not good. When you choose assisted living, you move into a category that covers a broad scope. Sometimes I think I need assisted living in that I sure wish one of my kids or grandkids were there to help me build a rock garden or put a heavy box on a top shelf. But I'm not ready for true assisted living. As we age and our abilities diminish, our connections with the larger world also break down. Before we know it, we want help and don't know where to turn. Often, we pay for help, hiring maids, gardeners, and out-of-work fellows who bill themselves as handymen. Often, we don't get what we bargained for; sometimes we get unquestionably cheated.

"It's hell getting old," I hear my peers moan.

I wish no one else would say that. I'd rather keep it a secret, so when succeeding generations face their challenges, they might have a blueprint for courage. I'd like to find better ways to address aging instead of just complaining. Art Linkletter, that wonderful guru of 1950s reality television, told us many years ago that old age isn't for sissies. The process is inevitable. We need to be tough—and creative.

Inspired by the day's observations, I retired to my room to make a list. If you're lucky enough to live past middle age, you'll find yourself experiencing a series of losses. At first you don't even notice. Or you don't care. So what if you're not easily turned on sexually like you were at eighteen? That may be a blessing. So what if you can't see as well as you used to? That's what glasses are for—and Lasik, and then cataract surgery. So what if you're telling someone a story and you can't remember the name of the famous person the story's about? That happens to everyone, and we all laugh about it. And then there comes the time when you decide you're not going to hike with the family anymore, or take part in the volleyball game, because you're just not up to it. And then you can't hear what the grandchildren are saying. It's okay. All kids mumble.

The breakdown of systems is a given; the tortoise pace to which we are now able to hold the erosion of our bodies is a modern miracle. But eventually, if you study the road map, one would benefit from a plan. So I, as I said, made a list. I started by naming the losses that really diminished life. It looked like this:

Driving
Seeing (This comes and goes in stages.)
Moving (This includes everything from being able to stand up without holding on to the wall to being able to polka or waltz when the music starts playing.)
Hearing (Like seeing, it can be helped. But most people I know with hearing aids don't wear them.)
Mental Clarity (a moveable feast)
Continence
Sex

So that's my list. Maybe someone else would come up with more. Maybe I'll add one later, but seven is a good number. I decided that driving and sex were the easiest to do without, and that shows just how gritty this gets. But they're important, so on a scale of 1 to 5, the loss of driving and sex gets a 2. Seeing and hearing are crucial, though they can be helped, so being past help—almost blind or deaf—gets a 3. Not being able to move freely, like depending on a walker or one of those marvelous scooter chairs, is painful for me to envision, so I give it a 4, as well as continence. That leaves mental clarity at 5. How does one measure that loss? This is tough, but I'm guessing there comes a time when you don't trust your own thinking, whether it's judgment or memory.

I'm sure the list would be different for everyone, as would be the ratings, but this was mine. I had also decided that when you reach ten points, you should consider opting out. We could help each other. And this was what I planned to present soon to my dearest friends, after a nice dinner and sufficient wine.

VII

*L*ynn was enthralled with her painting class. She described her instructor as a small man with curly gray hair, rosy cheeks, expressive hands, and such energy that he seemed to dance across the studio. He was probably in his sixties, a world-renowned acrylic expert based in Guadalajara. The class, which consisted of a dozen middle-aged to elderly retirees, was held in a large, bare room with good light. Over time, Lynn came to know her classmates.

"Another woman in class called him an asshole, but I really like him," Lynn said. "She wanted to do the lake, and he told her everybody wants to do the lake, that she should do something else. She says she doesn't want to do something else, that she paid no small amount for this class and may ask for her money back."

Lynn was relating this story to us at dinner. "I told her that I had taken a lot of art classes and the most important thing a teacher can do is to make you stretch."

The lady had replied she thought she should get what she paid for.

"I told her she was exactly right, and today she dropped out of class."

"Leaving you more time with the instructor." Totie chuckled.

"Well, that wasn't my plan, but I can't say I mind." Lynn smiled sweetly.

She had a trip scheduled to Guadalajara to visit a couple of museums there and invited us to join her. Kitty and I signed on;

Totie declined. Everyone was happy, and that's when I chose to present the second part of my plan.

Grabbing the moment, I passed out copies of my handmade list, my seven deadlies, without my personal ratings. I asked them to make their own ratings and add or subtract categories as they chose.

Kitty questioned the sex category.

"Are you talking about one man and one woman—copulation and climax?"

Everyone jumped into the conversation that ensued. We decided there should indeed be room for interpretation, that sex is too complicated to be considered an isolated act.

That call to connect with the life process speaks to our bodies and minds with multiple voices. A peach at perfect ripeness, a saxophone calling out across a smoky room, a tale of romance, a full moon rising—all these and so much more have the power to evoke a visceral response. Being caught up in the sticky fullness of life, that's the sex we enlarged our category to. Those who lose that capacity for wonder or sensation are sorely diminished, we agreed. And after that conversation, I was rethinking my own rating.

Totie wanted to delete driving, since she didn't drive much anymore anyway, and wanted to add speaking, which would include the ability to talk and sing. She mentioned celebrities like Diane Rheim and Julie Andrews who had developed problems with their voices and were struggling to carry on. We agreed she had a good point and added the speech category, but we didn't delete the driving.

"I don't miss it," she said. "There's always someone to take me where I want to go. And sometimes they're as cute as Raul." She dimpled.

"So what is this all about?" Lynn turned to me. "I agree they're all bad losses, and I've seen people lose them all."

I hoped she wouldn't notice the quaver in my voice when I answered. "I'm thinking we should give a certain weight to each loss, and when we reach a given point, we could help each other check out."

Lynn threw her paper down in disgust. "I don't want to talk about this. I'll make my own arrangements, thank you, and I don't see why you'd even choose to bring this up."

"We need to think it through," Kitty said.

"Perhaps," Lynn said, "but boiling it down to some kind of checklist is barbaric. I accept the reality of dying, and I plan to live as well as I can until then, and I'll pay someone to take care of me when I can't take care of myself."

"How long do you think that might be?" I asked.

"How should I know?"

"Statistics are we'll need two to four years of assisted living due to some chronic or progressive illness. We don't just die anymore; we fade away. I'm thinking we could live as long as we wanted to and…" I drifted off.

"Want to, as long as we live," Kitty interjected the bawdy toast. I knew she wanted to defuse the tension between Lynn and me, but I wasn't going to back down without saying my bit.

"I read a medical blog the other day that said it was important to know what the active elderly were thinking and doing because we might learn from their experience," I told her.

"And?"

"We need to come to terms with the end of life. That's what I'm thinking. We're living longer—so much longer—and quantity is no exchange for quality. It's pitiful to watch once vibrant people slip into oblivion, 'sans teeth, sans eyes, sans taste, sans everything,'" I summoned up a Shakespeare quote to make my point.

"It's been going on since time began," Lynn pointed out. "All of a sudden, you're out to change the natural flow?"

"The natural flow has been significantly changed by modern medicine and technology. I just think a little dignity is called for, for God's sake."

"I thought you didn't believe in God," Lynn continued to challenge me.

"Not as some might define that word. But I believe there's a benevolent order in this human experience we all share and that we can find better ways to die. I want to be in control of my own destiny. Does that seem unreasonable?"

"She's right," Kitty said. "People used to be healthy; then they got sick and died. Now we have long, healthy lives, followed by years of chronic illness and disability. The medical profession sees death as failure, so they shuffle us between multiple specialists, hospitals, nursing homes, and home, keeping us alive at all costs. I've seen people hang on for as many as ten years, moving from one *event* to another, surviving from sheer will or meanness."

"Nobody wants to think about dying," Totie said. "Too depressing."

"Dying isn't the worst part. It's dying by inches that's depressing. All the little losses," Kitty said, "like lubrication, like tight skin, like thick hair, like…"

She hesitated for a moment, and we all began to fill in the spaces.

"Pretty teeth."

"Balance."

"Smell."

"I can still smell, but things don't taste as good as they used to."

"I miss eating apples," someone said.

"And popcorn."

"And berries. All those little seeds mess up my colon."

"I miss hearing the rain on my metal roof."

"You can't hear that?"

"Not usually. But I do hear crickets."

"Crickets?"

"All the time."

"Tinnitus," Kitty diagnosed.

"I miss tennis."

"I miss sleeping the whole night through."

"I miss rolling down hills."

"I miss long, soft, sweet, wet kisses."

We all groaned. Then we laughed.

Over coffee the next morning, Kitty brought up the subject again. "Suppose we do set a number beyond which we don't want to continue anymore, what then?"

I smiled. "Then we plan a party, bake a cake, and say good-bye."

"A cake with arsenic?"

"Or Seconal. Or we could drink a bottle of wine and stick our heads in the oven, like Sylvia Plath."

"Or put stones in our pockets and walk into the water, like Virginia Woolf."

"Those people were crazy, and so are you two," Lynn interjected. "Besides, it's a sin."

"You know Allie doesn't believe in sin," Kitty interjected.

"But some of us do," Lynn spoke up.

"What if one is ready and the others aren't?" Totie asked, ignoring our side argument.

Hallelujah, I had them thinking.

"This isn't a suicide pact," I assured her. "The one who is ready gets to choose her time and place, and the rest of us make it as nice as we can."

"So just what would be a nice time and place to die?" Lynn's tone was sarcastic.

"In bed," Kitty didn't miss a beat.

"In your sleep," I said.

"Actually, an Indian man I dated told me, in his religion, to die in your sleep meant you had lived a good life," Kitty offered.

"Stopping eating is supposed to be the easiest and least painful," I said, "but I think that's for extreme cases."

"Good Lord, that would be the hardest way," Totie said.

"Hanging's the hardest."

"Or slitting your wrists."

"Will you all just shut up?" Lynn said with a helpless grin.

VIII

*R*aul found Totie's credit card holder in his van.

"A passenger found it stuck in the backseat," he told us. It also contained her driver's license and some American cash.

"Pretty nice to return it," Totie said.

"Most people here are honest," he said, grinning, "and besides, not many places take credit cards."

We had noticed that. It was a cash economy, and we found ourselves running to the ATM, which Totie dubbed the peso store, every time we turned around. Raul had warned us to use only certain machines and to be discreet about entering our PINs because, of course, not all locals could be trusted.

We had come a long way from the clutching of purses and furtive over-the-shoulder glances that had characterized our first week. Perhaps we were getting careless, but how nice it was to feel safe.

Then Lynn disappeared.

She didn't come home from class one afternoon. At first we were indifferent, knowing she was probably visiting with one of her artist friends, or maybe they had gone to the local gallery, where a class for children was regularly held and locals helped out. But when she hadn't appeared by 7:00, we were getting worried. Very worried.

"She has my cell number," Kitty insisted. "She could call."

"Her phone doesn't work here," I reminded them.

"Well, she can find someone with a cell phone. Everyone on the street seems to have one. We should have set up some kind of alert system, some way to contact each other if we get stuck."

"The city's not so big she couldn't walk home if she got stuck somewhere," I said, wishing Kitty would be quiet so I could think.

"We should call the police," Kitty said.

"Raul says never to call the police," Totie said.

"Then call Raul and see what he suggests."

Raul showed up, pleasant and reassuring, but he had few suggestions. He sat with us and made conversation as we watched the sun set and darkness overtake the streets. We tried to stay calm and remind ourselves that worst-case scenarios seldom play out.

"I remember going out one Christmas Eve and not getting home until three a.m., and my father was pacing the sidewalk when we drove up," I recalled. "I was with Eddie Baker."

"One of the Catholic boys we dated from St. Thomas." Kitty nodded in remembrance.

"My father was furious. He had expected me home at twelve. But I didn't know we were going to midnight mass, and it was a high mass, and it lasted for more than two hours. I knew my parents would be worried, but how could I leave mass without making a scene? Then, when we got home, I discovered the true meaning of a scene. First, Daddy scolded me; then he turned to Eddie and told him never to call or come around again, or he'd 'beat the hell out of him.' I was grounded for a couple of weeks and thought it was terribly unfair."

"Until you had kids of your own and learned what it was to pace the floor waiting for a child who doesn't call and is way past due," Kitty finished my thought.

"Well, children are vulnerable, but Lynn can take care of herself," I said optimistically. We all hoped so, but how fast could she run, how hard could she kick, and how loud could she scream?

"I hope she has her mace with her," Totie said.

We remembered that she had found a hardware store and bought a little hand dispenser of pepper spray that one of her classmates had recommended. "A little safeguard," she had called it. "Not that I expect any trouble."

Waiting is so hard. You'd think we'd get better at it, since we spend so much of our lives in that mode. We wait for our parents to listen to us; we wait until we're old enough to drive; we wait for someone to call; we wait for grades and letters of acceptance and invitations to come. We wait for babies to be born and for our parents to die— once we realize it's inevitable. We wait for movies to start and football games to end, for friends to come, and for salesmen to leave. Sometimes we wait for friends to leave.

I once tried to make a list of ways to live in the moment, instead of always waiting for something to occur. My list included playing games, working puzzles, making love, hiking, and cooking.

"Maybe we should cook something," I suggested.

"While our friend is among the missing?" Kitty said morosely.

"Yes. We'll cook something we know she loves, and when she gets home, she'll be so happy."

"Hmm." Kitty wasn't convinced.

"Raul, dear boy, can you take me to the *farmacia/groceria*?" Totie said. "I saw everything we need right there yesterday. Get ready, girls, we're making fudge."

"Look what the cat drug in." Totie laughed as she and Raul returned from their shopping trip with a remorseful-looking Lynn in tow. "We found her at the *farmacia*."

"I got off the bus there and was trying to decide if I should get a taxi, even though I don't know our address, or try to find my way home in the dark," she said. "And then these two walked in—a sight for sore eyes."

She explained, sheepishly, that the class had gone on a field trip to Jocotepec, a city to the west, and she had fallen back from the group and they left without her.

"I guess they each thought I was in the other car."

She had walked down a long hill to the highway, at least a mile, and then approached people on the street, saying, "Ajijic?" And someone pointed to an eastbound bus with an AJIJIC/CHAPALA sign in its window.

"So I got on the bus and showed my change to the driver and he took out ten pesos, and I sat down and I was so relieved and tired I went to sleep and woke up in Chapala. I got off the bus and crossed the street and waited for the next bus to come, and by that time, it was dark, and oh well, anyway, I'm here and I'm sorry I worried you."

"We're making fudge for dinner," Kitty offered.

"Can we have beer with it?" Lynn asked.

"Whatever turns you on," Totie told her.

IX

Ajijic has many faces. Our previous visits to Mexico had been to resort towns—Cabo San Lucas, Puerto Vallarta, Acapulco, and Cancún. We had been across the border in Laredo on shopping expeditions but never to a community where expatriates lived and interacted with locals. Sometimes, as with Caroline, I am charmed; sometimes, it makes my head spin.

"It's great," the wife of a couple I met at the market told me. "We escape Canada in the winter and come down here—been doing it for years. You can live for much less. We've picked up some tricks of the trade." She winked and smiled.

I wasn't sure what she was saying, but if I ended up living here, I wasn't sure I'd be interested in her tricks. I wouldn't want to offend the native population. For me, they're a large part of the appeal.

"It seems there's a good relationship here between the Mexican locals and the expat retirees—where everyone has a better life." I tried to make my point politely. I had been here long enough to see that services were inexpensive compared to the States, but the quality seemed overall to be good and reliable. And I had discarded the suspicion that all locals were out to cheat me.

"Well, you're a visitor," the husband told me. "You'd think different if you lived here. Some of these people make out like bandits."

I wondered whom he was talking about. Was it the maid who worked for $400 pesos a day, touching essentially every surface of their two-thousand-square-foot house? Or was it the gardener who kept their grounds cut, clipped, raked, watered, and ablaze with a great variety of flowers, many worthy of a photograph? Maybe it was the chefs at local restaurants who bought and prepared fresh fish and chicken daily, who washed and treated those fresh salad greens, who created soups and sauces to rival fine dining in the United States? Or the waiters who left you alone to visit as long as you like and never brought a check until you specifically ask for it? Maybe he was speaking of the plumbers who didn't charge much but seldom got it right the first time; or the stone masons who were untrained artisans, or the guys who worked at the *hierromiento*, which I learned was the ironworks.

What do they do at an ironworks? I met an attractive young matron at lunch who had ordered a wrought iron stand for a vase to be constructed from a crude drawing. I commented that I'd never been to a *hierromiento*, though I'd seen signs everywhere. At her invitation, I accompanied her to pick up the finished piece. This particular establishment lay down a deserted side street, off the beaten path. As she clicked on a solid metal gate with her car keys, I was thinking perhaps I shouldn't have agreed so readily to come here with a stranger. A teenager with a shy smile opened the gate. I followed my new friend over bricks and rubble into a garage stall where, at the far end, a man worked with a welding torch. Sparks were flying, and two giggling, unattended four-year-olds jumped around, playing tag with the thrill of fire.

Two more young men were lounging about. When they saw us, they nodded and disappeared into a back storage area. They returned shortly with a curved iron base and the vase, which had been left with them. One set the base on a worktable, and the other two placed the vase upon it; then all three stood back to smile. They were obviously pleased with the finished product, as was my friend, who clapped her hands in pleasure. They pointed to a feature they had added to increase stability and invited her to inspect the feet, which had small felt pads to protect her floor.

"I told you I thought this would be good." She looked back at me with a grin and a flip of her straight blond hair as she paid them the equivalent of $12. "They weld iron—mostly big stuff—but these guys love to get creative."

I nodded in agreement.

She had wanted an audience, and I was happy to have been in her path. It's the kind of cool shop gringas here like to promote. I made a mental note of how to find that place again, should the occasion arise.

My friends and I were smitten, repeatedly, by experiences such as this that called us to reevaluate our definitions of complexity and simplicity. No wonder people wanted to retire here. No wonder Caroline had stayed rather than go back to Chicago and look for another husband. I also discovered that, despite good health care, most people went back to the United States or Canada within about seven years, usually for health or family reasons, often both. Seven years was beyond my vision.

"So what do you all think?" I asked at dinner one night. "Is there a chance we might move to Ajijic?"

We were pretty well in agreement that this seemed the best of all possible worlds. It was too influenced by expats to be authentic Mexico, perhaps—too "easy," the purists might say—but, for us, it was just enough. Even Lynn loved it but wasn't ready to commit.

We set out one morning in Raul's van to tour the area and check out real estate. Totie was humming the old Roger Miller tune "Trailers for Sale or Rent," and we began to sing along, all except Lynn, who didn't like looking foolish, especially in front of outsiders. Raul kept turning around, smiling at us, and Totie taught him to come in on the line "Ain't got no cigarettes."

Mexicans have a wonderful sense of play, I was noticing. Especially the men, I thought. They like a good laugh, even if it's on them. I loved watching the children at play as well. Along the walk at the lake's edge, I watched two young girls with their younger brother. They had a ropelike piece of blue woven string and took turns putting it on one another and pretending they were walking a dog. The little boy was the best puppy actor, and the bigger girls seldom let him be the owner, but he didn't seem to mind.

Children in Mexico are very sweet to one another. From what I understand, when they get to be teenagers, they talk back to their parents, whine for things they see on the television, and sometimes hit their siblings, but the younger ones are incredibly good-natured, and you will often see them walking down the street or across the schoolyard holding hands.

Perhaps they're mostly from large families and don't develop a sense of self, the idea of their unique personhood, until puberty and hormones kick in. We've all seen only children who get gobs of attention being terrors at age one, but there are few only children in Mexico. Kitty told me of a theory that correlates the development of the autobiography in the sixteenth century with the appearance of the mirror in society: When we begin to get a sense of ourselves as separate identities, our connections begin to break down. We seek self-reliance; we strive to please ourselves.

Self-indulgence seems to be one of the prices of an increasingly civilized society. Isn't that why everyone wants to be rich, so they can indulge themselves in all the pretties that are out there? I seldom find people aspiring to have "just enough," though that's a very nice rule to live by and one that has been around a long, long time. If we all settled for "just enough," there might be enough for everyone, but that has strangely become a dangerous philosophy. And how do I reconcile that philosophy with what we have in mind? I couldn't begin to try—unless you'll accept that a house that's "just enough" for these four old women is something quite grand.

Caroline had filled us in on the nuts and bolts of real estate in the area. Visitors and tourists had poured into Mexico in the '90s and early 2000s and had bought and built some lovely homes. Then came the market crash of 2008 and the devaluation of property in the States and in Canada. Everyone snapped their pocketbooks shut, and the market in Ajijic felt the pinch. That's when she had gone into property management, although she would be happy to sell us a house if we found one we liked. But she didn't push; she sent us out to explore on our own.

Some houses had been on the market for more than a year; some had sold for two-thirds their original price. Things were slow, especially in our price range. We saw some fine places, though most were too far from the village or too high up the mountain. We ran across people who, knowing we had significant money to spend, walked us through hillside homes with fabulous views of the lake and the mountains beyond.

"Most buyers of your means opt for something with a grand view," Caroline had told us.

"We've decided to take our views from ground zero," Kitty told her, "and closer to town."

"Well, that works to your advantage," she told us. "Some friends of mine have a place in La Floresta you might like."

X

"This is it!" Kitty exclaimed when we walked through the ornate iron gate.

The house sat on an oversized corner lot enclosed by six-foot walls dripping with masses of green foliage and those substantial purplish-blue flowers we had first seen at our place in town. They're properly called thunbergia, we had discovered, though almost no one recognized that name or seemed to care.

As we walked through the gate and down a stone path leading to a massive front door, we admired well-situated fruit trees, cacti, and an expanse of carpetgrass with tended borders, beyond which stood a line of matching rectangular ficus bushes, immaculately trimmed. Before us stood the house, with sandy-pink stucco and distinctive stone trim. Inside, we found not a fortress, as the exterior suggested, but a garden, all glass and light. We moved through a cozy interior sitting area, then past a huge kitchen with granite counters and a serving island. Floor-to-ceiling glass doors stood open, and we slipped by the protective screen doors and into a covered courtyard. Seating for both small and large groups was tastefully arranged around a kidney-shaped swimming pool of turquoise tile.

The building opened out, hacienda style, to include four bedrooms, five baths, and an office. Discreetly positioned a distance from the main house, a small casita sat at the back of the property, and the mountains rose lush and green in the background. Everything had been freshly painted and repaired. It appeared to be in perfect condition; everything worked, the water pressure was good, and the neighborhood was old and established. The price was just under $500,000, and we had been prepared to go higher, though we didn't even know how many would be in on the deal.

The economic climate of our most productive years, the 1980s and 1990s, was such that anyone with any assets at all—real estate, equities, bonds, mutual funds, or retirement funds—experienced exceptional gains. As a rising tide lifts all boats, we "girls" found ourselves edging toward prosperity, and as our kin passed on, we were doubly fortunate to inherit what they had so carefully put away for the next generation. There were also funds from past husbands, living or dead.

There was not a single Foolish Heart who couldn't afford to live well—some better than others. We found ourselves, almost unexpectedly, with expensive homes, nice cars, and the ability to help children and grandchildren. We could afford to shop at Nordstrom, belong to a country club, take fine trips, and support favorite charities. I could say we had all worked hard and were careful with our money, but mostly, we had been in the right place at the right time. We had been very lucky.

We inspected the house carefully, Kitty making notes, and then agreed we needed lunch and time to talk. This was not a decision to be made lightly, and I wanted to sit back and view it from another perspective. Caroline took us a few blocks down the street, possibly suspecting it would please us to find an interesting old hotel in the middle of the subdivision.

We made our way through the parking lot, up wide cement stairs, and into a large open waiting area, complete with leather chairs, glass-topped tables, and a variety of sitting spaces. In a corner, we saw a desk. Brick openings led to hallways with well-marked destinations: Meeting Area I, Rooms 102–185, Rooms 203–246, Bar/Snack Bar, Restaurant, and Meeting Area II. It had the ring of established authenticity. Lynn looked at me and nodded approval.

Lynn was very particular about certain things. She liked to sit in the best-available seat in the restaurant—not near the kitchen, or where the vent blew too hard on her, or where the music was too loud. She had been in enough quality establishments to know that there were better seats and lesser seats, and if someone knew your name, they would see that you got the better seats. It was that simple. She liked to go where they knew her name and treated her well.

Well, they didn't know our names at Hotel Chapala, but they might get to know them, and our lunch was part of the test—or so we thought. They couldn't have been less interested, even with Caroline there. We sat on the open patio, appreciating the hotel's position directly on the lake, with an unobstructed view. Birds played in the trees overhead and drank heartily from huge brass fountains. The sound of children enjoying themselves at a pool a distance away added a pleasant note. We could see waiters from time to time, serving a large party just inside the glass doors, but couldn't seem to get their attention.

"This is a big weekend and holiday retreat for Guadalajara," Caroline told us. "They've been here for years and aren't particularly involved in the general Ajijic scene." With an experienced hand signal, she finally managed to capture a gray-haired waiter's attention.

"*Algo que tomar?*" he asked, meeting some blank looks.

"Margarita," I said.

"Make that two—*dos*," Totie said, proudly displaying her linguistic ability.

"Do you have chardonnay?" Lynn asked.

"Beer?" Kitty said.

"Tea for me." Caroline smiled.

The waiter smiled too, as if he thought we might be fun—four older ladies with some desire to celebrate. Kitty, who had been ready to give him hell, ended up flirting with the guy in her companionable way.

"I noticed there are cabs at the door," I said, and Kitty nodded.

Cabs meant transportation was only a block away. We could also hang out at the restaurant when we wished. Totie even discovered there was an annual regional bridge tournament held there.

"It's a slam dunk," she said.

When we got back to our rooms, Kitty took a survey.

"So, who's in?" she asked, and no one raised a hand.

The last time she asked that, we were in high school. Well, actually, we opted in when it was the sorority, but the next time, it was about taking instructions to become a Catholic. My father had problems with Catholics. He also had problems with Italians, though he knew some in a friendly sort of way. But that's another story. This was about when we were freshmen in high school, and there was a place, innocuously named the Community Center, in our general neighborhood. For a brief time in my life, it was the most important place I had ever been. We danced. In the middle of the week, we came together and danced, and someone—I have no idea who—played all our favorite songs. The boys were well behaved, and the girls, at the brink of womanhood, were provocative, I suppose. What I recall is that we were quite young, and it was very sweet.

"*Ser cher maichen*," a cute guy blurted out some strange words to me as we danced. And when I shot him a questioning look, he blushed. I didn't know what it meant, but it felt like a compliment. He said his uncle had taught him that phrase, and it meant I was a pretty girl. I later wondered if it was really for me, or for the first girl he could summon up the courage to say it to.

The more I reach back to remember, the less certain I become. My memories, having lost the clarity of specifics, become gossamer. Sometimes, this offends me; sometimes, I rather like it. Our lives are but a moment in space; we are pieces of dust in the detritus of the universe, drops in the great blue ocean. But "some of the drops do sparkle," the poet says, and I am convinced it's true.

The Community Center sparkled for us for a year or so, which seemed a very long time. The sponsoring church was a Catholic congregation, and how we found our way there, I have no idea, but it had to do with boys. The boys of mention lived in the parish but attended a Catholic school, St. Thomas, and they had a certain mystique. A few were headed for the priesthood. Those had a sacred aura for us.

Other boys from our school came on Wednesday nights, but the Catholic boys were the excitement. My father thought it was another church having the Wednesday-night event. In fact, I believe we had him drop us off at the Episcopal church and then walked around the corner to the Catholic church. Eventually, some of the girls decided to take instructions.

I couldn't begin to tell them why I couldn't do that. I said nothing while five of them went to talk with the priest. They attended masses and learned rosaries and catechisms and could talk intelligently with the boys about such things. There was something mysterious and romantic going on and I felt I was missing out, but my father was a force to be reckoned with and I was reluctant to anger or hurt him.

One of our group became a Catholic, the one who married a Frenchman and became very cosmopolitan. The rest of us have struggled with religious attitudes. Well, at least I have. I remember a time we came together years later when we were in our forties. There were probably eight of us that weekend, and someone had brought some questions we were supposed to answer. The point was to invite intimacy. Granted, we already believed we were intimate. This particular question was about ultimate authority, and there was a bit of wavering in the ranks when someone said, "Everyone who believes that Jesus Christ is her personal savior, raise your hand."

If that seems extremely awkward, let me assure you that it was, even though that mind-set is quite common in Southern circles. By that time of my life, I had grown comfortable with my more liberal beliefs, but there I sat, with people I had known forever, nursing the warmest of relationships. None of us truly knew where the others stood on religious matters. I had my ideas; Lynn, actively involved with her church, was quietly devout; and Totie was loudly irreverent.

I didn't raise my hand. Neither did Kitty. Totie came to sit with us. The others moved into some gentle formation on the other side, and we quickly entertained another question.

⌒

I hadn't been in on taking instructions in the Catholic faith, but I was in on buying the house in La Floresta. I knew it wasn't the smartest of things to do, I knew my family might have concerns about my judgment, I knew that maybe only two of us would be in on the deal and I needed to get a lawyer I could trust, but I was still in. Totie said she was in, too, but she needed to negotiate. Lynn thought the house was wonderful and promised to visit regularly. Caroline took us to the office, and things began to bubble. We could close as soon as the down payment could be made.

Kitty called home for money to be transferred. I wanted to hold up a little while, but we were due to go home in a week.

"It's a good deal, even if it's just an investment in rental property," she told me.

I knew she was justifying the purchase, but what I didn't know was if she would move there with me next month. Or did I even want to move there next month? And would Totie come, and could we really make a life there?

"I need to think," I told her, but she wouldn't leave me alone.

"What better thing could you do with your money right now? Bricks and mortar," she kept repeating. "Bricks and mortar. You can't go wrong."

I thought I might go wrong but was willing to try, and if it didn't work out, I wasn't risking everything. Actually, we were assuming a seller's mortgage at 6 percent, and my monthly output would be well within reach. I had property in the States, and so did Kitty, and we knew to ask questions and get advice. I could sell bonds for the down payment—bonds that were giving me a minimal return. It felt right.

What are the repercussions of owning property in Mexico? I wanted to know. What happens when we sell? Do we need to change our wills? What are the property taxes, and can women do business here? I remembered when they couldn't in Texas.

I can understand the written word, but I will admit, with some chagrin, I don't understand a lot of legal documents I sign. I know it's important, but they're elusive and complex and sometimes poorly written. The print is often small and the pages numerous, and I challenge almost anyone to a contest on this issue. The courts are often brought in to interpret what these documents mean. The important thing, I have decided, is to know if what you're signing is standard and to have some level of trust in the people you're dealing with.

We ended up buying a house in Mexico, a fact that left us momentarily breathless. We found a lawyer in Guadalajara who had lived and practiced in the States. He assured us the contract was standard and that this transaction would be handled before a notary; ownership would transfer and papers would be recorded much like it was done in the States. We believed him and left after transferring an amount approximating $50,000 US. I flew home feeling like Karen Blixen in *Out of Africa.*

"I have a house in Mexico," I whispered to myself all the way home.

XI

*T*o do a business transaction so quickly was uncharacteristic of Kitty, but when I pointed out that fact, she told me she knew it and didn't give a damn. She had learned at her mother's knee about real estate. She had been careful all her life, buying fixer-uppers and then riding herd on someone to fix them up. She knew she had a good eye for a bargain, but wasn't looking for bargains anymore.

"Are you in an extravagant phase?"

"Something between a phase and a spell—depending on how long it lasts," she told me.

After ten days back in Houston, we felt exhausted from the sweltering heat, fighting the traffic, and being bombarded by morning, noon, and nightly news. We met for lunch and traded war stories about having told our friends, doctors, lawyers, accountants, and children what we had decided to do. We had been confronted with words like "ridiculous," "imprudent," "complicated," "foolish," and "dangerous." We had gotten our share of thumbs-ups and "You go for it, girl," which, if not genuine, were encouraging.

It took a long time to get past the stories of how our announcements had been accepted. Kitty's lawyer looked at the real estate contract and gave it an okay. Her accountant asked if she had any idea of the annual overhead, and she had a number ready for him (something like $10,000 a year), which he questioned, until she showed him the tax records and said homeowner's insurance wasn't the rule. When he raised an eyebrow at that, she told him masonry houses seldom burn down, plus we weren't in an area that suffered earthquakes or tornadoes, and liability laws in Mexico were much less strenuous and seldom taken into court.

"He was appropriately impressed that I had done my home-work," she told us.

We had done it together, but I gave her the credit. She takes the ball and runs. Sometimes you have to stop her.

"Hal also said," she added, referring to her accountant whom she calls by his first name, "if we rented the house part of the year, we could call it investment property and write off our travel."

"Are we planning to rent it?"

"Part of the time, maybe?"

"Can we just go with the idea of living there?"

She held her hands in the air. "Sorry," she said, "it was just a thought."

There's always something going on between Kitty and me, and always something going on between Kitty and Totie. Totie says she'll love me forever, but she's a fickle piece of work and she may ditch us both. Could I do it with just Kitty—live in Mexico? I don't think so. I needed my dear, funny Totie as a buffer. She hadn't said it, but I'm sure, in the back of her mind, Kitty was willing to buy me out if it didn't work. And that was a comforting thought.

Totie had proposed a great idea: She couldn't share in the pur-chase but wanted to be a permanent visitor. In return for her board, she would hire Raul to live in the casita, and she would pay him $1,000 US (a princely sum in Mexico). But his pay was contingent on being there when we needed him and being willing to do what-ever we required.

"Incredible," Kitty said, but I wasn't sure whether she liked the plan or not.

Totie beamed. "How much could three old ladies *require?* In addi-tion, I'll pay a thousand dollars more a month for overhead—you know, for food and wine and utilities, whatever. That's about the limits of my monthly budget, but I really like that place, and well, I don't beg," she said with a slow smile.

Kitty hesitated and I suspected she was thinking about Totie's wine; conservatively, a half bottle a day, at $200 pesos a bottle, would be $3,000 pesos a month. But that's less than $300 US, and the remainder would cover food and overhead—or close to it. Totie was being very generous to Raul, and that was a bit of a worry for both of us.

"I'm being very generous to Raul," Totie said. "But he likes me and I like him, and you could say I'm buying everlasting devotion."

"That's going a little far," I told her.

"The literary one speaks," she said.

I thought Raul would jump at the deal, and I also thought he'd treat us well for as long as he could put up with us.

"I wish he had a wife," I said. "Then we would have our couple in place."

"Maybe we can find him one," Kitty suggested.

Back at the lunch table in Houston, we shared our children's reactions.

"Bitsy thinks it's cool," Totie announced. Bitsy, a successful attorney, knew better than to criticize her mother. She had seen her off on many adventures and was always there to welcome her home.

"My kids think it's a little extreme," I said. "But they're okay with it."

"Mine are raving about me leaving the country and about investing money in Mexico. It's a third-world country, they have to remind me," Kitty said. "Count on anyone who lives in France to put you down."

"One of *us* lives in France," I reminded her, meaning Joanne of our original Foolish Hearts.

"We're circling down to three," she said, "and we better get tight."

I was worried. Kitty gets deeply involved with things, Totie doesn't, and I'm somewhere in between. Always somewhere in between, it seems. But it was too late to question the decision. That was the joy of the moment. We had acted on a whim—almost, except that all the groundwork had been laid. We went there and fell in love, and it felt very romantic and exciting and full of promise. We spent the months that followed making arrangements, deciding what to take and what to leave, gathering important papers, and finding reliable people to oversee our stateside holdings. And then we returned to Mexico for the closing and the move-in, which had been set for April.

April, among the loveliest of months in Texas, is not a good month in Jalisco state, or the area around Lake Chapala in particular. Everything was brown. The grass, the trees, the mountains—all brown. Flowers still bloomed, but against the brown background, they were less than breathtaking. The lake was still there—large, graceful, and all knowing—but without the green of the mountains, it was less impressive.

"Wait until the rainy season," Caroline told us. "You can hear the rainbirds calling already. It will come in June."

Totie looked at me, eyebrows raised, and silently mouthed the word *rainbirds*.

We had at least six weeks until June, but there was much to do. For a while, I thought we'd lose Totie. The temperature got up over 80 degrees Fahrenheit, although they measure in Celsius, but no matter the letter, we knew our limits without air-conditioning.

"We don't have AC?" she asked, as if she hadn't been a party to choosing our quarters.

"Use your fans. No one here has AC or central heating. It's like the beach in Southern California. The climate just doesn't require it. Maybe you're uncomfortable five days out of the year with the heat and five days with the cold. Does that really warrant the expense of installing and maintaining a heating-cooling system? Not to mention the fact that they're expensive to import and very few people are comfortable working on them." Kitty made her presence known.

"Well, I'm not real happy with this," Totie said, "and I may have to go home."

"Guess what?" I interrupted, hoping to change the subject. "Someone told me about a *divorceada* who owns her own salon, is very attractive, and is looking to date. I thought we should check her out and see if we could hook her up with Raul."

"We have to be subtle about this," Kitty said.

Before I tell you about Veronica and Raul, you must suffer, as we did, through the move. We had bought the house furnished, so there was not much to carry with us when we left. We all had houses or town houses we knew we'd return to from time to time. Neither Kitty nor I had pets we were attached to. Kitty had just put down a brown spaniel that she tolerated. I was waiting to have a love affair with a dog until such time that it presented itself.

Totie, of course, had to bring her two cats. It was no small hassle, and she made Kitty go through many of the motions of doing what was necessary to import cats into another country, but we both knew she wasn't coming without the damn cats.

We did bring suitcases filled with clothing and cosmetics and books and stuff we thought we needed or might want. We knew it was far from a primitive society but had discovered in our earlier stay that sometimes the simplest of things, like a needle, is hard to find. First, you have to know the word—*aguja*, if you're interested, a very awkward word. And then you have to know who deals in sewing stuff. Needle shops are not among those on the shopping trail. We had a lot to learn but had also cut down on the learning curve just by staying there awhile, and we were counting on Caroline and Raul. With all kinds of connections, she would guide us, and he would drive us to Guadalajara to buy what we couldn't find locally. Princesses, we would be.

We closed the deal and moved in, officially homeowners in La Floresta.

Come to the Homeowners' Association meeting on April 31, the announcement in the mail said.

Kitty went and came home with her new point of view.

"They have a lot of problems, but I've been in HOAs for a long time, and they always have a lot of problems. We're going to pay our dues and be friendly and claim old ladyness. We're not getting into those other responsibilities."

"Claim old ladyness?" I said in mock offense.

"Yes. I've been thinking. This is a pretty good position to come from down here. They may want our financial support or our vote, but if we claim ill health or confusion, they won't want us on the board."

"Done that," Totie said.

"You've been on a homeowners' association board?" I asked Totie.

"Once, for two weeks," she replied with a throaty laugh.

We were in Mexico for the long haul. We had bragged to friends and family about the perfect climate, but late April was disappointing and May was worse. The house had a cave-like coolness, and the fans kept a breeze going, and the swimming pool was indeed a blessing, but our patience was running thin. On the night of June 17, we awoke to thunder and lightning, followed by rain beating against the windows, dancing off the pool, and pouring from the gutters.

"Hallelujah," I said.

On the nineteenth, we had another rain, and again on the twenty-third, and every day after until the mountains turned green, reborn before our eyes. Everything glowed with freshness and color, and the lake gave up energy. When people gathered, their eyes said it all. The rainy season had come again. No one doubted it. The birds had been singing for it for weeks, and it was worth the wait. If the rainy season failed to come to Ajijic, I would be ready to check out, to drink the painless potion. Well, we didn't have a potion yet, or a magic sleep-forever pill, but I knew we would get one. At that precise moment, it didn't seem too important.

XII

$\mathcal{N}$ow, back to Raul and Veronica. We decided to try out her beauty salon. Located in a small shopping mall, it was tastefully decorated—slick and upscale, with mirrored walls and the fresh smell of expensive cosmetics. A flat-screen television installed on the wall played music videos, and in one corner, an interesting assortment of jewelry and accessories were displayed. Veronica was friendly and attentive and gave Kitty a flattering hair-cut while I had my nails done and Totie watched and chimed in on the conversation.

"Have you been to the casino?" Totie asked, nodding in the direction of a place down the block.

"It's safe, if that's what you're asking." She smiled. "As long as you're not looking to win."

"Well, I always like to win," Totie drawled, "but I stick to the machines."

After a number of weekly visits, we became rather friendly. She regularly recommended places to eat in town, and one afternoon, when we were the last customers, she closed up and invited us to have a glass of wine. We learned that Veronica had grown up in California of illegal parents and had moved here with her husband when she was twenty. The marriage had fallen apart, and he had gone back to the States. She dreamed of returning as well, but had stayed with a teenage daughter so the child could finish her schooling here. She wanted the girl to be perfectly bilingual before being subjected to a new setting. The daughter worked in the shop when she could, running the cash register and interfacing with the patrons. She was a darling, all agreed, bright and polite and very pretty.

Veronica touched a soft spot in our gringa hearts. This was a woman who wanted to improve her life. She seemed to befriend us as more than just paying customers. We believed she thought we had something to teach her, and of course, we thought the same thing. We liked Veronica and her spirit. But culture is so complex, and you can't mess with it. This is what happened.

We wanted to set up Raul. He had an ex-wife and a child he was supporting, but we knew he liked the ladies, and it was just a matter of time before he found another. We tried. We talked her up to him, so he stopped by the shop to get a haircut. He liked the way she looked, and asked her out. But he didn't like her, and she didn't like him.

She wasn't really divorced yet, he had discovered, and that made her a liar in his eyes. She had a friend who had a friend who had been in unpleasant business dealings with Raul and badmouthed him. Our Raul? When we heard it, we circled around him like a mother hen.

"What's the deal?" Kitty asked him—very brusquely, I thought.

"Raul, we trust you, and I'm thinking we should have kept our noses out of your dating life, but now we have some questions," I said.

"Yes, señora," he said softly. Between his attitude of sincerity and his stunning good looks, we were hard put to confront him with anything but affection and appreciation.

"There are people out there saying you cheated them in a business deal, before you started driving taxis."

"Señora, I can't say I don't have enemies, and I have made my mistakes, but today I'm an honest man. I need to take care of myself and my son, and I want to work for you and your friends. You won't be sorry. I will, what you say, keep a low head, and I will see to it that *nadie*, no one, will know anything about your life here. I will protect you from people that would cheat or harm you, but I can't keep people from talking. It's a small place."

Oh my God, it was like a pact. We were Foolish Hearts, with a partner. I accepted his explanation/apology/devotion the best I could but felt a sense of unrest. I wanted to share those reservations with Totie and Kitty, but didn't. We each had to find our own way here.

People who might cheat or harm us? What did that mean? I wondered.

This was a new world, and we certainly needed Raul as a guide.

And so we all lived together in a delightful house of deep-pink stucco, with terrazzo tiles and grand boveda ceilings of arched brick. Every day, I discovered more beautiful things about the house: the quality of light through certain windows in the mornings or afternoon, the proportions of the molding around the fireplace in my bedroom, and the garden view outside my bathroom.

And almost every day, something went wrong. The hot water ran out while I was washing my hair. Only three burners on the stove were operable. When the refrigerator motor kicked in, the kitchen light dimmed. The skylight leaked when it rained very hard, as it did from time to time. Granted, it leaked onto a tile floor and could easily be wiped up with a towel, but gringas in half-million-dollar houses want everything perfect.

The maid, Graciela, came too early in the morning for Totie. She needed to understand that Totie didn't want to see anyone before 10:00 a.m. We asked her to attend to our side of the house before she went to Totie's, and of course, she complied. Gracie managed to cover every surface of the house every day and did it with ingenuity and great good nature, though she clearly didn't like the cats or their poor bathroom habits.

"*Huele mal,*" she would say, holding her nose as she approached the door of Totie's room. The cats had not reacted well to their new surroundings and were peeing on everything to show their displeasure. I wasn't too happy about them either. They had chased away, or done away with, most of the birds in the courtyard.

"The cats have to go," I told Kitty.

She shrugged, as if to say she wasn't about to confront Totie on this.

We were disappointed that the heater for the outdoor hot tub wasn't very efficient. For a price, we put in a solar heater. We were easy, perhaps. I know this for sure—there were a lot of people living in the area who were pickier or less generous than we. We might have had a sense of privilege, but we hadn't come here to take advantage. We came, we saw, we loved. It was our intention to get everything like we wanted it, and we would deal as fairly as seemed appropriate. Caroline helped us choose workmen who seemed trustworthy, and Raul acted as overseer, making his presence known as the one in charge of keeping the ladies happy.

"Do you all accept that Raul is part of this deal?" Totie asked one night.

"I accept that he is. And I like him," Kitty said. "But I also know he's getting a lot—free rent in a lovely casita in La Floresta and more money than many Mexicans in the US get monthly. So, assuming he's as intelligent as we think he is, I have no qualms about asking him to do just about anything."

"You make it sound like he's sold his soul—made a deal with the devil," I said.

"Oh, Allie, that's bumbershoot," Totie said with a wave of her hand.

"Bumbershoot?" Kitty said.

"Something said that makes me nervous," Totie answered honestly. "By the way," she added, "he's going to find a home for my kitties. They're making my room stink and eating the birds, and they just won't behave."

Totie started painting; I pursued the study of Spanish; Kitty hooked up with an organic farm, and we began having company for dinner. It started with the brother of my Spanish teacher, one of many aspiring chefs in the area. The boy was very sweet and intensely excited about his dream. He was fun to talk with, and it didn't take long before he suggested that he could come to my house and cook dinner for some of my friends.

"We can give a cooking lesson, if you like, *la cocina Mexicana.*" He smiled, and that, too, sounded like fun. We wanted Caroline there, of course, and then decided each of us would invite two people from our respective studies. I chose a married couple I liked, Canadians who seemed quite down to earth and interested in the culture. Kitty chose an American woman who had come here in the '80s and decided to stay and start an organic farm, as well as a man who worked at the farm who had been a botanist in England and found his way here two years ago. Totie invited her art teacher, but he declined, so she settled for two older men, a gay couple with whom she had made friends.

We were excited at the prospect of our first party. Raul listened with interest and asked if we needed his help.

"Can't have a fiesta without a Mexican," we teased him.

"The gringas here do it all the time," he shot back, but I could tell he was pleased to be asked.

We greeted our guests with anticipation and brought them through the carved wooden doors, through the polished kitchen, and out to the covered patio, where Raul stood at a table mixing drinks.

"Mexicans don't really drink margaritas," he told us, "but we learn to make a good one for those who do."

The young cooks came in after we were all settled and getting to know each other. Four of them came with a hustle and bustle, arms full of sacks, talking fast, laughing, happy to be in such a nice showplace, happy for their gig. The *jefe*, Luis, who looked to be about twenty, was skinny, with large dancing eyes and a wide mouth. Caroline greeted him with a hug and told us she had known him since he was thirteen and had bussed tables at her restaurant.

"He may not be the best," she whispered to me, "but he's the most enthusiastic young chef you'll find."

With some fanfare and a broad smile, he announced that tonight he'd be cooking enchiladas, Mexican style.

Totie's look said, *I thought they were all Mexican style?*

And for dessert was *galletas con crema,* which turned out to be a variation on what we used to call Eagle Brand lemon pie.

What fun it was to gather with strangers, all with new and different stories, all who loved where they were, and all who had chosen to settle in this place for a while or the duration. How different from the life we had left, where so many of our acquaintances were disillusioned or angry at aging and at life. How nice not to know too much about these people, to still have things to discover.

We regrouped in the kitchen to observe the preparations and ask questions. After stretching our language skills for a while, we then wandered back to where the table was set with bright woven placemats and matching napkins Kitty had bought for the occasion. Our chefs served the meal, and Raul served the wine. When the sun had set, he turned on the evening lighting, tastefully hidden among the garden plants.

I remember thinking, *Life is good.*

"Life is good," Kitty announced to Totie and me when everyone had left, echoing my thoughts.

We nodded.

"It may not get any better than this," Totie observed, "but I'm willing to stick around and see."

And then things started going bad. During a fierce storm, *una tormenta,* a waterspout developed out in the lake, came ashore, and emptied itself in a subdivision to the west, uprooting boulders the size of cars and rolling them down the mountain, destroying whatever lay in their path. There was a robbery at the local casino—described as slick and professional. Our wonderful maid, Graciela, had gall bladder surgery and sent her sister, who wasn't nearly as thorough or as nice. We sent Graciela flowers and gave her two weeks of paid vacation, and prayed (hoped sincerely) she'd come back to us.

Raul was threatened over the phone that someone was going to hurt his son. He got up every morning and quietly followed him to school in his truck. When we asked who might be so cruel, he told us maybe it was just the doings of his ex-wife, who wanted him to come back home. I asked if he was afraid, and immediately regretted my choice of words. You don't ask a Mexican man if he's afraid.

"Worried?" I hurried to correct myself.

"Some," he told me, "but this will pass."

"That bitch," Totie said when she found out.

"Hey," I told her, "that's the best scenario I can think of for someone threatening his child. It's just a female power play."

And Totie nodded. We had all seen our share of these—just not Mexican style.

There were ups and downs in our Mexico life, hills and valleys, and days that had sharp curves. One day, I awakened ever so content and then went to the bank to find that my records had disappeared. Well, not really disappeared, but they couldn't be accessed that day and I wouldn't be able to get money until Thursday. That's bad news for someone who needs money today, but there is always the ATM card, and though they charge a fee, I could still get money. But the ATM at the market wasn't working, and when I went to the one at the *farmacia*, it was being filled, surrounded by stern-faced uniformed guards with pistols.

It was a bad start to the day, compounded by the fact that the pants I had left to be altered weren't ready. The lady couldn't come in today, they told me matter-of-factly, but she'd be there at 11:00 a.m. tomorrow. Irritated, I made my way to where we were all to meet for lunch. Raul had dropped us off in town and returned home to wait for the computer repairman.

"This is a bad Mexico day," I told my friends at the table as I watched a peacock freely wandering the garden and spreading its feathers as if to distract me from my self-involvement.

About that time, Kitty's cell phone rang, and though we could only hear her side of the conversation, we knew it wasn't good.

"That was Raul," she said very businesslike, sitting up. "The computer guy called and can't make it—again—and the van won't start."

"I told you it was a bad day," I said.

"Señora," the waitress interrupted timidly.

We all turned to face her.

"I couldn't help hearing. My husband is *mecanico*, very good with fixing cars. Maybe I can call him and he can help with yours."

Kitty hesitated a minute, moving her head back and forth as if weighing the pros and cons. "Sure," she said.

The waitress took a cell phone from her pocket, dialed the number, and spoke briefly in Spanish, then turned to Kitty. "If you give me the address, he will be there in fifteen minutes," she said. "And he is also very good with computers. He will look at yours, if you want."

Kitty looked at me, and her eyes said it all: *Isn't this an amazing way to live?*

It hadn't been a bad day at all, but simply a valley. I wondered if that was just my read on it or a part of the culture that was rubbing off on me. Certainly, there are a lot of bad days in Mexico. Poverty and debility are everywhere, but Mexicans remain among the happiest of people. They are quick to help each other, which so often makes life easier.

When Raul picked us up, we were raving about our good luck.

"He fixed my car, but it was very expensive," he said.

"It's okay," Kitty said, not sweating a few hundred pesos. "But did he get the computer working?"

"Sorry, señora, I let him go. I didn't think we wanted him in the house. I think he may be, how you say, looking around to steal."

"Casing the joint?" Totie piped up.

"Oh my God," Kitty said.

"I told him you had a big dog that was at the groomers."

"That's good," she said, getting herself together.

"Well, girls, I guess we need a dog," Kitty announced the next morning.

We set out together for the animal adoption agency in Ajijic. What a trip that was—cages of creatures needing or wanting attention, approaching with forepaws spread upon the chain link fence, tails wagging. Some cowered against the wall, watching us with sad eyes. Others wandered in the center with the pack, looking confused or agitated. A few seemed angry, even ferocious. Some looked malnourished or ill, with runny eyes and skin sores. The Chihuahuas were too small; the Great Danes were too large.

Dogs are plentiful in Ajijic. Many of the locals have dogs, and few of those are spayed or neutered. Dogs often seem to live on the street and, for the most part, are surprisingly well behaved. There's one that sleeps outside the butcher shop and waits patiently for the black truck that delivers meat. He is regularly rewarded with a hearty bone or two. Another dog I've noticed sits beside his blind master in front of the food market, and he also gets treats without asking. The societal urge to pet ownership hasn't been lost here. Many of the expats we see have brought dogs from home or have adopted here. Almost everyone has a dog, and soon we would as well.

We wandered through the space provided, perusing our options. Strangely enough, none of us had ever done this before.

"What about that guy?" Kitty asked, pointing to a good-sized dog, mostly black, with brown muzzle and paws.

He stood alone—rather proudly, I thought—and I could swear he was watching us. The person in charge said he was perhaps a mixture of Doberman and Lab, and I immediately voiced concern.

"You said you wanted a smart dog," she told me, "and sweet and protective. You couldn't do much better than that mix. Take him home for a week and see how it goes. He's neutered and had his shots. He'll need regular exercise, of course."

So we had our pick of dogs, and we picked Sammy—or maybe he picked us. We had no clues to his past except that he seemed to have an aversion to tile floors. He loved being outside, which was an added bonus in our search for a protector. We had a cozy and attractive house built for him near the casita, from where he could stretch out in the doorway and survey his domain.

Sammy, our wonderful Sammy, was able to bond with all four of us and seemed to understand his role. He particularly favored Raul, but was loving and obedient to each of us, as desired. He knew who wanted to pet him, who just wanted him to lie at her feet, who would tolerate growling if she sensed something amiss, and who didn't like growling. If he noticed something he thought needed attention, he would find the appropriate one of us to check it out. If he hadn't been a dog, he could have been a Foolish Heart.

Now that we have Raul and Sammy, are we actually still Foolish Hearts? I asked myself, wondering if there was a better name, but there was no better name. *Aren't we all Foolish Hearts? Don't we all have expectations for our lives together that can fall at the turn of an ankle?*

If, for instance, one of us were to get sick, or in any way change in the role she had accepted, the whole deal would break down.

Be still, my foolish heart. Change is the only constant. But I would dream on and not bother anyone else with my worries.

"I'm so glad we have Sammy. We're like a family," Totie announced. "We don't need a wife for Raul. He can have his girlfriends, and we can have our buddy Sammy."

At the sound of his name, Sammy wagged his tail and appeared to smile.

XIII

A year flew by. We had guests. Family nodded approval, and the few friends who were still traveling came and marveled at our new lives. Lynn came down for the March bridge tournament and again for most of August, when Houston's heat is so draining.

Each of us returned home twice that year, at separate times, to visit family, check on our property, and transport things back and forth. Someone in the States wanted a drug that was sold over-the-counter in Mexico; someone wanted alpaca silver jewelry; someone wanted tequila liqueur. Returning to Mexico, we brought dog treats for Sammy, favorite brands of underwear and cosmetics, and extra-strength Excedrin. We all visited our doctors and returned with similar stories of our MDs shaking their heads, asking what the taxes ran in Mexico.

We were definitely thriving. Kitty played doubles tennis in the subdivision three days a week and worked with the organic farm three days as well. Raul took me to the gym on Mondays, Wednesdays, and Fridays at 9:30 a.m., which allowed me time to shower and dress for my daily afternoon Spanish classes. Totie painted T-shirts, Frieda Kahlo style, with burning beds, birds in hair, and evocative images on black backgrounds—a cross between exciting and disturbing. She had changed her daily pattern and now arose at a reasonable hour and started painting. She decided she needed to exercise, and bought a used treadmill—an ugly thing—and set it up on the patio. When she decided to take a break, she'd walk on the treadmill.

Sometimes she chewed on cherry cheroots when she was walking. It helped her get new ideas about her painting, she said. When her stateside doctor declared her health markedly improved, she told him he ought to move to Mexico because he would love it there, and they would love him, and he wouldn't have to deal with all the bullshit in his brand of medicine.

On New Year's Eve, when the last of us had turned eighty, we threw a party. After almost two years, we felt we had seen the good and the bad Mexico had to offer. We reveled in the one and could live with the other. Gringas, we would always be, but we felt a bit more connected to this new place every day, month, and year that passed. Sometimes, I worried what would happen when the first one went down, whether we'd want to stay on, but we never talked about it. Why spoil the moment, anticipating something bad down the road? Of course there's something bad down the road. You can sit and wait for it and worry about it, or you can go down the best path you can find and take a drink of life.

Instead of talking about another year passing, we had a party where everyone was to come as their secret desire. Some invitees resisted the idea, but Kitty insisted.

"Everyone has secret desires," she declared, "and if you think not, perhaps it's time to uncover one."

Mine was to be a cello player in a symphony orchestra. At a resale shop, I bought a long black skirt and a beautiful white high-throated blouse, and decorated myself with appropriate jewelry. I had someone make me a large cardboard cello, which was placed on a stand on the patio, and I borrowed a real bow, which I carried all evening and irritated people by tapping them on the shoulder with it. At one point in the evening, I put a piece of cello music on the sound system and sat at my instrument, as if performing. People stopped, listened, and applauded.

Kitty chose khaki—a long skirt and a wide-brimmed floppy hat with a yellow flower. She wore boots and carried a stethoscope borrowed from Dr. F. It had been her secret desire to do important work in a third-world country, she announced, something between Dian

Fossey and Mother Teresa. The stethoscope was a big hit. Everyone wanted to check someone else's heart or lungs—even Sammy's.

Totie came in black, as herself, claiming she had no secret desires, though she had always wanted to be in the circus. And then she turned to reveal a complete circus scene in vivid color on the back of her long cotton-knit gown. She had been working on it for weeks, and two of the ladies at the party asked if she would make them one—the first of her special orders.

The guests, some sixteen in number, were again a mixture of our contacts. Raul chose not to bring friends, but to be there, observe, assist, and be beautiful. It worked. He, like Sammy, knew a good thing.

Kitty had invited a man she met on her daily bus ride from the organic farm to La Floresta. An American with no family, he had moved here with his wife, and she had died last year. He was spending some time each week at the local orphanage, working with the children. Ever soft of heart, Kitty invited him to our Secret Desire New Year's Party, and he came as a clown.

"I never really wanted to be a clown," he confessed to me, "but when I painted this smile on my face, I realized no one could see how I'm really feeling, and somehow, that eases my pain."

The party was a smashing success. It was a new year, full of promise. We wouldn't have wished to be anywhere else. Perhaps the feeling was contagious, for our guests lingered on until the early hours. So when Kitty came out of her room the next morning and told me that the clown was dead in her bed, I was struck speechless.

His name was Benjamin, and he had identification on him, and other than the uncomfortable fact that he was in her bed, there was nothing more to report. We called Raul, and without a grin or a grimace, he took care of it. He called the police, telling us that's when you have to call the police, when you have a body, and we answered questions. Kitty told them he had drunk too much at the party and that she had put him in her bed, while she had slept in the sitting room with a blanket, and when she went to wake him, he was dead. She didn't know him very well, and this was the identification that was on him, and if they had any more questions, they could talk with Raul.

She was obviously under pressure, but I also think she did the old-ladyness thing. It's a good way to opt out of uncomfortable situations. And having a dead man in your bed is definitely an uncomfortable situation.

"I know you want to know what happened," she told Totie and me. "But I can't remember. I put him to bed. I brushed my teeth. I lay down beside him. He rolled over and spooned against my back, and I realized he was surely in limbo land thinking I was his wife, and that's it. All I remember."

"Oh, come on," Totie said. "No sex?"

"We have to be respectful," I said.

"I'm just curious," Totie went on. You did get in bed with him, and you're such a softie. I know if he wanted—"

"He was a unique human being, and this is all we can say about his passing?" I was suddenly sad and uncomfortable with the direction of the conversation. "In a certain way, 'Any man's death diminishes me.'"

With a wistful look in her eyes, Kitty picked up on the John Donne poem. "'Therefore, never send to know for whom the bell tolls; it tolls for thee.'"

"I'm not diminishing him or you," Totie said impatiently. "I just wanted to know if there was anything juicy going on I was missing."

"Sadly, no," Kitty said.

"You guys are impossible," I told them.

Raul dealt with the police and reported back what he had learned— that the formal investigation of an incident involving the death of an elderly person at the home of another elderly person could sometimes be avoided by some kind of order that would cost $1,500 pesos. That sounded fair to us, so we gave him the money and he paid the police, and that was the last we heard of the clown. We always thought of him as the clown. The *payaso*. In fact, that's what we started calling them—the men who spent their final hours with us. And there were quite a few.

XIV

$\mathcal{I}$t developed this way. Kitty was in Houston on a doctor/shopping run and met a man who invited her to a Right to Die meeting. He had offered to pick her up, but she agreed to take a taxi to meet him there. Driving in Houston is not for the old or faint of heart, and she hardly trusted herself, much less a stranger.

They went to a coffee shop after the meeting and talked.

"I'm all for this Right to Die thing," he told her, "but I don't see why one has to be a basket case before you can check out. I've had a good life," he said with conviction, "but I have prostate cancer and a bad heart, and I'm on blood thinner and I can't get it up anymore. If I drink too much, I have gout, and if I travel, I may have a meltdown in a foreign land, and today I found out that I have the beginning of Alzheimer's. Hell, I have Alzheimer's, and it's only going to get worse from here."

Kitty shook her head in sympathy, not quite knowing what to say to this almost stranger.

"In Mexico," she said, "it might be easier."

"Alzheimer's?"

"Checking out," she said.

"Yeah, who's going to do it?"

"I might," she said. "Do you have family?"

"No. Well, brothers and sisters, two still alive, one in a nursing home, but my only son died last year in an offshore accident, and my first wife lives with children from another marriage."

"Maybe you're just depressed," Kitty told him.

"I wasn't until I heard about the Alzheimer's."

"Maybe they're wrong."

"True. But I failed the fifteen-animal test. There's another test on Friday."

"Call me after that," Kitty told him, "and we can talk."

Kitty had heard about the fifteen-animal test before when someone she knew had been to the doctor after his eightieth birthday. When she heard about it, she went to the doctor and requested that she have it.

"You're not old enough," he told her.

"Well, at least you can tell me what it entails," she demanded.

"Name fifteen animals," he said with an emotionless voice. "If you can do that in a sitting, you probably don't have Alzheimer's."

"Good God," she said. "Lions and tigers and bears, and dogs and cats and mice and men and"—she paused for a moment in panic—"horses and cows and chickens and pigs and goats and sheep and turtles. Do turtles count? Llamas, and what do you call those striped things? Oh well, giraffes and elephants. That's enough. Zebras, that's what you call those striped things."

Her new acquaintance called to say he had failed the second test and to ask if she would meet him at his house, because they had told him he shouldn't drive anymore.

"You don't just stop driving in the middle of a Wednesday because you failed a stupid test," he told her. "And they didn't tell me I couldn't. They just said I should think about it, as they sent me out to my car. Lucky I found my way home."

"Do you get lost sometimes?" she asked, and he nodded.

"Tell me about the test," she said.

"The doctor drew an empty circle and told me it was a clock, and he asked me to put the hands on the clock to show twenty minutes to five or something—some time I can't remember. But I remember that I couldn't do it. I sat there and tried, and I used the eraser, and I tried again and it didn't look right, and my mind kept spinning around."

"Did you put numbers on the clock?"

"No."

"Did you think about drawing a rectangle in the middle and putting four forty on it?"

He looked blank.

"So, James, would you like to talk about Mexico?"

It must be a secret, she told him, but they could do it together. So she changed her airline tickets and, without mentioning it to anyone, moved in with James for a week, during which time they prepared for his final trip. She helped him get his papers organized, with keys to bank boxes and names and numbers for advisors, as well as a letter explaining that he was going away and didn't intend to return, and please not to worry about him, that he was happy to have had such a good life and to be able to make decisions about his final wishes.

"That should put everyone's mind at rest," she told him.

She bought tickets on her credit card for Guadalajara, and even if they traced him there, she was certain they would never be able to follow him to Ajijic. On the plane, she wore a red wig and acted like they were newlyweds. Happy with the attention, he quickly lost track of the premise of their game.

"Do you speak Spanish, James?" she asked.

He didn't.

"Well, just smile and say *gracias* whenever anyone asks you something, especially if they're smiling."

He smiled and practiced. "*Gracias.*"

He seemed to be having a good time, and it crossed Kitty's mind that he, like the Foolish Hearts, might be able to find new energy and health in Mexico, and the idea of bringing this man down here to help him check out was dangerous and ill conceived.

"I don't have to drive down here, do I?" he asked when he saw the Guadalajara traffic.

"No. Do you remember why we came down?" Kitty asked.

"Remind me," he said. "It seems like a nice place."

The first clown was a mistake, and the second clown was difficult. Very difficult. I was irritated with Kitty when she arrived with James. What was she thinking, bringing a stranger back without telling us?

"It's more complicated than that," she said. "He came for the potion."

"We don't even have one yet," I barked at her. "That was your department, and now you're converting recruits when we don't even have a potion."

"I know. The timing isn't exactly right, but we've had a death, and it wasn't so bad. James needed help, and I thought we could give it to him. I can't see that anyone else will."

"We can't have another death in the house," I told her.

"I know," she said. "I've been thinking about that, and I talked to Raul this morning. You know the new road, up in the mountains, the really steep one under construction?"

I nodded.

"Well, if Raul could transport a body to the new road and cover it as necessary with the soft diggings of the day, then the next day, when the bulldozer drivers showed up, they would deposit their diggings on top of the previous day's, and therefore, our man would soon be six feet under—or more. Raul has a cousin who works as a guard on Sundays, and he'll let him on-site with his truck. He will go late in the afternoon and tell him he's expecting a girl and wants to set up a surprise for her, so please stay and watch for her to come, and to call loudly when she shows up. And then he'll dump the body and cover it up and tell his cousin thanks, guess you just can't trust women, and come home."

"Raul would do this?"

"He suggested it as the best place to get rid of a body. With luck, it will never be found."

"You said he had sold his soul."

"I simply explained the situation to him, and he understood. He's a smart boy."

"Do you think they're having sex?" Totie asked me one afternoon about Kitty and James. She wasn't completely clear on why Kitty had brought him home, but she was used to Kitty's men.

"He's another *payaso*," I told her, and it took a minute to soak in.

"He's going to die?"

"Wants to."

"And we're going to help?" she asked, with a light of recognition. I nodded.

"*Payaso número dos.*" She lifted her wine glass.

We all actually became quite fond of James, including Sammy. He seemed so happy to be with us, though he couldn't always recall how he had gotten here or why. Being removed from his regular routine and surroundings had exacerbated his confusion, Kitty explained, and it was important that we all make him comfortable so he didn't get depressed.

He remembered much from the past and liked to tell us stories about being a veterinarian in West Texas, inoculating for blackleg disease, birthing calves, and performing massage therapy for horses. Kitty cooked for him and rubbed his feet at night, and he spent a lot of time around the swimming pool, talking with whoever passed by. He tried to talk with Graciela, but she didn't understand English and avoided him when she could. He talked nevertheless, and she learned to stop and listen and nod when it seemed appropriate.

"What are we going to tell Gracie when he leaves?" I asked Kitty.

"That he had to go back home," she said rather snappishly.

"And when might that be?"

"I don't know. I'm working on it."

Kitty seldom does anything carelessly, and I could tell she was giving this her best attempt. She spent hours on the computer researching drugs, I supposed. She asked James what he would use to euthanize animals, but he couldn't remember. She visited the local vet as a concerned animal activist and got an answer. Barbiturates, she was told, delivered intravenously. Painless and easy. Well, she could do that. All she needed were the barbiturates. Briefly noting the irony of being in a drug-infested country yet unable to get ahold of what she needed, she sent Totie to a doctor in Chapala to say she wanted some phenobarbital to help her sleep.

The doctor frowned. "There are better sleep drugs than that in today's market."

Kitty had told her to expect that response. "I know," she said, "but it works for me—always has—and some of those others don't. I've used it for years, Doctor, and the liquid form works best for me. Just a little at bedtime. I'm past the age of getting dependent on a drug. Gracious, I'm past the age of almost everything, which is part of my problem."

"Why do you think you are sleepless?" he asked. "Are you depressed?"

She paused. "Well, this is a bit embarrassing, but I have a man interested in me, and I'm trying to decide if I should encourage his attention."

The doctor smiled slightly. "This is a problem?"

"He's younger than I am, and I know he only wants my money, but it would be an adventure, no? You see, I just need to calm down and get some sleep, and I'll be able to figure it out."

"I think you've already figured it out. This man is not for you."

"Then, Doctor, I really need my medicine, because without his attention, I'll be quite depressed, and when I'm depressed, I can't sleep at all."

Totie was sipping a margarita by the pool as she related her doctor visit.

"He looked at me and shrugged his shoulders, and I could hear him thinking that I was too old to argue with. If he didn't give it to me, I'd find someone who would, so he broke down and wrote a scrip for ten days, with no refills. Is that enough?"

Kitty nodded.

"Enough of what?" James asked.

"It's your medicine, sweetheart. I picked you up some medicine today," Totie said.

"*Gracias.*" He smiled sweetly.

My assignment was to buy syringes. This was no problem, as there are many diabetics here who inject themselves daily with medicine. I believe Kitty gave me a job with the idea that we all needed to be involved. I understood her reasoning, but this hadn't been part of my original plan. I wanted death with dignity for myself, but somehow this rang of Dr. Kevorkian, and we all knew how that ended up.

"We need to test it out," she said. "The idea of a magic potion is fine, but it doesn't quite work that way. And someone needs to administer it. And isn't that why you brought me into it? Because I had the training?"

"I'm sorry, Kitty," I told her. "You're exactly right, but I never thought of it that way. Maybe we should reconsider."

"Reconsider Mexico? Our pact? Or just James? And if we don't have James as a learning tool, do you want to take a chance that we might botch our own deal? We need to get this down to an art."

That was Kitty—ever a scientist.

"Well, I haven't been thinking much about dying lately."

"It's always in the back of my mind," she said. "Ever since you first brought it up. What if my turn comes before yours? What are you going to do for me?"

"I just thought there'd be something simple we could take," I told her, realizing how stupid that sounded.

"Nothing's simple." She smiled and brushed at a fly.

We needed to get this over with so she could get back to enjoying herself. So we set a date for the next Sunday and planned a last supper. We picked up grilled chicken, potatoes, and onions from our favorite street vendor, and Kitty made a flan. Raul fixed margaritas, and we played Mexican music and dressed in bright colors and took turns dancing with James. Kitty poured him a second margarita, with an extra dose of tequila, and took him to the room. It was about 4:00 p.m., and Raul wanted to be at the construction site by 6:00.

When Kitty appeared on the patio at 5:15, she looked pale and concerned.

"I'm still getting a faint pulse," she said. "And he's jerking. I know that's natural, but I can't watch anymore. It shouldn't be long now."

"I'll go," I said. She seldom asked for help, and this was a clear call.

He was on the bed, on a sheet, with a blue tarp beneath the sheet. He seemed to be in a deep sleep except for the involuntary motions of his body. I had seen this before. My grandmother used to wring the necks of chickens, and my cousin and I laughed as they ran around the backyard without heads. Snakes move after you cut them in half with a hoe. And so do people, I guess. Kitty said it was to be expected, but she had never experienced it before. I calmed myself and watched for maybe fifteen minutes until he was still. In that time, I separated out the man who had been James from the body that had housed him. I don't think he felt any fear or pain, and I know his last days were happy ones, in a beautiful place, surrounded by people who were good to him and interested in his welfare. Maybe it wasn't socially acceptable, what we had done, but it was kind and it was what he had wanted. "Kindness is not a bad religion," my mother used to say, "no matter what name you have for God."

It was after 5:30 when we called Raul in to help us roll the body in the tarp. Then we had to move it into the truck. He was very heavy. In the movies, people pick up dead bodies all the time, but let me tell you, it was hard. Kitty and I still have enough upper body strength to move a piece of furniture together, but it took all three of us to manage this long 180-pound roll of lifeless flesh. Once he was in the tarp, it ceased to be gross and just became a chore.

We pulled him along the tile floors; through the patio where Totie sat, quiet for a change, with wide eyes as she held Sammy; and then out through the back door to where a strange truck waited. Together, the three of us heaved the package into the back of the truck.

"I borrowed my brother's truck," Raul said. "Told him I had to haul something."

He piled some tools and old bricks and cardboard boxes on top of the tarp and climbed in the truck.

"See you in a while," he said, looking serious, but not worried.

"Can you get him out alone?" Kitty asked. "I can come."

"Then you mess my story about meeting a woman," Raul said. "This will be okay, señora. Leave it to me."

Kitty and I made our way back to the courtyard where Totie and Sammy waited. I sank into the sofa and tried to wrap my mind around the evening's events. It was all very clear, but I felt no emotion—no fear, no revulsion, only an overwhelming desire to stare into space forever. I wondered briefly if I was in shock.

Kitty brought a bottle of wine and three glasses. "We need to process this," she announced, "tonight, while it's fresh in our consciousness."

"Well, I'm feeling pretty strange," I told them. "We've broken a cardinal rule of society, and we've basically hired an accomplice to clean up our dirty work, and we may all end up in prison."

Totie reached over and patted my knee. "Well, darling, it all started with you."

"I know," I said, resting my face in my hands. Maybe I was feeling shame. "What in the world was I thinking?"

"Your thinking was fine," Kitty said. "You're just having a spell of remorse."

"Thou shalt not kill," I mumbled. "What about that?" I asked, strangely reverting to a biblical admonition.

"There's a difference between killing someone and helping them die. We did the latter, and we did it with kindness and forethought, and personally, if something goes awry and we get caught,

I'll take a stand for what we've done. I'm keeping a journal in case my memory fails me. And, just for the record, I don't think there's a chance they'd put us in prison."

"Well, that wasn't exactly my primary concern."

"So what is?"

"It's like we've fallen off the morality chart. We're making our own rules."

"Yes, and you know, I like that a lot," Totie piped in. "We're seniors, and that means we've lived the longest and should know the most. Why should young doctors and lawyers and judges and politicians be making rules about how we choose to check out? What do they know about living at eighty and more? I think, after eighty, you ought to be able to choose—and you don't have to be sick. You could just wake up one day and say, 'This is a good day to die.'"

"But, what about the social contract?"

"What about it?" Totie said. She loved to play dumb, but I knew she knew what I was talking about.

"We honor the social contract," Kitty said in her most comforting voice. "But we're ready to redefine it. Control over one's own life is a natural right, not something to be given up to a governing body."

"I always thought it was kind of silly that it was against the law to commit suicide," Totie said. "How funny is it to punish someone who doesn't want to live? *If things were bad before, we're going to show you just how bad they can get.*" She chuckled at her imaginary scene.

"So you don't think we're being lawless or immoral or irresponsible?" I pressed.

"Lawless, almost certainly; immoral, by some people's definition; irresponsible, absolutely not," Kitty shot back. "If we live long enough"—she laughed wryly—"I think we'll see a swing of the pendulum, at least in the United States. There will be so many old people who need personal care and expensive medical help they'll overburden the system, and suddenly, someone will make the case that a lot of these people are ready to die, and wouldn't it be kinder to give them an option?"

"I can imagine that," I said. "Suddenly, it would be compassionate medicine."

I began to feel better about our evening's work. Kitty was right. I was feeling remorse, but when I ran it back through my playbook, it all made sense.

"You're going to have to come up with a better way," I told Kitty. "That twitching has to go."

She gave me an offhand salute.

I helped Kitty clean up the bedroom and then took Sammy for a walk. It was dark by then, and I was anxious to see Raul, needing reassurance that all had gone well with him. I didn't like this disposal plan either. We needed to improve on that as well.

Walking past the lighted hotel entrance, I caught the fragrance of flowering fruit trees and the sound of music from the ballroom that overlooked the lake. Sunday evenings were long in Ajijic, as weekend visitors extended their revelries. I stopped to watch a family deposit three sleeping children in their car and take off for what I imagined to be a comfortable home in Guadalajara. I remembered going through similar motions once, long ago, and I sent my blessing with them for safe travels and a happy life.

There's a lot of work and a lot of luck involved in family life. And then, one day, the marriage—or the romance—is over and the children are raised and one must reinvent oneself. Well, you don't have to. But many do. And then, one day, you're old.

It happened to me at seventy-five. I had steadfastly asserted that numbers—my age, weight, IQ, or bank account—wouldn't define me. I had all sorts of rules about what it meant to be old, but when the fact is that you've lived for seventy-five years, you do fit that category, even if you're a "young" seventy-five. It's okay to be old, I decided, and it was nice to put away some things, but better not to talk about them. That was my new rule—discretion and dignity. I was always making up new rules.

Suddenly, the awareness of a vehicle following slowly behind me broke my reverie. I quickened my pace, even though Sammy wanted to go back in the direction of the car.

"Señora Ollie," Raul's voice called out his version of Allie.

I slowed and turned to find Raul and a young woman in the borrowed truck.

"Hola, Raul," I turned on my most pleasant and surprised face. "*Como está?*"

He laughed and said he was well and introduced me to Esperanza, a beautiful young woman. "I wanted to show her where I live." He smiled, cool as an airline attendant after a stormy flight. "And maybe we'll have dinner at the hotel."

"You've had a good evening, I hope," I said casually.

"Oh, yes," he told me. "Tell Señora Kitty I was able to take care of her business. Esperanza even helped me," he added, and I had to hold my face together to keep from registering concern. "She met me at the gate and talked with my cousin while I was taking pictures."

"He's so much help to us old ladies," I said to the girl. "*Mucha ayuda a las ancianas,*" I tried in Spanish, and she smiled in recognition.

Raul smiled, too—the beautiful, innocent, and captivating smile of one who had sold his soul.

XV

" $\mathcal{I}$ 'm worried about Raul," I told Totie. I knew Kitty wouldn't listen.

"He takes care of himself," she told me. "He let us court him. He just didn't suspect where it would lead or how devious we could be."

"You think we're devious?"

"No. Well, we didn't set out to be, but we're doing a pretty good job of it. I even thought we might change our names from Foolish Hearts to Black Widows. What do you think?"

When I didn't answer, she began to giggle. "You ought to see the look on your face. I thought you were over your problems with our latest adventure."

"I'm not certain I'll ever be ready to joke about it."

"It's done and you're a member of the club, like it or not," she announced. "Come here"—she motioned me into her bedroom— "I need your advice on what to wear today. I have an important interview."

"An art showing?"

She gave a mysterious smile.

"I like your tie-dyed caftan with turquoise," I said. Totie always wore black pants and sturdy rubber-soled loafers, so deciding what to wear was a matter of choosing a top and jewelry. She had amassed a fine collection of necklaces, rings, and earrings in every color imaginable. With a box of well-placed hooks, she had decorated the walls of her room with the things she wore daily, and it was both whimsical and beautiful. Her closet, now empty, had become a mini-kitchen for the days she didn't want to leave her room. There were still such days, but fewer and fewer.

Nevertheless, I was surprised to see her going out and apparently excited about it, but refrained from asking. I would know soon enough. Totie was poorly programmed for keeping secrets.

"Is Raul taking you?"

"Yes, and you can stop worrying about him. He's handled a lot of dead people, and he's not bothered by it."

"How do you know that?"

"He told me. He ran away to the States when he was fifteen. Snuck across the border, stole cars, worked for anyone who would hire him, learned English, rode the rails as far as Detroit. He was in a gang for a while. He's seen a lot and done things we can't even imagine."

"Like what?"

"I told you."

"No. Like what could he have done that I can't imagine?"

"Well, he delivered his first child in the back of a milk truck in Mazatlán."

"How do you know all this?"

"He told me."

"Well, of course, but why would he tell you?"

"I don't know. People tell me things. I ask and they tell me. He shot a man once. It was an accident, but he was just a kid and that's why he ran away to the States. He won't carry a gun now, but he's good with a knife."

I walked away, shaking my head.

"He almost drowned one time," she called after me.

My days had taken on a lovely pattern, and I was surprised to find that, much as I had always disliked the rote and the predictable, my Mexico life was rich and rewarding. No longer feeling the need to address the world's ills, I didn't follow political issues much. My Spanish was coming along, but not to the point I could follow the news, nor did I care to. Once a week, we picked up a copy of the *Guadalajara Reporter*, which gave an English version of what had transpired in the area over the week. Often, things that might have caused me concern had been resolved by the time I read about them.

Mornings began by walking Sammy. We stopped along our path to greet other early risers, most of whom were watering their gardens, sweeping their driveways, or walking their own four-legged friends. We exchanged smiles and common greetings and felt no need for further conversation, even if I had been up for it. I appreciated that most of our neighbors were Mexican and off the path of the bustling social life of Canadian and American expats.

After my morning walk, I circled the garden to cut and arrange fresh flowers for the day. By that time, Gracie had arrived, and we talked, after a fashion, in Spanish. If it was my turn to plan the evening meal, we discussed what I would take care of and what would be left to her. I liked trying new recipes, and what a luxury it was to have her in the kitchen to chop and stir and watch after things once I got them started.

Three days a week, Raul drove me to the gym, where I did the circuit of machines for a couple of hours, taking time to visit with other regulars. That's where I got my dose of local gossip, of which there was plenty. Someone's house was broken into; someone's pet was poisoned; someone had left his or her partner and was dating another. The chef from a favorite restaurant had gone out on his own in a new place in the village, just above the music store. The Lake Chapala Society was sponsoring a '50s night at $200 pesos a head, with local art for door prizes. The party boat got stuck on Scorpion Island, and some fishermen had to ferry all the passengers to shore. There was a grease fire at the casino, but no one was hurt, and a carjacking in the parking lot at 2:00 a.m. Nothing good happens after midnight, my father used to tell me and my sisters, and

I had adapted that proverb to Spanish: *Nada bueno occurre después de la medianoche.* Mexican friends nodded in recognition and smiled at my efforts at their language.

I would come home from the gym and slip into the hot tub, then from there into the pool, all while our gardener's young grandson, with music plugged into his ears, smiled and nodded as he clipped and tended the plants in the courtyard. Sometimes Gracie's music from the kitchen seeped into the area, but often, I was entertained by the calls of the various birds that were attracted to our garden. Around noon, I would wander into the kitchen and find a bite to eat, either something left over from the day before, or fresh fruit and yogurt, bananas and peanut butter, tomatoes and avocado, goat cheese and anything. And every afternoon, I went to Spanish class, where we had conversation and field trips and only recently had started reading *Pedro Paramo*, an early Spanish novel.

Kitty didn't like language classes, but she watched movies on television, where the dialogue was in English and subtitles were in Spanish. She said she could pick up a lot that way. Totie watched *Bob Esponja* and *Dora la Exploradora*. She said she was learning new words and phrases every day, but I think she just liked to watch cartoons.

I tried to recall my life before Mexico. It seemed to involve a lot of dressing, driving, returning phone calls, checking e-mail, and a multitude of things I felt required to attend to. It seemed there was much concern about investments and politics, and there were many more decisions. Life was simpler here—perhaps because we had actively chosen to simplify, or perhaps it is indeed a magical place. In almost three years, none of us had seen a doctor, not counting routine checkups and minor issues, and we were all feeling quite healthy. I did have reservations about our agreement, our pact, but the decision had been made. We were all in it together, and *que será será.*

"Guess what?" Totie challenged us as we shared our evening bottle of wine.

"You got a part in a play," Kitty said with an air of prescience.

Totie's round face drooped in disappointment. "How did you know?"

"Raul told me he had dropped you off at tryouts before he picked me up."

"I asked him not to tell."

"Well, I insisted. It wasn't his fault. You so seldom go out I was afraid you had a problem and were sneaking off to the doctor."

"I'd check with you first. You're my first line of defense." Totie pouted. "Well, you were."

"So tell us about the play." I tried to move them past their tiff.

"It's very close to home," she said. "It's a classic, and I'm perfect for the part. Now you must guess."

"*The Man of La Mancha*," I guessed.

Totie shook her head. "I'm a little long in the tooth for Dulcinea."

"*African Queen?*" Kitty said.

Totie stuck out her tongue.

"*What Ever Happened to Baby Jane?*" Kitty continued.

"I've got it," I said, though I wasn't sure I wanted Kitty's reaction. "*Arsenic and Old Lace?*"

Totie nodded with delight.

"*Mierda.*" Kitty had picked up a Spanish curse. "You can't do that."

"I most certainly can and I will, and it will be great fun, and maybe we'll learn a thing or two."

As a matter of fact, we did.

This wasn't Totie's first venture into showbiz. The earliest I remember was in seventh grade when she was in an operetta—Gilbert and Sullivan's *H.M.S. Pinafore*, I believe it was—and she stole the show. With her short blond curls and that perky little bow in her hair, all eyes were on her, even when they weren't supposed to be. As the curtain came down, she turned her back to the audience, then looked over her shoulder and grinned as she flipped up the back of her sailor skirt. She was a scene-stealer, and though seriously called down by the teacher after the fact, she was the hit of the show.

Years later, I saw her in a community theater performance in some little town outside of Houston where she was living briefly with a fellow.

"Allie, you've got to come see my dramatic debut," she called, and I went.

I can't remember the part, but it was a serious play, and while she was still a presence onstage, I remember thinking she needed something comedic to best showcase her talents. She forgot her lines twice, and the action onstage froze momentarily until someone picked up the pieces and continued on. This happens regularly in amateur theater; nevertheless, drama was not Totie's forte.

Despite Kitty's horror, I thought *Arsenic and Old Lace*, a play about two sweet little old ladies who poisoned lonely old men with elderberry wine laced with arsenic, was perfect for Totie. No one was going to suspect us. But she did have a problem learning her lines, and this time it bothered her.

"I hate being old and not able to remember things," she fumed one day when I was helping her with the script.

"You've never been much on memorizing things," I reminded her.

"You're right." She brightened. "Remember that damn periodic table in chemistry? No connection, no clues, you just had to memorize that Na was salt or something like that."

"Something like that." I smiled.

"Oh, I know that you know. You and Kitty always know that stuff."

"But I don't know the words to 'The Rose,'" I said.

"And I don't either—not anymore. Ever since I had that spell in New Mexico and they said it was a little stroke, my memory has played tricks on me. Truman says it doesn't matter, that as long as I keep the action going and understand the direction I'll be fine. He thinks I'm perfect for the part."

"Who's Truman?"

"The director."

"Interesting name."

"Interesting man. He's married, of course."

"Of course."

"Not that I'd be interested," she said quickly.

"No. But you can't even flirt with them if they're married," I commiserated.

"Exactly. At least, that's what Kitty said."

"Our Kitty?"

Totie nodded. "She said I'm breaking out of our living pattern and there's a lot of social stuff that goes on here and a lot of jealousy about colorful people and I should be careful not to get on anyone's bad side because it's a small community and a lot of gossip and the worst thing you can do is look like you're interested in someone else's man."

"Well, that sounds like some good motherly advice," I told her. It was particularly unusual, considering the source. Kitty had seldom allowed what other people thought to influence her course of action, especially where men were concerned.

"I think this whole theater thing is a mistake," Kitty told me when we were alone in the kitchen. "Totie's unpredictable, and there's so much that can go wrong."

"Like what? Surely you don't think she'll let something slip about the *payasos*."

Kitty threw her hands up in a gesture of helplessness. "Who knows what she'll do?"

I laughed. "That's why we love her."

Kitty frowned. "I think it's trouble."

"I hope you're wrong."

Kitty had drawn a glass of water and was stirring baking soda into it.

"What's up?" I asked, looking at the concoction.

"Oh, I've been having indigestion all week, and my chamomile tea isn't helping."

Kitty frowned on prescriptions for chronic ailments and had a bagful of home remedies. She swore by common things like baking

soda and Listerine and was ever on the alert against artificial sweet-
eners and high-fructose corn syrup. She used castor oil regularly
as a lip balm, a nighttime facial moisturizer, and a treatment for
corns. When bitten by bugs, she relieved the itch by cutting a yellow
onion in half and rubbing the cut side over the bites. She said the
sulfur neutralized the chemicals. (I personally would rather itch
than smell like onions.) She used chamomile tea for an eye soak,
along with yogurt for sunburn, green tea as an antihistamine, and
cayenne pepper for cuts.

"Any pain?" I asked.

She rubbed her side and shook her head.

"That's not very convincing. Why don't you go see our favorite
doctor?"

"Because it's either a gallstone or diverticulitis or a hernia or—"

"Or maybe it's your way of dealing with our recent test case.
Your stomach always reacts to stress. Remember when your kids
used to come to Houston to visit?"

"I guess you're right."

"And if it's something that needs tending, let's tend to it. You're
in good shape, and a little surgery never hurt anyone."

"Ha-ha." Kitty grimaced.

"Drink your bicarb, and then let's have a glass of wine."

"I've been avoiding wine all week."

"Well, now we understand the problem."

"If this is a liver problem, I shouldn't take alcohol."

"Kitty, if this is a liver problem, we'll find out tomorrow. Tonight
I want you to relax."

It was seldom that I talked to her like that, especially considering she had the training, but she had a propensity to overthink. And
she knew enough to be dangerous. Basically, she was quite healthy,
and I was hoping this was something easily manageable. So we had
a light supper and a couple of glasses of wine, and Totie joined us
and told us more about Truman.

He had been involved in theater for years, going back to the
old Alley Theatre in Houston in the '50s, which we all remembered

fondly. He had acted back then and gone on to directing, which he had done all over the country, even for a while off-Broadway. New York, that's where he met Vanessa, his third wife. Vanessa was ten years younger than Truman, but she was no spring chicken, according to Totie. She was cast opposite Totie but mostly sat beside Truman, conferring during rehearsals, and sometimes she missed practices completely. There was something wrong with her that Totie hadn't been able to figure out yet. He treated her as if she were made of porcelain.

"Maybe that's why he likes me." Totie laughed. "I'm sure as hell not fragile. Anyway, I want you to meet them, so I've invited them for dinner."

XVI

*D*r. Ferrano, wearing his Crocs and a multicolored sport shirt, was scattering birdseed in the courtyard of his office when we arrived.

"*Momentito,*" he called to us with a wave and a smile as the receptionist seated us.

We watched as he snipped some faded blooms from a hibiscus plant and carefully selected two beautiful full blossoms, one red, one yellow, then brought them into the office and presented them with a flourish—the red one to Kitty, the yellow one for me. I tucked mine behind my ear, willing to look a little foolish in order to honor his thoughtfulness. Kitty arranged hers in a buttonhole.

"Take time to smell the roses, my friends. That's my best advice," he said, "but I imagine you're here for something else."

Kitty leaned forward. "I've been having some stomach distress," she told him.

He nodded. "This is common. People who relocate here get bacterial infections, and I recommend a good cleansing every six months." He was writing a prescription as he talked.

"Let's get a stool sample and a blood test, just to be safe, but start on this." He handed her the prescription and the test orders. "Take it for a week and you should be feeling fine before long." He looked at me. "You should take it too."

"I don't have any problems," I told him.

"You will," he said.

We walked out onto the street and blinked against the brightness of the day.

"He didn't even take my blood pressure, much less examine me," Kitty said in a tone between confusion and irritation.

"I'm sure he would if you asked."

She ignored my attempt at lightness. "Don't you think he handled me peremptorily?"

"He knows you're medically trained. Maybe he thinks it'd be a waste of time to go into detail with you. Get some tests, take the medicine, get better or get worse, call if there's a problem—sounds pretty standard to me."

"I guess so," she said.

"You didn't really want to talk about your bowels, did you?"

"Actually, I did." She looked at me with a wry grin.

Kitty has been talking about her bowels since I first met her. Her mother was fixated on bowel movements and grilled her daughters daily on their activity. She was given laxatives and enemas with great regularity, and my friend grew up thinking this was how everyone lived. When she discovered that some of us didn't realize we were constipated until we had a bellyache and that some didn't examine their stools before flushing, she was amazed. She gave us lessons on proper eating and always had a Fleet enema handy if someone needed help. It became a joke among the Foolish Hearts, and Kitty learned to laugh at herself. She also learned to let up a little, though we seldom completely get over our childhood training in things so intensely personal.

A week later, Kitty was feeling much better. Her sample had shown positive. We had both taken a round of the prescribed medicine, and things around the casa were back to normal. Kitty told Totie she should take the medicine too, and Totie laughed.

"Oh, he put me on it a long time ago. Said he could tell I was going to be one of those who had trouble because I was the self-indulgent type, and they aren't as careful with what they eat or how often they wash their hands, so he just started me on it right after we came and I do a round twice a year."

"Why didn't you tell us about it?"

"Well, first, it was kind of fun knowing something you didn't know, and second, you didn't seem to have a problem and I didn't want to make one for you."

"If I'm your first line of defense, medically, I need to know what you're taking," Kitty said. "So we're going to make a pact."

"A what?" Totie and I said in unison. It was an old joke.

"An agreement," Kitty said, ignoring us, "that we share with each other when we go to the doctor and what meds we're on. We may need that information sometime. I'll make a chart, and we'll keep it taped to the inside of the spice cabinet."

Totie and I looked at each other in mock surprise.

"A pact and a chart," I said.

"Fancy that," Totie said.

Like the promise of a rainstorm, the anticipation of a dinner party with Totie's theater friends brought a tingle of energy into our days. We had long discussions about the menu and finally decided on appetizers of cantaloupe and prosciutto (*melón y jamón*), a grilled pork loin, white rice pilaf with corn, roasted chilies and fresh cheese, stuffed zucchini, and Gracie's wonderful flan for dessert. Raul would grill the meat for us, Kitty would do the rice, I would take care of the zucchini, and Totie would prepare the appetizers. The guest list was more difficult. We searched for some personalities to balance the colorful Truman and Vanessa and chose Caroline, of course, along with Polly and Andy Nixon, a middle-aged couple who were enthusiastic about living in Mexico and had been quite active in attracting other expats to the area. It was Totie's idea to invite Lauren, another member of the cast. She described her as young, attractive, and bilingual, with a built-in connection to Truman and Vanessa.

"And I think I can talk Raul into joining us," Totie added.

"You're not playing matchmaker," I cautioned.

"Certainly not," Totie said innocently, but she was.

The gardener and his grandson were instructed to spray early in the day so no flies, mosquitoes, moths, or other flying creatures would disturb our evening's pleasure. Much of our life in Mexico was spent outside, and though we had learned to live with the occasional fly in our soup, we opted—for tonight—to take precautions. After spraying Kitty's homemade organic insect repellent, the two worked on through the afternoon so that when our guests arrived the grass was cut, the hedges trimmed, flower beds raked, and fresh flowers floated in the pool's sparkling water. I had never seen the garden looking so beautiful, and when I thanked them, they smiled shyly, as if it made them happy to make us happy. Gracie was the same, giving special attention to the front entrance. She polished the massive wooden front door and shined the brass; in the foyer, she dusted the overhead fans, moved throw rugs, mopped every surface, and arranged a tall vase of flowers Kitty had brought from the village. Raul helped explain their excitement. It had been some time since our last party, and such a beautiful home, they felt, needed a small fiesta from time to time.

Raul and I chose a mixture of music, some American, some Latin, and we stacked enough on the CD player to keep it going for hours. We stationed candles, round, thick ones, throughout the house and garden, set on mirrored coasters to reflect warm light everywhere.

"Is there something special about these people I should know?" Raul asked.

"No," I told him. "We just haven't had guests in so long; we're ready to go all out."

"I hope you well," he said.

"I *wish* you well," I corrected as gently as I could.

"*Gracias,*" he said, missing my intent. "No problems?"

"Not that I know of."

"No sickness tonight?"

"I hope not," I said, confused by our exchange, and then I realized what he was asking. "No, everyone is quite well, and we expect them to continue in good health—at least for tonight."

He nodded and smiled, noticeably relieved.

Truman and Vanessa Baddeley were a striking pair. They came thirty minutes after the appointed hour. He was attired in a tweed sports jacket and an ascot, and she, pencil thin, wore a long, black jersey sheath, adorned with an exceptionally large silver cross.

"Christopher Plummer and Vivian Leigh," Kitty whispered to me as Totie moved them through the foyer and out into the pool area. Raul and the Nixons were engaged in conversation about the Chula Vista Golf Club and the driving range/restaurant across the street where you could practice your game while enjoying a Sunday brunch of eggs benedict and champagne. Truman immediately jumped into the conversation.

"I once saw a combination motorcycle repair and gift shop," he said, "run by a mother and her son, but this has more imagination—and, frankly, more class. They make a damn good martini there."

Vanessa stood quietly, hands folded, looking around.

"Totie tells me you came from Houston," she said to Kitty, and as they began a conversation about our hometown, I studied Vanessa. She had an ageless beauty and grace: dark hair, well past her shoulder and streaked with gray; creamy white skin, so thin I could see the blood pulsing in the veins at her temple; and sad eyes. She spoke in a near whisper and with little animation, but seemed alert and pleasant nevertheless. Totie was right. Something was wrong with her, but it was hard to put a finger on it. I studied her, briefly mesmerized, thinking of the different paths we had taken and how interesting it was that we had all arrived here at this moment in time. Was there something we were to learn from each other? Was it all just coincidence?

At that moment, the music changed from a Latin beat to a familiar old song from my youth, and a fresh young thing came through
the arched entrance to the patio.

"Hi there," she said. "I couldn't get anyone to answer the door,
so I just followed the voices and the music."

We all looked up, caught by surprise. Like a luscious peach, she
appeared there on the other side of the pool, dressed in a pink sun-
dress with a white sweater thrown across one shoulder, searching in
the low light for a familiar face, then coming to rest on Raul.

"I'm Lauren," she said, looking a little unsure, as if she might
be in the wrong place. "Totie invited me." It came out more like a
question than a statement.

"LAUREN," Totie roared, exiting the kitchen with a platter of
appetizers.

There were introductions all around and apologies from Lauren
for being late.

"I couldn't find the address. This is my only complaint with
Mexico—that I can't find the streets or the street numbers. It's
always an adventure and almost always worth it. My God, this is
beautiful." She spoke with a natural spontaneity so charming in the
young, and all the time, she was looking at Raul and he at her.

"How do you like my little girl?" Truman put a fatherly arm
around her shoulder. "We were having a hard time finding someone to play her part and then she just walked in and we all knew
she was perfect."

"I was nervous trying out, because I've never acted before, but
my aunt sent me over, and it worked out just fine."

"She's Patricia's niece," Truman interjected. "You know, the artist on Colón Street."

"I'm here for a year to help her out and try to learn the business
so I can help with the buying and maybe start an outlet in Santa Fe."

"Are you an artist also?" Kitty asked.

"I'm moving that way," she said.

My God, I thought. *When I was her age, I was married, teaching
school, and had two small children and a husband in graduate school.* I

was overcome with envy for all the possibilities that lay ahead for a girl like Lauren, then sadness that never again would the world be open to such possibilities for me. I silently chided myself for being pitiful, and passed around the melon.

Truman Baddeley was the kind of personality that fills up a room. When he spoke, everyone listened, and he spoke a lot. To his credit, he told good stories and kept the party moving, and from time to time, he would look over at Vanessa, take her hand, and pat it. He called her "Butterfly," and she called him "Tru."

"We're going to Cuba when the show is over," he announced. "It's one of the last places"—he hesitated—"we haven't been."

"Of the places we'd like to see," she explained. "So many tourist spots are overrated, and one can't get an honest feeling about the place or the people. Tru and I want the real thing."

"And you think you'll get something honest in Cuba?" Polly Nixon asked pointedly.

"We've hired an outstanding guide, and he assures us this will be a trip of discovery. We're staying a month in Havana at the Hotel Nacional, and we'll venture out from there."

"Vanessa's father actually played with a music group at the Tropicana in Cuba in the forties, and she's always wanted to go back." As he spoke, he held her hand and looked at her adoringly.

Vanessa reached into her handbag and pulled out a cigarette holder.

"Does anyone mind?" she asked, looking around as she fit a cigarette into the holder.

Truman reached into his pocket for a lighter, and as the table watched in silence, the two reenacted a scene from movies of old— the long, sensual lighting of a cigarette between two lovers.

The next morning, over coffee, we were still talking about Truman, Vanessa, and Lauren. The Nixons, interesting and pleasant as they were, were no match for the other three.

"When she pulled out that cigarette, I eliminated pneumonia, lung cancer, and emphysema," Kitty said.

"Maybe she's a vampire," Totie said. "She sure seemed to come alive the later it got and the more red wine she drank."

"I'm sure she's in serious decline, something mysterious and incurable, like an autoimmune malfunction, or an inability to produce pathogens, or one of those diseases that are all letters," I said, "but I also think they're playing it to the hilt."

"And that little Lauren is a precious thing. I think she took a serious shine to Raul."

"Well, I knew that would happen." Totie smiled. "He's been looking forlorn these days. I just thought we could sweeten the pot."

"Will you never learn?" I asked.

Totie smiled innocently.

Gracie came to me a few days later with an apologetic look on her face and a pair of small lacy panties in her hand.

"Fernando found *en la alberca*." She motioned toward the swimming pool with measured distaste.

"Whose?" I asked.

She nodded toward Raul's casita. "*La señorita.*" And then she launched into Spanish so rapidly delivered that I couldn't follow, but I caught words here and there and was able to piece things together. I knew that after the dinner party, after the others had left and we had gone to our rooms, pleasantly exhausted and exhilarated from our efforts, Lauren had stayed on to visit with Raul. Visit was apparently too gentle a term for what I was now privy to. I took the offending panties from Gracie's hand, shook my head in what I hoped was appropriate shock and frustration, and searched for a proper response.

"*Los jóvenes,*" I said, blaming it on youth, though I, too, was offended by what seemed a brazen disregard for the sanctity of our home.

"*Raul no es un joven.*" Gracie reminded me that Raul wasn't a kid.

I nodded, thanked her, and said I would talk with him.

I wasn't sure how to approach this and considered having a group meeting in which the three of us would confront him and make it clear this was unacceptable. However, I had to accept that Totie had more or less set him up with Lauren, and we weren't sure what she had told the girl. I also had to consider that my position was a bit unreasonable—that our house rules were amenable to death by poisoning, but could not tolerate abandoned panties.

"Raul," I began slowly, "I need to talk with you about Lauren."

He slapped his forehead with the palm of his hand. "Loca," he said. "She is crazy. She want to see my casita, and then she take off her clothes and run in the garden, and when I try to find her, she jump in the pool and I jump in and she takes off her other clothes and I go for a towel and she runs around to make me catch her and I tell her *shhh*, not to disturb you, and she laughs and says I must do something to make her be quiet—like get her a drink—and I know she has enough to drink already, but I go and get more and get her out and put her in the towel and take her inside my casita again so she won't bother you, and she tells me she has run away from her church group that came to Mexico to help a village in Chiapas. She rides on a bus here because it is as far as her money will take her, and she is working in Señora Patricia's shop, but she isn't going to set up a shop in Santa Fe and that was all a story. She say she wants to live here with me because she only have a little money left and she can't stay with Señora Patricia after the month is over. She isn't really her aunt. I told her that was not possible, but I would try and find her a place to work and stay, and she cried until she went to sleep. And later in the night, she got up and put on her dress, with nothing under, and said good-bye, I was a good man, and she hoped I would come see her in the play."

"Wow," I said. "What do you think about all that?"

"Loca," he said, and shrugged. "Maybe she won't come back."

"And if she does?"

"I'll take her to Ms. Totie."

"He certainly sounds innocent," Kitty said when I told her about the conversation.

"He attracts women like flies," I said, "but his first duty is to us and I think he handled it about as well as he could. And to think, I was so envious of her youth and all that was open to her."

"I was too," Kitty said, in a rare admission. "I guess there's a lesson there."

"Shall we tell Totie?"

"Let's see how long it takes for her to find out."

"That silly little Lauren that I thought was so cute is a manipulative piece of work," Totie announced at dinner later in the week. "She told me Raul came on to her after the party and she thinks he may have drugged her because she couldn't remember how she got home and she hoped there were no hard feelings. I asked Raul, and his side of the story was completely different, and frankly, I think he's telling the truth. But I worked something out."

"Like what?"

"Well, I didn't want to put her off completely, because she could sabotage my part in the play. You know, there's all kinds of things one actor—or actress, if you could call her that—can do to make another look bad, and even though her part's very small and mine's crucial, I still wanted to keep her feathers smoothed. I think she's a little off her rocker, but anyway, I talked with Truman and he said she could stay with them until the play is over and house sit while they're in Cuba."

"You think she'll behave herself at Truman's?"

"Who knows what she'll do?" Totie said. "Crazy little twit."

XVII

Caroline arrived at our door early one morning, looking worn and worried. We were in the courtyard having coffee with Lynn, who had come the night before for a holiday visit.

"I've been up all night, needed to talk with someone, and then I thought of you—three hundred and twenty two years of experience." She wiped her nose and managed a weak laugh.

Kitty handed her a tissue and, with a blend of care and impatience, demanded that she tell us what was bothering her—and start at the beginning.

"Just a minute," Lynn said sweetly. "Let me put on a cup of tea and come sit at the kitchen table so Raul will know it's a private conversation. Are you okay, dear?"

Caroline took a deep breath. "Sure, I'm fine. Just confused."

"It must be a man," Totie said, and Caroline nodded.

"You told me once you didn't have time for a man in your life," I said.

"And I didn't, but—"

"He swept you off your feet," Totie interrupted.

Both Lynn and I shot her a look intended to shut her up.

Caroline's drawn face melted into a smile. "He's trying," she said, "and I can tell I'm not thinking straight."

"So tell us, from the beginning," Kitty repeated.

He was originally from Mexico City, a wealthy man, recently divorced, with two children in private school in Guadalajara. He had his eye on a piece of lake property and was looking to develop it as a restaurant and nightspot. That's how she had met him. He had walked into the real estate office. She was on the phone at the time. When someone asked if they could help him, he said he'd wait until she could talk with him.

"He's very attractive," she confided, "tall, graying at the temples, nice shoes, crisp suit, beautiful smile."

"But you don't even handle commercial real estate," Kitty said, as if that were important.

"I know. He says once he saw me, he didn't want to talk with anyone else."

"How long ago was this?" Lynn asked.

"About a year ago."

"He's been courting you a year?"

"Uh-huh."

"You never mentioned him," I said.

"Well, I wasn't very encouraging, and frankly, I never thought he'd stick around."

"Have you checked him out? Is he really divorced?" Lynn wanted to know.

"How about his business credentials?" Kitty asked.

"Why are you suddenly so upset? Did he hit you?" Totie continued the questioning.

Caroline shook her head, smiling at the suggestions. "He's a good friend of my boss, and he checks out on all counts. The problem is, I don't want a serious involvement," she said with authority, and then her lovely face melted again. "Except I do."

The four of us looked at each other, and Lynn spoke first.

"We understand," she said. "Women love to be wanted."

"And men exist to want," Totie said.

"I knew you'd understand. I've been going over it all night." She pressed her hands together and held them childlike under her chin. "Please tell me what to do."

"Ha!" Totie said. "Don't give up your house."

"Or let him move in," Kitty offered.

"Don't commingle your money," Lynn said, "or get involved with his children."

"Don't leave Ajijic. You love it here," I reminded her.

He wanted her to go with him on an extended motorcycle trip, into Ecuador, where he had other business interests. She was reluctant to leave her various enterprises, all of which needed daily tending. He offered financial support, saying he would set her up in her own restaurant when they returned. He offered adventure and protection and promised loyalty. There was no pressure for marriage, but he would marry her if that was what she wanted.

"He said as long as I was with him, I would never be bored."

"That's a big plus," Totie agreed.

Kitty spoke up then. "Go home, Caroline, and get some sleep. When you're rested, and before you talk with him again, make a chart. List the pros and cons—everything you can think of. Feel free to come back tomorrow and go over it with us. No one can make this decision for you, and just because we've lived a long time doesn't mean we're blessed with wisdom. But we've been around the block and back, and we're happy to be your sounding board."

For the rest of the day, I couldn't put Caroline out of my mind. My head was spinning with memories of my own—and Robert Frost's poem about the road not taken kept bubbling up. There are times in life you feel your future lies in an exquisite balance and that a given decision will make all the difference. In truth, I question whether a person can change the course of their life with a single decision, but in moments like that, everything seems crucial, and you find yourself looking for signs. I think we all sensed that Caroline was in such a place. She was a steady young woman with a clear head, suddenly thrown off center by an outrageous possibility. What would she decide? She had already made a courageous move to come here with her first husband. Is that part of what's eating at her? Should she dare once again, or just play it safe?

Over wine that evening, we shared our thoughts. Naturally, everyone had a different take. Totie had decided it sounded too good to be true, and therefore, Caroline would end up hurt, or at best, disappointed.

"He's offering a lot," Kitty said. "She's been on her own a long time. Think how nice it would be for her to have someone to lean on? Not to mention sleep with?"

"I've been thinking of the men who have swept me off my feet," Lynn said, "and there's nothing like romance."

"Even when it doesn't last?" Totie asked.

"Nothing lasts"—Lynn smiled—"except the memories."

"If I were her, I think I'd take the adventure rather than always wonder what I had missed," I said.

"She can take the adventure—just not buy into love forever and all that jazz," Totie said.

"I don't know why you're so sour on men," Lynn confronted Totie.

"Just too much trouble," she told her. "Always needing attention. Now, if I could find a man like Sammy, I might go traveling with him." She reached out her hand, and Sammy, at the sound of his name, came over to lay his head on her knee.

Lynn, who wasn't particularly fond of dogs, shrugged. "You have to give in order to receive, Totie."

"I know, and that's a big problem."

XVIII

There were a lot of strange stories in Ajijic. People moved from the States and Canada to reinvent themselves or escape a troubled past; others came to invent their past. There were criminals aplenty, living here like ordinary citizens, I was sure, and on the other side of the coin, self-proclaimed specialists who had done very little special in their lives. There was a plethora of people with interesting backgrounds and laudable talents as well, but we had learned to be cautious in forming opinions. Tales abounded and it wasn't easy to separate the gold from the dross.

Perry Marsh was an Illinois lawyer whose wife was found dead under unusual circumstances in 1998. A year later, he moved, with his children, to Ajijic, where his father, a retired army colonel, had settled. Perry started a financial consulting business and a restaurant, then moved in with a young Mexican woman and her three children. Later, the two were married. All seemed to go smoothly until Perry's former in-laws, seeking visitation with their grandchildren and retribution for the death of their daughter, pursued him into his new life. Eventually, he was extradited, tried, and imprisoned. His beautiful local wife stood by him and carried on with quiet dignity.

Considering stories of wrongdoers in our midst, I was conflicted. Part of me wanted to disagree with criminals escaping the law. And then I realized I was one of them. Sure, when I reflected on our course, it was respectable in my mind. But was I truly on the right side? Do-gooders often came to no good end.

I was suddenly questioning everything—not just our plan and its tentacles, but also my whole liberal attitude of wanting to help those in need, hoping I could make a difference. I was confused again—still.

I approached Kitty just before our third anniversary of moving in.

"How are you feeling?" I said.

"Fine," she said

"So life is good?" I asked.

"I have to think about that," she said.

"It's been three years," I said.

"I know," she said. "I have no regrets. How about you?"

"No regrets. Just checking up."

Every day, one or the other of us dealt with losses, both physical and mental. Maybe it was a level of incontinence, a sudden catch in the knee or hip, the inability to complete some once easy task. Sometimes it was hard to think clearly—to make change, to find the right word, to remember where the dog's leash was, to complete a favorite recipe without leaving out the seasoning that provides its zest. Mental sharpness, something I had always taken for granted, was slipping away, and nothing could change the truth of that or take me back in time.

Kitty was still on course, and Totie was totally involved with her play, and I, for the thousandth time (which means the thought comes to me about once a day), chose to continue. There were hours spent pondering a new ache or lump, days I arose and struggled to get myself together, nights I considered how nice it would be to simply lie down and wake up dead. Then I awoke in my most comfortable of beds, looked out an open window to a beautiful garden, heard the birds singing, considered my options for the day, and hoped that nothing would happen to upset the apple cart. Not today. Certainly not today. While I knew our situation could only deteriorate, I willed myself not to look ahead. I comforted myself in our pact. We weren't a problem for our children, we understood each other, and best of all, we laughed together.

Totie regularly regaled us with rehearsal reports. Now that we knew some of the characters, it was even more entertaining. Lauren had apparently latched on to the young man who has the part of her fiancé in the play, so hopefully she would be leaving Raul alone.

"I returned her panties," Totie told us. "It was hard to keep a straight face, but I told her I found them in the garden and wanted to protect her reputation, so I didn't mention it to either of you. Ha! Like she'd care. I put them in a Walmart sack, but I doubt that she got the innuendo."

Truman had taken Totie aside and explained that, because it was hard for Vanessa to walk steadily, he wanted her to do most of the moving about, and when they needed to exit the stage, that she should offer her arm to her sister so they could move off together.

"I think she's getting weaker daily," Totie said. "I hope she can make it through the play. Oh, and he wants to take us to dinner."

Truman had chosen a restaurant out from the village, one in a row of spots situated along the western curve of the lake. Raul drove us there, waving at the cast of parking attendants, males of various ages who stood along the roadside, snapping red cloths with a certain flair, waving us in as if each restaurant were our chosen destination—or should be.

"Do you know these guys?" I asked, impressed with the warmth of their responses.

"I know their type," he said. "It's a simple job, but if you do it really well, you might get someone's attention."

The weather, regularly delightful, was particularly splendid that evening. Flies and mosquitoes, sometimes a bother, seemed to have taken a vacation. The ambience of a sunset over peaceful waters, romantic ballads playing softly, savory food, unobtrusive service, and interesting company was just right, and a peacefulness and appreciation of life's simple pleasures enveloped us all.

"Vanessa sends her regrets, but she wasn't up to it tonight," he said wistfully.

"Is she okay?" Kitty asked, a foolish question, but I knew she was trying to create an opening for him to talk if he wished to. And it seemed he did.

"She's dying," he said.

"I'm so sorry."

"We're going together," he said, "when we get back from Cuba— unless we find some magical cure. There's a doctor there who has had some success with her illness, which is quite rare."

"And it is…?" Kitty prodded gently.

"CJD," he said.

"Umm," Kitty said, and the table grew quiet.

As well as I knew Kitty, I still couldn't tell whether it was too fatal to discuss or if it was something new she wasn't familiar with. Lost in private thoughts, we all stared into the water, watching a heron perched on a post. I was wondering what he meant by "going together."

Truman took a sip of his tequila. "Did you know our play was based on a true story?"

"*Arsenic and Old Lace?*"

"Yes. Sister Amy's Nursing Home for the Elderly, in Windsor, Connecticut, was the site of numerous poisonings, somewhere between five and forty-eight. Sister Amy apparently murdered her second husband—after he signed over his assets to her—and then went on to do the same with residents of the home. Finally, someone got suspicious. They exhumed some bodies and found evidence of arsenic poisoning. Quite a scandal in the early 1900s. Now it's fodder for laughter."

"Well, it's not quite the same, Truman," Totie piped in. "We're not after their money. We just want to put them to rest gently." She was enjoying a tequila too.

I cringed at her comment before realizing she was talking about the characters in the play.

"Don't mistake me. Butterfly and I see the humor. In fact, we're elevating the irony by making this our final play."

"And when you return from Cuba?" I asked.

"Well, we'll see."

"No, you said you were 'going together.' What might that mean?"

He hesitated. "I misspoke."

I didn't think he had. He had just let down his guard. He was about to tell us something, wanted to tell us something, but then he thought better of it.

"Might I have an amaretto?" I asked.

"Of course." He signaled for the waiter, ordered my after-dinner drink and another tequila for himself, as I had hoped would be the case.

The conversation wandered for a while, and we all continued to relax under the spell of a creamy moon that spread its glow across the lake.

"Nice to have mature company," he said. "You ladies are refreshing. So many don't seem to know how to age these days. All they can talk about is their ailments and their forgetfulness and how good life *used* to be. Doesn't anyone want to go out with style?"

"We certainly do," Kitty said. "That's one of the things that brought us here."

I looked across at her, wondering what she might be up to.

"Oh?" Truman said.

Kitty leaned forward and spoke in a conspiratorial tone. "We had heard there were doctors who might help one make comfortable end-of-life choices."

"Ha!" he said. "We thought so too, but the Hippocratic oath was apparently translated into Spanish. The Mexicans hold to strict ethical principles, I've found. Their approach is much gentler, more patient-oriented, and there have been some attempts at a legislative bill to decriminalize active euthanasia, but the Catholic Church opposes it, of course."

Kitty sat back and Totie headed for the restroom while I toyed aimlessly with the silverware.

"You don't need a doctor," Truman said. "You need a veterinarian."

"We have one," I said.

"Ask him about pentobarbital."

"It's a form of Nembutal," Kitty said.

"Smart girl." Truman nodded at her like a teacher bestowing a compliment on a young student. "They use it to put down large animals, and it'll put a person down painlessly in less than an hour."

"A potion?" I came to life.

Truman nodded, smiling slightly—at my enthusiasm, I supposed.

"How do you know about this?" I asked.

"PBS story on suicide tourism a few years back. Tour groups bringing people to Mexico from halfway across the world to buy the stuff. Government got wind of it and cracked down, but it's still available."

"And how would one get this potion?" I asked, trying to be casual.

"If I had a Mexican driver like you girls do, I'd put him on the trail."

Raul came around to pick us up at the restaurant, and on the way home, Kitty outright asked him if he knew how we could get some of the medicine veterinarians used to put down large dogs.

"Not for Sammy," he said, half question, half denial.

"Of course not."

He was silent for a while. "For old man friends?"

"That's an interesting way of putting it, Raul, and the answer is yes, perhaps. It's a drug called pentobarbital."

"I know," he said. "I used to work in a clinic for animals."

"Is there anything you haven't done?" Totie laughed.

"I've never been in a play," he said.

"Well, you are now." She laughed. "It's called *Raul and Las Tres...* How do you say old ladies?"

"*Ancianas.*"

"*Raul y Las Tres Ancianas,*" she repeated, chuckling with pride at her Spanish joke.

XIX

Our schedule had suddenly become quite crowded. Totie's play was three weeks away, I was leaving for ten days in the States to visit children and grandchildren, and Kitty's family was coming to Mexico for the first time. Because they had chosen to come as a group, it was convenient for me to be gone in order to free up another bedroom, and frankly, I was happy to be absent from what would surely be a chaotic time. Much as I loved Kitty and valued her children's talents, the family dynamics were painful. She did things they didn't want done for them and then felt slighted that they didn't appreciate it. They professed affection, but she got on their nerves and they snapped out at her, or ignored her, or took advantage of her desire to look good in their eyes. I couldn't help but want to take her side, but once I had expressed a position, I became drawn into the situation.

"Traitor," Totie called me when she found out I was leaving.

"You'll be busy with the play," I told her, "and besides, you handle it all better than I. You just tease them out of their bad humors."

"I think I'll be spending a lot of time in my room."

It was early April when I left, a good time to be gone from my Mexico setting, where the mountains had turned brown, the ground dusty, and the rainbirds had begun their plaintive call for the earth's renewal. As I had hoped, it was a near-perfect time to be in Central

Texas. Flying into San Antonio, I looked down upon random fields of pink and yellow, with bluebonnets and Indian paintbrush sprinkled along the highways, all against a canvas of bright green. My grandson, an aspiring medical student, met me at the airport, looking so mature I almost walked by him.

"Dandy?" he called out, and I stopped, embarrassed.

I had dressed with care, hoping to look attractive, alert, and capable, and here I had failed to recognize my own. Damn.

"I almost didn't recognize you," he said, giving me a reserved hug. "I was looking for someone older and more shriveled."

I laughed, relieved. "And I didn't know who was picking me up, but I certainly didn't expect someone so tall and handsome," I told him. "I think you've grown six inches since last year."

"Three," he said. "A late growth spurt, they say."

"Well, it looks good on you."

"And Mexico looks good on you," he said, smiling, and what a fine moment that was.

I had always valued independence and freedom, for myself and my two daughters, and though that might not have been the family life they would have chosen, they had adapted well. I had taken the mother cat approach to child rearing—protect them, teach them, and then let them go. It was a far cry from the helicopter style of hovering motherhood I had later observed. As a result, we all missed a lot of warm moments, I suppose. What I did have—or tried for—was an honest relationship with these individuals I had brought into the world.

I didn't expect anyone to love me just because I was family, and I didn't want them to worry about taking care of me in my old age. We had gone over this when I moved to Mexico. They felt I was holding them at arm's length, and I was. I could take care of myself financially, and I would make my own decisions about where and how I would live. They might have thought they wanted to take care of me, but they hadn't really considered what that might entail: feeding someone, changing diapers, visiting a smelly nursing home, not being recognized, seeing a familiar and once active body shrink and decay, or enduring groans of pain, bursts of anger, and tears of confusion. Maybe it was pride, but I didn't want them to remember me that way. Better to say, "Mother's wasting away in Margaritaville."

After they had come to visit in Ajijic, their concerns seemed somewhat allayed. They had relaxed and, I hoped, taken some relief in the fact that I wasn't on their to-do list. As long as I could make it home every six months, we could communicate regularly by phone and e-mail, and they could pop down for a weekend now and then. We had come to peace with it. The grandchildren, busy with other activities, had never made it down. I regretted that but hoped they would remember me as an adventurer. I preferred to be a role model rather than a responsibility. Of course, I hadn't told any of them about the pact.

My ten days in Texas were crowded. There was shopping to do. I carried a list of at least twenty items I needed to look for, purchase, and pack into the suitcase I had brought loaded with Mexico items I thought would please my family and friends. I brought textiles, jewelry, art pieces, and liqueurs, and carried back kitchen gadgets, cosmetics, books, and various favorite foodstuffs that were either hard to find or ridiculously expensive, like Bisquick and graham crackers.

Going through customs, almost invariably uneventful in Mexico, is considerably stricter in the States, a fact I learned the hard way. Once, I carried a harmless white powder into the United States for a friend who wanted to try an animal remedy for her own asthma, and ended up spending an uncomfortable hour in a guarded room, feeling quite foolish as uniformed agents tested the material.

I had doctors to see in the States. While I liked and trusted Dr. Ferrano and had found a wonderful dentist in Ajijic, I still liked to maintain my contacts in the States. So there were visits to the dermatologist, the cardiologist, the podiatrist, the rheumatologist, and the internist.

"You're in great shape," they told me. "Should live to be a hundred."

God forbid, I thought.

The aspiration to a long life has eluded me. Of all the elders I've known over the years, only a handful remained happy or productive. What pride or pleasure should we take in just living on? Like Kitty says, if I live to be a hundred, I bet a potion will be available on demand. But I don't want to wait that long.

On the other hand, it was exhilarating to travel home (I still called Texas *home*) and to enjoy brief visits with my daughters and their husbands and children. We drove to Houston, my youngest and I, to see the older girl and her family. I had forgotten about Houston traffic, but fortunately, I wasn't the driver. I sat back and felt pleased with my daughter's coolness and competence.

"You're amazing," she said.

"I was just thinking that about you."

"Well, you can eat anything you want to and stay the same size, and you don't have to pee as often as I do."

"The golden years," I joked.

"Mother," she said, taking on a more serious tone, "Karen and I really want you to come home. You're just too far away, and though you seem to be doing really well, anything could happen and we don't feel capable to handle a problem in Mexico."

"That's the point," I said. "You don't have to. I've got it all covered—doctor, hospital, friends, communication, attorney, will, cremation."

"They have cremation in Mexico?" She knew I was strongly opposed to having a cemetery plot where people could visit and put stuff on my grave.

"Yes. And they'll ship you my ashes, if you wish."

"My God, I hate this."

"Come on, it's only natural. Ashes to ashes, dust to dust. I'm perfectly okay with it, and I want you to be too."

"Hmm," she said, and I wondered if, in all good intention, I was just being a pain in the ass. I have a friend who once told me she knew her daughter would end up taking care of her, and she planned to be totally agreeable so that it would be as easy as possible. What a lovely thought, I told her, but I've taken another route.

In Houston, I was received warmly, but when I saw the girls with their heads together, I suspected another conversation about my welfare. I didn't expect it to come from my son-in-law.

"Allie," he said, "your daughters want to be closer to you these days. You're active and fun to be around, and they want to enjoy your company, and they want you to be more of a presence in their lives and in the lives of your grandchildren."

"They sent you to soften me up," I joked.

"This is serious," he said. "I feel the same way." And then he hugged me. Damn.

"I'll think about it," I said, avoiding eye contact because mine were teary.

My twin granddaughters in Houston came by for dinner. They were young professionals, sharing an apartment, dazzling in their beauty and energy. Their conversation, punctuated by phone calls, text messages, and God knows what, was brisk and barely decipherable—the part I could hear. Impressed as I was, they made me feel very old.

"They exhaust me," my daughter said when they had left in a bustle of chatter. "They're easier to take one at a time, but together, they're almost overwhelming."

"I thought it was just me." I relaxed a bit. "Do you think they really might come see me in Mexico?" I asked, referring to their last-minute promise to visit.

"I wouldn't count on it," their dad said. "They want to do everything, but beautiful as Ajijic may be, those two seldom end up in places where there are no *hotties*."

"Poorly equipped as I am to recognize a *hottie*, I wouldn't want to disappoint them, but they're always welcome," I said. "And, of course, there's always Raul."

"Raul," my daughters repeated in unison, smiling at their memory of our houseman, while my son-in-law frowned.

"We're not promoting that, Allie," he said.

"Just wanted verification that I hadn't lost my ability to discriminate," I told him.

I stopped by to see an old friend, Lulu, in the retirement home. She had moved, or been moved, to the fifth floor, a memory unit, and wasn't happy about it.

"I need to get out of here," she told me repeatedly. "The play's about to begin, and they need me." Her hands shuffled nervously, alternately smoothing her dress, then her hair.

"Totie's in a play in Mexico," I told her.

"Totie?" she said.

"Our friend Totie. She was a Foolish Heart."

Lulu thought for a while and nodded.

"You and Totie used to sing together in high school. You dressed up like sailors, remember?"

She nodded and then smiled, though I wasn't sure if she actually remembered or just wanted to.

I reached in my purse and brought out a colorful bracelet I had bought her. She held out her wrist, and I put it on.

"Did you know that Mama died?" she asked. "And Sam, too."

"I know, and I'm so sorry for your losses," I told her, taking the easy way out. Kitty says it's helpful to try to orient the disoriented. Remind them what day it is and who you are and what your connection is. I think she read that in a journal, but it didn't seem the right thing for me to do just then. Maybe it's good for regular caregivers, but I didn't want the little time I had to spend with my friend to be tutorial, so I asked if she'd like to sing a song.

She nodded, and I took both her hands, looked into her eyes, and began softly, a bit self-consciously. "*The night is like a lovely tune.*"

She started humming with me and then, on the second line, came in with "*My foolish heart.*"

And so we continued there, in the open room, while others sat and stared at Lucille Ball on television or nodded in their chairs as we sang through that incredibly sentimental piece—twice—and briefly wandered back into young womanhood together.

"Now, can we go to the play?" she asked. "I'm all warmed up, and they're waiting for me. I'm singing, you know."

All in all, it was a good trip home, but I was tired when I reached the Guadalajara airport, and happy to see Raul's beautiful face smiling at me when I came through the door after customs gave me the expected green light.

"Señora." He reached down to brush both cheeks in a traditional Mexican greeting among friends. Then he took my bags and told me to wait at the front door while he brought the car around.

Why was it, I wondered, that I could love allowing this young man to pamper me, but felt such a strong need to be self-sufficient with my own dear ones. *Mexicans really do revere their elders*, I thought. It's built into the culture. Besides, we pay him well.

XX

$\mathcal{B}$ack at the casa, there was much to catch up on. Kitty's visit with her children had started well but ended in disaster. Her daughter and two granddaughters from Houston arrived first, followed by her son, daughter-in-law, and granddaughter from France. There was some wrangling over the space, but Kitty agreeably gave up her room and moved in with Totie so that the others could be more comfortable. The girls badly wanted the casita and asked why Raul couldn't find another place, but Kitty put her foot down on that one.

"He's just hired help," her daughter had said, and Kitty closed down the conversation, saying she thought she had taught her better.

Despite her warnings, the granddaughters had insisted on eating on the street and had gotten quite sick, with vomiting and diarrhea throughout the night. Kitty was prepared with medicine and advice, but the girls were spoiled and thoughtless despite their elite private school training in the States and abroad. Gracie made them fresh chicken soup, and they turned up their noses, then sent Raul to the Walmart in search of Campbell's, the only thing they knew and the only thing they were sure their stomachs could tolerate. They complained about Mexican Coca-Cola and hated the saltines. That was the second day.

The third day, they lay by the pool in bikinis, moaning over how weak they felt, calling for pasta, sorbet, tomato puree, and french fries, all the while texting each other and comparing how flat their stomachs had become. They sent Raul to buy a scale to compare how much weight they had lost, which was minimal. The next day, they were feeling better and went into town, where they had pizza and ice cream, and came back with bellyaches. During this time, the four adults had rented a car and driver and taken off for Tapalpa, an alpine village a few hours away. It was so appealing they decided to stay the night.

When the parents returned, they were anxious to visit Tlaquepaque, an artisan's marketplace in Guadalajara. Kitty had arranged and paid for a private van and driver, and since the girls were feeling well enough to go at the last minute, there wasn't room for her. They took off for the day without her and came home laden with expensive gifts, too large to take on the plane. Kitty was left to arrange for packaging and mailing these items back to Texas and France. They asked her to tell them what they owed her when she had a price, not something she was likely to do.

On the last night, she took them out to dinner, and they complained about the service and the menu.

"I had hoped to take you to the organic farm where I work," she said, and her daughter-in-law reminded her that she was familiar with organic farms in France.

"You see one, you've seen them all," her daughter said jokingly.

"Thanks, Mother, for the visit," her son said as he left. "I'm glad if you like living here, but it's a little dirty and inefficient for my taste."

Kitty was furious—and obviously hurt. She had decided she would leave the house and her other Mexico possessions to Raul.

"Wait," I said. "The house is half mine."

"I know. But I want to buy out your half and leave it all to him."

"Wow," I said. "That's a major diminishment of your kids' inheritance."

"I've given them about all I'm going to," she said. "I've helped with fine schools and camps and horses and dressage lessons and God knows what for those self-indulgent young women, and I've invested in homes and remodeling and professional growth for the adults, long after they were married and out on the world on their own. I've been an enabler so long I don't even know how to act with them any longer. It's time to cut the purse strings, or the apron strings, or whatever strings remain."

"Are you going to tell them?"

"Not necessarily."

"Do you think they'll come after Raul, like a legal suit or something?"

"Not if I do it right. Change my will. That's what I'll do—change my will and send them a copy. For Christmas."

I had seldom seen Kitty so upset, and the entire time she talked to me, I noticed her massaging her stomach.

"I wanted to show them this wonderful life we have, share with them the beauty and interesting culture here, and all they could do was complain."

"That's not true," Totie said. "I think they had a good time, but you know, when you get to a place that feels like home, you tend to indulge yourself. You're their mother, after all, not their hostess."

"Hmm," Kitty said, unconvinced and unwilling to let go of her bruised ego.

"Now, can we talk about my stuff?" Totie grinned. "The play is coming along, and Vanessa is much improved, thanks to vitamin B12 shots she's getting daily, and Lauren has moved in with her newest boyfriend and is much nicer than I thought she was, and I found a gun in Raul's car, and Lynn is coming to visit with a friend."

"Whoa," I said. "That's a lot to digest."

"Well, you shouldn't go away for so long."

"Let's talk about the gun."

"I found it in the glove compartment the other day, and when he saw that I had seen it, he said he had meant to keep that locked up. He said he had a permit and he needed it, and when I tried to pin him down, he said he felt he was our bodyguard and needed to be ready to protect us."

"Wait! I thought he didn't do guns. And who's going to hurt us?"

Totie shrugged.

I turned to Kitty. "Have you talked to him?"

"He said there are people in town who are suspicious of—or jealous of, not quite sure which—his relationship with us. And something about obtaining that drug we asked him for. You know, sometimes I'm not exactly clear what he's saying, but I've chosen to trust him and I ask you to do the same."

"I trust him, but I don't want to get caught in a gunfight."

"I agree. So I found a gun and he's going to teach me how to use it and I'll carry it in my purse whenever we all go out together."

"Kitty!" I was horrified. "Where did you get a gun in Mexico?"

Totie sat, giggling.

"The first *payaso*. He had it in his clown suit. I don't know why. Maybe he was going to kill himself; maybe he was going to shoot us all. I found it when I cleaned up his clothes. Wait, I'll get it." And she disappeared down the hall toward her room.

I looked over at Totie. "And when is Lynn coming?"

"Day after tomorrow, and she's bringing a friend and she wants us to help her."

"Help her what?"

Kitty returned before Totie could answer. She was, rather gingerly, holding a smallish black revolver.

"I put it in a closet and forgot about it until this came up," she said. "It's a very unusual gun, Raul says, and perfect for someone like me. It's called a shotgun pistol—or a revolving shotgun, can't remember which. You don't have to aim very well. Just point it in the general direction and it'll stop anything, at a fairly close range. They call it the Judge, Raul told me, *el Juez.*"

I walked slowly over to the bar and poured some very fine tequila into a glass.

"My dear friend," I said when I had sat back down, "I've never known you to be interested in guns. Whatever made you think this was a good idea?"

She slumped into her chair and looked diminished. "I know it doesn't sound like me, but when Totie found the gun and I remembered the other one and I showed it to Raul and he was impressed and promised to teach me to use it, I got carried away. Poor impulse control, I guess. That's one of the early signs of Alzheimer's."

Something happens when Kitty and Totie are alone together for too long. I looked over at Totie, who was still grinning.

"You're not serious about this idea?"

"I just think it's wonderful how much freedom we've taken on ourselves. Most old ladies just become victims; we've got a body-guard and a serious equalizer." She nodded at the gun, which I was now holding, checking to see if it was loaded. "We could be avengers," she said, exaggerating the word as we knew it from the television series.

Actually, peacenik that I am, the gun felt good in my hand. It has been my observation that nothing brings out the animal in us—some of us—like a gun. I guess Kitty was feeling that too.

"It'll stop anything within about twelve feet," she said.

"And what might that be for us?"

"An intruder?"

"That's what we have Sammy for," I countered.

"What if he shoots Sammy?"

"Mexican intruders don't usually carry guns. They want to get in and out without being noticed and carry off as much stuff as they can. We've taken precautions against that."

"Well, what if we find a snake in the yard, or a big rodent," Totie teased.

"We'll call someone."

"What if we get caught on the highway and they want to take our car and—"

"You guys are just making up what-ifs. We have a dog and a bodyguard of sorts. We don't need to be carrying a revolving shot-gun around. Period."

"You're right," Kitty said, "but I'd still like to learn to shoot it." As she spoke, she turned the gun over in her hand, put her finger on the trigger, and cupped her hand around the grip.

"Tell her why," Totie said slyly.

"It makes me feel powerful," she said in a confessional tone. "I don't have sex anymore, and this seems like the next best thing—something that goes off that I can control."

After the laughter had subsided, we agreed that Raul could teach us all to use the gun. Then it would stay locked up in the glove compartment, replacing the one Totie had found, and would only come out for shooting practice and real security emergencies, of which I hoped none were in our future.

XXI

*L*ynn's appearance on the scene was imminent, and we scurried around in preparation for her visit. She hadn't told us much, only a phone call to say she was coming, wasn't sure how long she would stay, and needed our help. She had made reservations at a downtown hotel, but we weren't having that, so she would stay with me in my room and her friend would take the guest quarters.

"Is this a woman friend, or a man?" I asked, but no one had a clue.

"It isn't like Lynn to spring a visit with a friend," I told them. "Maybe she met someone and wants to run him by us."

"No, her call sounded more serious than that," Totie said.

"More serious than a potential man in her life?"

"Just different," she said. "I think she wants to join our club."

"No way," Kitty said, "though it would put a different spin on things. I don't think she'd let us practice anymore. She's pretty adamant about thou shalt not kill."

But that's close to what Lynn had in mind. We met her at the airport, Raul and I, and she was pushing a wheelchair. I couldn't tell if it was a man or a woman, for the poor thing was so bent over I couldn't see the face, only the top of an old soft fishing hat and a pair of sturdy black tennis shoes. Raul did his job beautifully, positioning the car as close to the curb as possible, lifting the frail body into the backseat, and folding and packing the wheelchair, along with two good-sized bags. He greeted Lynn warmly and tucked her into the car as well, then slid smoothly into the traffic pattern that would take us across the hills and back to our paradise.

Lynn arranged a pillow behind her friend's shoulders so he could lean his head back a bit, and I saw the wan and wrinkled face of an elderly man. He was of an indeterminate age, his face colorless, his white hair unkempt, and his body small and shapeless beneath baggy pants and a shirt many sizes too large. His eyes fluttered and closed.

"Theo's tired," she told me. "He'll rest on the drive, and then you can have a chance to meet him properly."

On the drive home, she told me his story. He had been a Catholic priest for twenty-five years and then, in a crisis of faith, had left the church and went on to teach. But he missed it—the loving community, the reverence for life, the reading and study and discussion—even though it had become increasingly meaningless to him.

"Theo says we can be cocreators by sifting through all the ways of looking at the world and choosing that which most rings true to us," Lynn told me, her brown eyes shining. "I've tried so hard to accept what others told me was the truth, the only truth, even when I found contradictions and what seemed like concocted arguments. He's actually set me free."

This, coming from Lynn? Was she inviting my thoughts on the subject?

"I don't believe anyone understands the mystery of creation any more than we understand the vagaries of human nature or the secrets of a seed," I said. "We can be in awe, we can seek enlightenment, but questioning is very threatening to those who believe in a big daddy in the sky."

"It's okay to say God," she told me with a slight frown, and I could see that my irreverence still bothered her. "Theo taught philosophy after he left the priesthood. He says the search is important, because the closer we can come to living in tune with our beliefs, the more at peace we'll be. And that peace, he says, is like being saved or the dream of everlasting life."

"I think I live in tune with my beliefs," I said.

"Do you believe in the value of all living creatures?" she asked.

"Sure."

"Then why do you eat meat when other protein is available?"

"Well, I like it, and even if I stopped, people would still eat meat. Have you gone vegetarian?"

"Not yet," Lynn said, "but I'm thinking about it. It started back in ancient India and was more about nonviolence to animals than any particular diet program. It all ties in with respect for the environment. Do you know how much carbon went into the atmosphere for Theo and me to fly here?"

I shook my head no. This was a new Lynn talking.

"More than anything else I'll do for the rest of the year," she said.

"But you chose to come," I said, trying to figure out her point.

"Yes, on one-way tickets."

I had seldom seen Lynn so imbued with enthusiasm. She loved her art, she had loved a number of men, and she had always read widely, but she wasn't one to pick up a new set of values and take off like a skyrocket. She had long been a devout Christian, without beating anyone over the head with it. Although she hadn't taken instructions with the other girls, she had romanticized those Catholic boys just like the rest of us. That is not to imply that Theo resembled a boy in any way.

At the house, she hovered over him, making certain he was comfortably arranged in his room and, later, bringing him out to visit with us all around the pool. He walked with the help of a walker, which had yellow tennis balls on the wheels, along with a light and a horn.

"Just so you'll know I'm coming," he joked softly.

Lynn hadn't told us much after they arrived other than to assure Totie that he wasn't a potential boyfriend.

"That's the farthest thing from my mind." She smiled mysteriously, almost beatifically.

"So what are you two up to?" Kitty asked bluntly.

"I want him to tell you," Lynn said.

It was wine time before the two were settled in and introduced to Gracie, who nodded a brief hello and scurried back into her kitchen. Sammy had taken a great liking to his man guest and sat quietly at his feet, licking the hand Theo offered.

"You're very gracious to accept me into your beautiful home." He spoke hoarsely, but his eyes danced about, taking in everything with clear appreciation. "You may not feel so welcoming when you find out why I'm here."

"And that is?" Kitty asked. I could read the impatience in her tone, but perhaps he couldn't.

"I want you to help me slip away into the next adventure. Lynn says you three have a pact and that you've thought this through. I'd like to be your test case."

"Too late," Totie whispered.

Lynn looked at me, questioning. We hadn't told her about the *payasos*, hadn't told anyone, but why was she telling this sweet old man our private business?

"I know I was against it when you all came up with the idea, but then I met Theo." She reached over and patted his hand. "And he's taught me so much and he's so wise and…" She paused then, and he took over.

"I've decided it's time to go, and my last act as a rational being will be to arrange my own passage. My body is disintegrating daily from osteoarthritis and complications therefrom. The pain is intense, and I'm taking increasingly stronger medications, which render me worthless for most of the day. There's no meaningful work I can do and no relief in sight."

"Family?" Kitty asked.

"None left," he said. I was the eldest of a big family, but I've outlived them all—two brothers, three sisters, and eight wonderful dogs over the past eighty-nine years." He patted Sammy, who wagged his tail vigorously, as if volunteering for something.

"Does this fellow have a ball?" he asked, and at the word, Sammy ran off to see if he could find one.

"He's tried everything," Lynn said. "Oral drugs, injections, topical treatment, acupuncture, mud packs, glucosamine—"

"And I'm down to morphine. There will be no more procedures and no more experiments. I shall simply slip away, with your help."

"Theo brought his own medicine. He has loads of pills that he's been hoarding," Lynn said, "but he wanted—"

"One last party," Theo said, rolling Sammy's ball as far as he could manage across the pavers that surrounded the pool.

"Now you're talking." Totie grinned.

"I'd like to go fishing," Theo said, "in beautiful Lake Chapala."

Lynn had discovered Theo in a nursing home where she was doing volunteer work. She recounted their meeting after he was settled in his bedroom for the evening.

"'What's a beautiful lady like you doing in a place like this?' was the first thing he said to me and won me over immediately."

"We're all suckers for flattery," Totie said.

Lynn ignored her. "So we started talking, and the more we talked, the more fascinated I became. He has the brightest of minds trapped in that shrunken little body. Reminds me of that British genius guy who's so disabled."

"Stephen Hawking," Kitty filled in. "One of the smartest men in the world?"

"I don't know where Theo ranks," Lynn said in exasperation. "I only know that he's the smartest man I've ever come across. And he never complains. When the pain gets too bad, he kind of disappears into a trance, something he learned from his Buddhist friends."

It seemed that Lynn had spent increasing hours in conversation with Theo, and he had convinced her to let him come with her to a warm and beautiful place where he could go fishing one last time. "He's changed my idea of God and Heaven, and even good and evil," she told us.

"You're in love." Totie laughed.

"This isn't funny. Will you all help me help him?"

"Of course we will, sweetie," Totie said. "That's what we're here for."

I looked over at Kitty.

"If he has enough morphine, it should be easy. We only have to figure out how to get rid of the body."

"He has an idea for that," Lynn said. "He wants us to tie a weight to him and roll him out of the fishing boat."

It was decided that Theo's fishing party would take place after Totie's play. Finding great pleasure in the irony of her performing *Arsenic and Old Lace*, he spent a few minutes each day going over her lines and laughing together at her ad-libs. He spent as much time as he could in the garden, with Sammy by his side, and each evening at dinner, he entertained us with stories of eating a hibiscus or chasing a hummingbird, from Sammy's point of view. He talked to us about the religious implications of democracy, the relativity of worldviews, and the limitations of language. And he told us jokes.

"Sammy's a very smart dog, but I bet you didn't know he has a sense of humor. He told me he once applied for a job as a secretary at a multinational corporation. Passed the typing and computer tests with flying colors, and got a private interview where they asked if he spoke any foreign languages. And his answer was, 'Meow.'"

Having Theo around was surprisingly joyful. He seemed to have let go of his ego so that the frailties of the body, while so limiting, were neither an embarrassment nor a source of anger. He found pleasure in everything: Gracie's Mexican ballads, Lynn's sketches, church bells, frogs in the swimming pool, Kitty's vegetables, firecracker eruptions at dawn, Fernando's soft whistle, Sammy's kisses. He never left the compound, by design. It would be easier, he thought, if no one but those who came inside the walls knew of his presence. Less to explain, he said, when he was gone.

Down the road, toward the next village to the west, was a dock where fishing boats could be rented. Kitty passed it on the way to the organic farm where she was helping teach sustainable farming methods to the locals. She had Raul stop one day, and they found a party boat that could be rented for the day for a reasonable price. Raul, of course, knew how to drive it.

"You're wonderful," she told him.

"I thought you'd be mad since I haven't been able to get that medicine."

"What medicine?"

"The one for the big dogs," he told her. "I thought you'd be needing it for Mr. Theo, and señora, it's hard to come by. I have someone working on it."

"Oh, yes, that medicine. Well, you can keep looking for it, but we have another plan for Mr. Theo. And Raul, did I tell you I'm going to leave the house to you?"

Raul came to me in confidence.

"Is Ms. Keety okay?"

"I think so. Why do you ask?"

"She ask me to get big medicine and then she forgets, and then she tells me she wants to leave the house to me. What exactly does that mean?"

"She's talking about buying my half of the house and changing her will so she can leave the house to you. Her children don't seem interested, and you've done so much for us."

He smiled, suddenly relaxed and back in charge. "Sometimes I wonder where we are going and how it will all work out, and I know I must trust, but sometimes old people—forgive me, señora—get confused and sometimes it's hard to tell, especially when the language is different, and the way of life, that's different too."

"I know, Raul. We're all tied together here with a thin thread, like painting on a ceiling, and if someone takes the ladder away, we'll be hanging by the brush." As I spoke, I acted out the vision I was describing, and I saw, by his smile, that he understood. Whether he made the connection with our tenuous relationship, I'll never know.

Totie had a panic attack on opening night. Raul knocked on my door two hours before showtime and motioned for me to come to her room, where she lay, fully dressed, in the fetal position.

"Can't do it, Allie," she croaked.

"Get up, Totie."

"I can't," she insisted. "I'm paralyzed with fear."

"What could you possibly fear at this stage?"

"Making a fool of myself."

I laughed.

"It's not funny," she said tearfully.

"Only because making a fool of yourself is something you do regularly, just to see people laugh."

"I know."

"So what's the deal?"

"What if I forget my lines?"

"Just act like the old lady you are in the play. If you forget your lines, throw in something and scratch your head and let Vanessa help you out of it."

"Throw in something? Like what?"

"What's that word you use when you don't like what we're talking about?"

"Bumbershoot?"

"That's it. Just throw in *bumbershoot*. That should be good for a laugh."

"What if I forget *bumbershoot?*"

"Then we'll have to shoot you. Now, get up and get going."

When I left the room, she was touching up her makeup and practicing her newest favorite word, which she did *throw in* a couple of times, to the delight of the audience.

"I didn't forget anything," she told me later, "but I used the word anyway, just for fun."

Totie was the toast of the town for the run of the play, a period of two weeks, during which time Kitty was operated on for colon cancer, Theo perked up, and Lynn fell in love. I was the only one functioning normally, thank goodness, for there was much to observe and record.

XXII

I had noticed that Kitty didn't seem to be eating much and her face looked thinner. When I asked her about it, she changed the subject. When I suggested a visit with Dr. Ferrano, she scoffed.

"Remember how he dissed me last time?"

"You're overly sensitive. And when you did what he suggested, you felt better," I reminded her.

Still, she postponed going. I raised the issue again, insisting I could tell she wasn't feeling well.

"Half the world's work is done by people who aren't feeling very well," she shot back.

"That sounds like something your mother would say."

"Did say. We weren't allowed to mope around, feeling bad. Either you're sick and you go to bed until you get well or you get up and get going, like most of the people in the world."

I had no answer for that, except that I was sure she'd know when it was time to get some help. When she did finally go, she got more attention than she wanted. Dr. F. sent her that day to a hospital in Guadalajara for tests and kept her there for surgery, which involved resectioning and removing the diseased part of the colon and reattaching it to ensure normal bowel function. It happened so fast the household was put into a spin. Kitty was certain she would die on the table. She even wished for it openly.

"I've seen resectioning gone bad," she told us. "Colostomy bags, infection, putrid smells, total loss of privacy, someone looking up your butt all the time."

"Hush," Lynn told her. "You're in good shape, and you have a good doctor, and all you need now is a good attitude."

Lying in the hospital bed, Kitty looked small and chastened. Her face was drawn, colorless without makeup; her usually bright eyes, slightly glazed from medication, seemed to plead for reassurance.

"Dr. Ferrano says your chances for a complete recovery are about ninety-three percent."

"If I survive the anesthesia," Kitty mumbled. "And I never changed my will to give the house to Raul."

"I know that's what you want, trust me," I told her. "Our pact is about taking care of each other. You just never thought you'd be the one to be taken care of. Relax and let us keep things going for a while."

She finally closed her eyes and drifted off. Kitty had always been a flurry of activity. It was strange seeing her lie there, helpless and frightened. I had seen the others take to their beds for various reasons, but never Kitty. If I had believed it would help, I would have prayed to some god or goddess to miraculously heal her, but what I knew in my heart was that something's going to get each of us, and it may not be pretty. If she came through this, but then got home and had an infection or complications and said she was ready to cash it in, could I do the deed? Give her the potion? Hell, we didn't even have a potion yet. And Theo was waiting in the wings.

"Raul," I said on the way home, "we need to get that medicine."

He nodded and kissed the cross he wore around his neck.

Three days later, we brought Kitty home. She had come through the surgery quite well, and Dr. Ferrano agreed to her coming home a little early because he could stop in at the casa daily to check on her. The colostomy bag was a problem, however.

"This is what I get for always being involved with my bowels," she grumbled, but she learned to clean and change it herself. The procedure was reversible. If all went well, she would only have it for twelve weeks, and neither radiation nor chemotherapy were called for. They had gotten it early. The good doctor stopped in every day and urged Kitty along. She came, grudgingly. He checked on Theo as well, consulting on his medications and offering various suggestions for relief from the pain with which he struggled.

In the mornings about 10:00 and afternoons around 3:00, Theo and Kitty could be found sitting in the garden, talking. There was little Kitty loved more than a good conversation, and to that end, Theo was a godsend. He also brightened at finding an inquiring student who sat, quite literally, at his feet, smiling up, asking questions, formulating what-ifs, and repeating responses in a new format, just to be sure she had understood. They had created an ideal meeting area where Theo could stretch out comfortably on a chaise, lying on his side with a pillow between his knees and others behind his back. Kitty, still agile, rested on the ground on a cushioned throw, sitting or lying so that the two could easily maintain eye contact as they talked philosophy.

It was too much talk for Lynn, who had already experienced the joys of Theo's beautiful mind and wasn't much for prolonged conversations. She had started volunteering at the local orphanage three days a week, and often, on those days, she brought home a child to swim in the pool with her, play ball with Sammy, and share an ice cream cone.

Totie, who had dedicated her last performances to her dear friend Kitty, was resting up from the pressures of her stage life and busy shuffling numerous social invitations. Everyone, it seemed, at least those on the social scene, wanted her to come to breakfast, lunch, or dinner.

"I had no idea there were so many clubs and events and parties here," she said. "This is as bad as Galveston. When I first moved there, I felt like fresh meat."

"Don't tell us you don't like it," Lynn said.

"Of course I like it," she said, "but been there, done that. I *vant* to be alone." She put the back of her hand on her forehead and closed her eyes.

"I don't believe that either," I said.

"Girls, I don't know what I want other than for Kitty to get well and us to keep on having a good time together." She slipped from her dramatic role easily. "But Truman has asked me to go with him and Butterfly to Cuba, and I'm thinking of doing it."

"Why?" I asked, amazed she'd consider it.

"Well, he needs some help. She wants me to go too. Says I make her laugh. And if I get away for a while, these people in town will forget about me. Besides, I've never been to Cuba, and I've always wanted to go. Tru said he'd take us dancing at the Tropicana. Isn't that exotic?"

"And when might that be?"

"Next Friday."

Somewhere during this time, I tried to recreate our original vision. We came to Mexico with the idea that we would take control of our lives, but they were flying about in many directions, and I didn't even know if it was a good thing or a bad one. Lack of control is always unnerving, but Kitty, the control freak among us, was the most detached. One morning, after my walk, I sat down with her and Theo.

"I've been wondering about Theo's last party." I turned to him and smiled, and he smiled back sweetly. "I don't mean to bring up anything unpleasant."

He waved away the idea. "It's very much on our agenda."

"Oh?"

"Well, since Dr. Ferrano has been visiting Kitty regularly, and me as well, it's going to be hard for me to just disappear."

"I was thinking about that."

"So we have another plan." Kitty beamed. "Theo believes that whatever the body desires and the mind focuses on can be manifested. He has tons of examples, and we've been experimenting with some simple projections, and well, look at me. He's got me believing. Me, the biggest cynic, doubting Thomas, and doom-and-gloomer you know."

"She's not really all doom and gloom," Theo spoke up protectively. "Her left brain was scientifically trained, and no one ever opened her up to other possibilities, which she had characterized as magical thinking."

"Until now," Kitty said. "But the mind is more powerful than we think. We just haven't explored it sufficiently."

"And your plan?"

"It's not exactly a plan," Theo said. "Just an affirmation."

"And I'm his partner, helping along the affirmation," Kitty said. "There's significant evidence that two voices are more than twice as good as one in influencing outcomes. Here"—she reached up and took hold of both of Theo's hands—"we'll show you."

They closed their eyes and repeated in unison the following words from, of all places, *The Gambler*:

Every hand's a winner
and every hand's a loser
and the best thing I could wish for
is to die in my sleep.

Then they opened their eyes, looked at each other, and laughed heartily.

"It will work, I'm sure." Theo smiled. "Kitty came up with the words, and we say it at least three times a day."

"It feels very peaceful," Kitty said. "Much better than taking a potion."

"But what if it doesn't work?"

"Oh, it will work," Theo said. "Part of the concept is that you let go of doubt."

Later that evening, I talked it over with Lynn, who wasn't surprised. Theo had discussed it with her as well, but she wasn't willing to be a party to it.

"You can't orchestrate your own death," she told me. "That's why I brought him down here, but it looks like he's won a convert."

"Jealous?" I asked.

"A little. I wish I could have brought him the pleasure she's brought him, but the timing wasn't right. She got sick and needed something new to concentrate on, and honestly, she's a more devoted pupil than I was. I just loved the person and felt bad for how alone he was. I wanted to pay him back for freeing me from all that religious baggage. But when he said he drew from all spiritual teachings, I didn't suspect that included country and western songs."

"Do you think it will work?"

She shrugged. "I have no idea."

"I still think getting rid of the body will be a problem," I said, remembering that we had already called the authorities for one elderly gentleman stranger. While the police were fully enmeshed in their own system, they weren't stupid.

"I guess so, but I'm leaving that up to them."

Lynn was jealous. But she also had something new and wonderful in her life, and that was Julia (*Hoolia*, in Spanish). This was Lynn's new orphan friend, a young eleven-year-old whose grandmother had brought her to the orphanage because she felt it would be a safer place for her. The mother had died from a respiratory infection, and the father had gone to Mexico City to look for work. The grandparents lived in a three-room, dirt-floored house at the lake's edge, where two young uncles also lived and raised fighting cocks. The girl, coming of age, was a problem in a household where young men at the edge of the law came and went at all hours of the day and night.

Julia was thin, with high cheekbones and long hair as dark and shiny as a grackle's wing, and she was just budding into womanhood. In spite of all she might have seen, she gave off a shy innocence. She spoke a little pidgin English, but Lynn was determined to help her speak and understand properly. They spent hours together, swimming in the pool, dancing on the lawn, catching crickets, and raiding the kitchen for snacks. Lynn bought clothes for her, washed and braided her hair, gave her vitamins, read to her from English-Spanish picture books. Soon, it became a problem at the orphanage that Julia was getting special attention, and Lynn was asked to limit visits to on-site.

"My other option is to take her for the next seven months," Lynn said.

"We can't do that," I told her. "Not with everything else that's going on here."

"I know." She looked forlorn. "But Kitty's doing really well, and so is Theo. Totie's off for a while"—she raised her eyebrows—"and said I could have her room until she got back. The people at the orphanage can only keep her until she's twelve, and then she goes back to either the grandmother or whoever will take her. Just think what we could do for her in that time."

"Let me think about it," I said.

Later that night, I took out a piece of paper and started to make a list of all the potential problems of adding Julia to our household. The worst thought that came to me was that the child might witness a death. One of us had cancer, one of us was praying to die in his sleep, and the other two were eighty-plus-year-old gringas who didn't drive and could barely speak the language. We were inefficient, but we had deep resources and some very loyal helpers, and nothing terrible seemed to be looming on the horizon. On the plus side, Julia would decorate our days, as only a sweet child could do. She was quiet and well behaved and devoted to Lynn. Still, a young girl has interests and energies we couldn't keep up with. What if she took a liking to the gardener's grandson? What if she slipped out at night and we couldn't find her? What if she invited children in to play in the pool and we couldn't make them leave? What if she played loud music while Theo or Lynn or Totie were napping? Where would she stay when Totie came home? Frankly, I didn't want a child in my room. Shouldn't we ask Totie? Would she go to school? Then Raul would be responsible for taking her and picking her up. Shouldn't we ask him? And Gracie would be cooking for her. Shouldn't we ask Gracie?

⌒

My mother, the youngest of five children, had an older sister (born in 1900) whom her brothers and their families referred to as Aunt Wee. When I was a girl, I thought it was a derogatory bathroom name. My mother called her by her given name, Della; to my sisters and me, she was Aunt Della. I later realized she was called Aunt Wee because she was quite short. Wee, as a term of size, had gone out of favor by the time I was hearing and pondering the word. Actually, I think they called her Wee to distinguish her from another sister, also small, whom they nicknamed Peewee. It wasn't a very gentle family. But that's another story.

In my middle years, when I was married with children, there was a buzz in my mother's family that my cousin's marriage was coming apart. His wife was going to Hollywood to pursue fame and fortune, and she was taking the ten-year-old girl with her. This left a boy of about eight, whom Aunt Wee had regularly kept over the years and was quite attached to. Della was unmarried and lived a quiet church-driven life in a small house on Mercer Street in West University Place, a city of modest homes within the city of Houston. She knew my boy cousin, the father in this tale, quite well, and though she was fond of him, she had good knowledge of the ways of men, especially men in their middle years, especially men who carried her family's name. They had animal tastes—of that, she was sure—and Della, well into her sixties, decided she could care for the boy child much better than his father. She wanted to adopt him.

My mother and my aunt Edna were against it and talked her out of it, and I agreed with their reasoning, though I thought it a very romantic idea—a childless woman and an abandoned boy finding a haven together. But I knew that raising children was hard work and not always satisfying. Boys without a strong father figure seemed particularly troubling, or so I had learned from divorced friends.

They play with themselves, sometimes at inappropriate times and places. They're interested in sex and naked women and will seek out whatever sources are available to satisfy this craving. They will rifle your liquor cabinet and medicine cabinets in search of promised thrills. They play in the street. They climb trees and fences and jump off bridges and often break their limbs. They love to play with fire. They are hungry to explore life and will slip into trouble at the slightest reckoning. They like to belch and fart and pick their noses and stash the residue under the bed, along with their chewing gum. They have little respect for tidiness or cleanliness. I didn't see how Della could possibly deal with such things. But beyond being intellectually and emotionally unprepared for raising a child, a woman her age lacked the stamina. Raising children involves many sleepless nights.

I shared my concerns with Lynn, who had been thinking about it as well.

"You're right. I let myself get carried away. We're too old to take in a child, unless she has no other options," she said. "And Julia actually likes it at the orphanage. Sure, she likes it here better, but it's causing a problem for her and so I'll just visit her there. I'll visit them all. There are many children there I like, and I've been neglecting them. I got carried away with the beauty and freshness of her. Nothing like little girls before they become big girls. I wanted to protect her from what lies in her future, probably a life of hard work and despair. If she could postpone getting pregnant, find a good man, and get trained in a profession, just think what she might become." Lynn sighed.

We both knew that life was demanding, intensely so for women and children who are poor.

Lynn did an amazing turnaround. She immediately stopped bringing Julia to the house and returned to visiting the orphanage three days a week. She walked in the mornings and painted in the courtyard in the afternoons, when the light was soft. I passed by one day and saw that she had sketched Theo and Kitty, philosophizing.

"You've really captured something," I told her.

"I know," she said. "I wish I could give it a name."

"*Energy*," I said. "*Radiant* would work too, but I think that was used to describe Wilbur the pig in *Charlotte's Web*."

She laughed. Bless Lynn.

Later that afternoon, when the two of us were alone, Lynn tried to describe the conversation she had overheard between Kitty and Theo.

"They were so intent, something about inviting a god to tea."

"I recognize that. I've even done it—invited Mara to tea. It's like when things are so bad you can't deal with them and you accost the bringer of bad things—Mara, in this case—and you say, 'Oh, here you are, and I see what you've brought. Would you like a cup of tea?' Actually, it's so very civilized, so in touch with the vagaries of the universe, so woo woo, I can't quite get there, but I salute the idea."

"I think I've invited Mara to tea a couple of times myself," Lynn said.

"I bet you probably have, and I'm impressed you recognize it in the Buddhist format. I had to read a whole book about it."

"Well, it works everywhere," she said, and took another sip of wine. "Sometimes you have to bring the enemy to the table."

So here we sat. Kitty was in recovery. Theo was in remission. Lynn was in resolution. I was in recognition. And Totie was in Cuba. She had flown there with Truman and Vanessa, and the plan was to return on a private sailboat. It was only a short sail from Cuba to Cancún, and they would fly back from there. She had called from Cuba to say they were having a wonderful time and that Truman and Butterfly were headed into the countryside the next day to see some farms. She had no interest in local farms and intended to sleep late and investigate the Hotel Nacional. It had great coffee shops and gift shops and lots of interesting characters. She also reported that she had never liked rum before, but mojitos were very light and she could drink two without a problem.

"That means she's tried at least three," Lynn said.

"She's not going to let alcohol become a problem," I said.

"Not unless she falls down and breaks her hip," Lynn said. "And then we'll all have to come to the rescue."

"That's what we do," I said.

She looked up and smiled. "I know."

Totie didn't fall down after four mojitos, although she spent the better part of the evening in the bar, having discovered a wonderful little trio for whom she insisted on buying drinks, and purchasing a large supply of their CDs to bring home to everyone she knew. What did happen to Totie on that trip that was unexpected and truly noteworthy was that she fell for Truman.

"Girls, I'm making no apologies," she told us when she had us alone together. "I'm just telling you, this is it. He loves me, unconditionally, and I can't resist. I've had a husband and a lover and heaven knows how many short-term connections in between. I thought I was through with all this man stuff, but Vanessa died on the boat. She was already seriously ill, and then she came down with an awful fever for a couple of days, and then she perked up a little and we thought she was improving, so we started out on the sailboat, and the first day, she died. And there we were, Truman and me together, with his wife dead on the boat, and the captain didn't have an icebox to put her in. That's what they do on cruise ships. Lots of old people die on cruise ships, did you know that? They have iceboxes to put them in, but anyway, this was a sailboat and there wasn't an icebox and she was just *dead*. And none of us knew what to do, but we managed. And that was so wonderful. To have a problem, and there's two of you, and you hold on and manage it. The captain was a player, but it was mostly us, Truman and me, and we thought about everything, talked about everything, about what a beautiful person she was and what she would have wanted, and of course, he was in the lead on this. He loved her, and she was gone, and I was there, and well, there it is. I know I don't have a very good track record, but I'm going for the gusto, girls, and he thinks I'm wonderful, and how often does that come along?"

Totie came back and moved into Truman's house. She called Raul every other day and had him bring her over to visit us. She sat with Kitty and Theo at times; other days, she spent her time with Lynn and me. She was aglow, disgustingly so. The lines in her face seemed to diminish, her eyes were alive, and her gait—well, it was certainly neither halting nor tentative.

Kitty dismissed Totie's romance as just another of her whims. "She'll be back in a few months," she announced.

Lynn found it ironic that Kitty couldn't see that she was under a similar spell with Theo. With interest and amusement, I watched the shifting positions of my compadres and tried to make sense of it all.

XXIII

$\mathcal{I}$ walked in the village, crossing the cobblestone streets with care, and found a bench in the square, beneath a blooming jacaranda tree. Here, the world was encapsulated for me, reduced to simple elements that spoke volumes. Workmen were attaching garlands of fresh flowers to the gazebo for Cinco de Mayo, the celebration of a victory against overwhelming odds. There would be fireworks and music and dancing here tomorrow night, another fiesta, another chance to revisit the essence of Mexican life and history.

Schoolgirls in plaid skirts and white shirts held hands as they skipped along the path that led to the church across the way. Bells high in the tower rang out the hour, competing with a stirring tenor voice from the loudspeaker on the bandstand that cried out another tale of undying love, the pain of separation, the heartbreak of deceit. Farmers with fresh vegetables manned their portable stands, tables with awnings to protect from the afternoon sun. Weathered women sat with crossed legs on their blankets, beaded jewelry displayed at their feet. Lavender blossoms that had fallen from the tree accented the brown feet of a barefoot child, no more than five. He passed by my bench, offering fresh raspberries for sale.

"Please." He looked at me plaintively, speaking the one word he knew in my language.

"*Cuanto cuesta?*" I asked, knowing I'd pay whatever price he quoted. I'd rinse the berries with Microdyn to kill potential germs, then crush them with olive oil, garlic, and balsamic vinegar to make salad dressing for tonight. I was already making a mental note to stop by the vegetable table and pick up fresh greens and tomatoes and maybe some green beans and an onion. Gracie knew I'd bring back something. I could never resist.

I wandered over to the outdoor café and ordered iced coffee. It was warm today, getting up toward 80 degrees, I would think. I didn't follow the weather much—not as a steady diet like I did back in Texas, where we were always anxious about rain, either too much or too little. Here, we knew the rain would come and there would be plenty. If you listened, you could hear the rain-birds singing.

The tables of the café were filled with gringos, mostly white-haired and tanned. As always, you could tell the tourists from the regulars by their dress and their cameras. I couldn't hold it against them, for the place was so full of beauty, so filled with Kodak moments, if you didn't have a camera with you, you wished for one. But I had become a regular here. Ernesto waited on me.

"*Café helado?*" he asked, knowing I took it cold when the weather was warm.

I nodded and smiled.

This village had become my home. Almost. I looked around at other regulars, and though I might not have known their names, we recognized each other. Sometimes, we sat at one another's tables; sometimes, we sat alone. Today, I sat alone. I watched a group of women walking out of the cultural center, fresh from what I knew was a Zumba class. Wet with perspiration, they laughed and chattered. I wondered what the Indian woman on her blanket thought as they stopped to check her wares.

Mexico would never be my home, but it was my refuge. I would always be a gringa, but I could love this place and honor the lake and the mountains and draw strength from them, bask in their peace and beauty. I could respect the people and treat them fairly and try to learn their language and accept their customs, even though waking up to those damn firecrackers to scare away the spirits was hard to take with a smile. I wondered, yet again, if this was where I wanted to spend my final days, and the answer was still yes. However, the priorities were shifting.

I thought back on my original rubric, my list of things without which life loses meaning: sex, driving, hearing, sight, mobility, clear thought, and continence. My seven deadlies, as it were. And I thought how wrong I had been. For instance, with Raul, none of us drove anymore. It wasn't a deprivation; it was a release. Granted, our financial situation made this possible, as it did the best technology in devices to improve hearing and sight. Barring unusual circumstances, we could all enjoy an acceptable level of both to the end of our days. There were technicalities that could also improve mobility, replacements for knees and hips, and aids like the motorized wheelchair we had rented for Theo. Thinking of Theo, I had to admit that it wasn't a lack of mobility that had brought him to desire a way out, but the constancy of pain. I needed to make a place for that.

And continence, or lack thereof? Look at Kitty. She had wanted to die rather than have a colostomy bag, but she'd learned to live with it. And she'd be getting rid of it soon. What was I to make of that? Was old age about learning to suck it up? Seeing how much you can take? I had already rejected that. I didn't have to, nor would I, be the toughest old bird on the block. But if it was about acceptance, the loss of ego, opening up to whatever came my way because I might find a new idea or a new friend or a new path to some level of bliss, then I must not rush into a premature ending.

I was seeing a paradigm shift, both in myself and in my friends. We had brought it on by changing our setting, pleasing ourselves, seeking new and even outrageous adventures, and here we all were, evolving still. Perhaps it was just stagnation that I had found so frightening. Hopelessness? Craziness, too. I had yet to deal with that.

The brain is an amazing regenerative organ. Stories abound where people relearned skills after injuries or strokes, yet the phenomenon of Alzheimer's remained astounding. Lulu had it now, full-blown, and whenever we went home, we heard about other friends who just weren't with it anymore. Could I leave instructions with my friends that when I could no longer remember a conversation we'd had within the last thirty minutes that it might be time for me to take my potion? Today, that seemed a reasonable test, but considering how my feelings had changed about my so-called tests, I was reluctant to put it into print. However, it could be like the Do Not Resuscitate papers we all had in our wills. If I lost "consciousness," as it were, then it would be time to throw a party and say good-bye. If only I had the potion.

I was on my second *café helado* when I saw Raul across the square. He walked toward me with casual elegance, and the young women's heads turned as he passed. A few of them knew him and called out his name. He responded with a wave, a hug, and a friendly *hola*. Since Kitty's operation and Totie's move, we hadn't needed him so much lately, and he had started a small business in the village, a custom jewelry store run by one of his female cousins. They designed and made silver jewelry, set semiprecious stones for pendants and bracelets, and repaired jewelry. He had first asked our opinions of what kind of store we thought would be appealing to the expats in the area, and when we had put our heads together and come up with the idea, he asked our permission to allow him to spend some time getting it started. He assured us he wouldn't let it interfere with his regular duties, and had been true to his word. He was always available by cell phone and seldom more than a few minutes away. It was rather fun for us to feel we had a connection to the latest new shop and had even offered some of our own stones to be reset and put on display in the windows.

Raul had stopped to talk with a young woman who looked quite familiar. I was struggling to place her when the two arrived at my table.

"Señora," Raul began, "you remember Lauren." He said it as a statement, not a question, and I appreciated his gentle assistance in the memory department.

I did indeed remember Lauren, the striking young woman whose youth and fresh beauty I had so briefly envied before the after-party swimming pool fiasco.

I held out my hand. "Hello, Lauren," I said coolly. I didn't really want to deal with her and wasn't too happy about Raul's seeming welcome.

"I'm so excited," she said. "Raul has agreed for me to sell my jewelry at *Las Joyas.*"

I looked up. "Oh?"

Raul nodded and smiled as if to say he could explain himself. "She has much talent at designing jewelry; she speaks good Spanish and has worked in shops before. I said I would let her try, but I cannot pay. She will work on, how you say, omission?"

"I know I was rude and just a mess when I was at your home," Lauren interjected, failing to take time to correct Raul, "but I had some serious problems that night."

"It would seem you did," I said.

"Ms. Allie, I had run away, I was frightened, I was out of money, had to find a place to stay, had lied about everything, and was frantic. That night, I had taken some prescription drugs for anxiety and started drinking, and I didn't even remember how I got home, especially in the condition I found myself. I'm so sorry. I have a wonderful boyfriend now who comes from a good family. He helped me straighten my life out, and I just want to apologize and tell you I'm not the person you met that night."

That was an understatement. I thought about my first impression of the young woman, how it seemed she had the world on a string, when she was actually, if she was now to be believed, holding on for dear life. How little we really know about each other, especially our first impressions. What would it cost me to give her another chance? Totie said she had turned around, and Raul seemed convinced. I guess we all go a little loco from time to time.

"Keep an eye on her," I told Raul on the way home.

He responded with a smile and the Spanish proverb *No hay mal que por bien no venga.* His message was that something good comes from everything bad that happens. He's a practical young man and not much of a philosophizer, so I wasn't sure if he was testing my Spanish or simply offering a rationale.

When we returned to the house that afternoon, I found Kitty and Theo in their places in the garden, softly chanting their mantra about him dying in his sleep. Kitty was recovering nicely, but Theo's upturn had reversed. He seemed paler and weaker than when he first came, and seldom ate more than a few bites at a time, despite Gracie's finest efforts to tempt his appetite. He did seem to enjoy *nieves*, fruit ices made of pureed fruit, sugar, and water. She always had a sherbet ready for him in a variety of flavors: lime, mango, blackberry, strawberry, peach, and even one made from the fruit of the cactus, the tuna. When he joined us at cocktail time, he would hold a serving of this in a margarita glass and sip from it as it melted.

That evening, after the chanting, Raul moved Theo's daybed over to the pool area, and I described for them the Cinco de Mayo preparations I had observed in the village.

"I've been here six weeks," Theo mused. "Never expected to stay so long. Used up most of my long-hoarded morphine." He looked over at Kitty. "But won't need it, after all."

Lynn reached over and patted his hand. "We're glad you're comfortable."

"Can't thank you ladies enough," he said. "It shouldn't be long now."

There was nothing to say, and so we all sat in silence for a while, sipping quietly, watching with respect as he slipped away from us and into a state somewhere between sleep and meditation.

"Hola," Totie's voice rang out, and Theo twitched.

"Shhh." Kitty put a hand to her lips.

Totie walked over and kissed Theo on the top of the head. "Hello, darling," she whispered, and he fluttered his eyelids. "Anyone have a hundred pesos for the cab?" She looked around. "I'm fresh out, and where's Raul? I need him to get my bags."

Totie was back, and sooner than we had expected. It had only been three weeks.

"It doesn't take long to figure out what's what," she said. "He adored me on the boat when we were playing that death scene, but when we got home—at his home—I was supposed to fill a different role. And, frankly, I didn't like the part he gave me. Too much about him—his granola for breakfast, his sore shoulder that needed a rub, his favorite restaurants, his need for absolute quiet after ten o'clock. My God, you know how I like to wander around in the night. Oh, no, we would have none of that. And he wore socks to bed. Argyles. I know, he's almost ninety and his feet were cold, but we all have our little prejudices and I don't like to see men wearing socks to bed. It's just wimpy."

She soon had us all laughing.

"And that's something else," she said. "He didn't laugh at anything I said. I even resorted to jokes, told him about the dietitian who asked her audience what single food caused the most grief and suffering for years after eating it, and the seventy-five-year-old man answered, 'Wedding cake.' He didn't go for that one. I know, he was mourning Butterfly, but you know I can't put up with too much mourning, and I've got a sore shoulder too, and I need to get in the hot tub and get a massage. My goodness, it's nice to be home."

Raul put Totie's bags in her room and carried Theo off to bed, and Kitty told us about a package she had received. There was a handmade card from one of the granddaughters, with a drawing of Petey, the large yellow-and-gray Social Flycatcher that graced our cupola every morning, securing his breakfast. It was quite an excellent reproduction, dubbed "framable" by both Lynn and Totie. The other two granddaughters had written a joint letter saying they had a good time and were very proud of their tans, and it was nice to come home from vacation thinner than they went, and they sure wished they could have some more of Gracie's flan, and thank Raul for taking them out in the boat. He was a *hottie*.

Her son had written a letter as well. It included a check to cover the cost of shipping their packages to France and a story about running into someone on the airplane who overheard they had been to Tapalpa and was very impressed. He also said that he liked Raul very much and felt that we women were safe and in good hands with him there.

I hope you'll do whatever is necessary to keep him satisfied with his job, he wrote. *Thank you, Mother, for a surprisingly successful trip. As I said, Mexico isn't my cup of tea, but you seem to have made it yours and I'm happy for you.*

"That's about the nicest thing he's said to me in years." Kitty wiped a tear from her eye. "Aren't people strange? When they were here, they acted disinterested and uncomfortable. You just never know."

"Maybe they got to thinking about you when you had the operation, and this was their way of voicing loving concern," I said.

"I didn't tell them about the operation."

"Don't you think you should?"

"What could they do? Make phone calls? Come back to sit with me?"

I nodded. They weren't likely to make her feel better, but I was surprised she hadn't told them.

"If you hadn't come through as well as you have, they'd really feel guilty."

She nodded. "That did cross my mind. Would have served them right."

"Now, Kitty," Lynn said in her disapproving voice, "you can't take pleasure in the pain of others."

"But you can celebrate when karma steps in," Totie piped up. "We all know what goes around, comes around, but it's rewarding to see it in living color."

"It's irrelevant at this stage," Kitty said, "now that they've surprised me with all this." She fingered the thank-you letters.

Lynn came to us the next day with an idea for Theo. He had wanted to go fishing, and we had made plans for a final fishing party on the lake, but things had changed and the shape of our plans had shifted. He had offered Kitty his remaining morphine, determined to prove that one could orchestrate one's own peaceful death. He was fading before our eyes, but it was difficult to watch.

"He needs a defining event," Lynn said. "We need to go fishing."

That night at cocktail hour, we advised Theo of our plan, set two days hence. He brightened and said he hoped he could join us. The next day, Raul went off to arrange for the party boat that docked west of Ajijic. It wasn't intended for fishing, but it met our needs well. We would be protected from the sun, and it easily handled the wheelchair. When Lynn worried aloud that they wouldn't let us bring our own food and drink or that fishing from the boat would be prohibited, Totie laughed.

"Darling, this is Mexico. Almost anything goes. That's why I love it so much."

"Surely there are rules," Lynn insisted. "The boat must be licensed and inspected and in good repair."

"It probably will be," Totie said. "Things work around here pretty well, but they work on a different game plan than ours. I always want to laugh when people want to fly American or United down here instead of a Mexican airline because they think it'll be safer and more efficient. I've never had a safety issue on a Mexican airline, and seldom a delay, which tells me they tend to the important stuff."

"But things do break down," Kitty said.

"And when they do, there's always someone around to give you a hand."

"So all I have to do is hope the boat doesn't sink?" Lynn offered sarcastically.

"Raul will check for life vests, and be sure there are plenty."

"Wouldn't that be great? All of us floating around in the lake in life vests while we wait for someone to rescue us." Totie laughed at her own suggestion.

"You're not putting me at ease," Lynn said.

"Sweetie, you just have to trust. This is Mexico. Anything can happen and sometimes does, but we have Raul and he runs interference for us, and it was you, after all, who wanted to plan a fishing party. What did you have in mind?"

"A good-sized covered boat, comfortable, with music and food and drinks, where Theo can enjoy the lake and we can drift and troll and spend a happy day together. I expected it would cost a pretty penny, but that's irrelevant."

"Well, you got it, and he figures it will be about a hundred bucks for all day. What's bothering you?"

"I thought it would take more arranging, and it should be one hundred dollars a head."

Totie looked over at Kitty and raised her eyebrows.

"Look at it this way, if we go down, we all go together."

"You too?" Lynn looked put out.

"They're teasing you," I told her. "This isn't Houston, and the locals aren't out to take advantage, especially if you have one of them on your side."

Lynn, apparently tired of the conversation, wandered in to coordinate food with Gracie, who always brightened at the idea of a party. Together, she and Lynn came up with a plan for chicken wings, fresh melon, chips and salsa, guacamole, cucumbers spread with fresh goat cheese, and cupcakes. Totie had taught Gracie to make cupcakes by pouring the batter into ice cream cones before baking. It was distinctly American, but Gracie had taken to the idea and always jumped at the chance to prepare them. They would be served with raspberry ice, Theo's favorite. Lynn then focused on decorations and other plans.

"I don't think Theo will be much into decorations," Totie told me, "but she wants to go all out. Me, I'm bringing the music."

Raul was in charge of getting fishing poles and bait. Kitty was mapping our course, and that left me with nothing to do.

"You're in charge of games," Lynn said.

XXIV

Thursday, May 7 dawned clear and warm. It was a comfortable 21 degrees Celsius when I walked Sammy, but I worried that, by afternoon, it would be uncomfortable. However, with protection from the sun, we wouldn't suffer, especially on the water. Theo also must have awakened earlier than usual, for he whistled to Sammy as we passed his door.

"How are you this morning?" I stood in the breezeway, speaking into his darkened room.

"Excited," he said in a husky whisper.

"That's the perfect answer, Theo."

"You have all been so kind to me."

"No more than you deserve."

He didn't answer, and I waited a moment, then moved away. On good days, he could dress himself, but it was much easier when Lynn helped him. I went to alert her that he was awake.

"He's up too early," she said. "He'll be tired before we leave."

"He'll take a nap and be refreshed," I said, trying to calm her.

Interesting, I thought, how small our lives had become. Once upon a time, we played our stories out on a big screen, flying across continents, making business decisions in seven-figure numbers, dancing all night, climbing mountains, nursing babies, planning huge parties, meeting deadlines that seemed ever so significant. Today, we were going on a fishing trip, and it was all consuming. Nothing else was more important, and that was an incredibly comforting thought.

A similar thought had come to me the night before as I was planning "games." Regardless of the age of the participant, games on a fishing trip must be simple. I Spy was on my list, as were cloud pictures and the memory game: "I'm going on a trip and taking a fill-in-the-blank." We would add to the list in alphabetical order, except that ours had to be Spanish nouns. No aardvarks would be allowed, but an *amiga* would be accepted, as would an *aspiradora* (vacuum cleaner).

The morning dragged by in spite of the bustle in the kitchen. Theo sat in the courtyard, dressed in a bright-yellow gown. Lynn, the lover of colors, had bought him some at the market, and he had immediately taken to wearing them because they were easy, cool, and comfortable. He wore beads as well, seeming to enjoy his new playful attitude toward dressing.

"I wore a priest's frock for years," he observed, "and crosses around my neck. It all made a statement to the public. Now, I'm just enjoying the freedom and the decoration. What used to confine me now sets me free."

I never knew if he was completely serious or just trying out new ideas on us, but it was always a pleasure to see what he had to offer. This morning, I confessed I was anxious to make the time pass, and he suggested I try to catch some butterflies, nodding in the direction of a net that hung on the wooden post of an arbor near the pool. I had seen that net many times, thinking it was something Fernando used to clean the pool, but Theo pointed out, with a twinkle, that the long windsock shape was intended to catch flying insects. With a little guidance, I quickly became adept at trapping butterflies by laying the net over them on the ground and then, as they rose to the top, grabbing the net from below. When I had succeeded in my first capture, I brought it over to where he was sitting, and working together, we transferred it to a clear plastic container.

"Ah, a Variegated Fritillary," he cooed, and I suppressed a giggle.

"Are you teasing me?"

"No, that's the real name. Isn't it wonderful?"

I nodded. "Do you know them all?"

"Actually, only a few, but some of the names are so playful I couldn't resist making their acquaintance, like the Theona Checkerspot and the Painted Lady. My favorites are the Swallowtails."

"One of my favorite writers was a butterfly enthusiast," I told him.

"Nabokov?" he asked, and I nodded. "So lovely to come across pure genius," he said. "Truly an affirmation of life's possibilities."

"Most people feel insignificant in the shadow of greatness," I offered, thinking of myself.

"Most people don't give themselves credit."

I suddenly realized this was my first real one-on-one lesson with Theo, and I was falling under his spell. As we transferred butterflies, our hands touched, and though his were cold, there was nevertheless an electric current that passed between us. I looked into his eyes and wanted to drown—well, at least swim.

"Ever been married, Theo?"

"Only to the church, and that turned out badly. I was quite reluctant to commit to anything after that."

"I'm sure you were sought after."

"Oh, yes. Women love a challenge, but I was elusive."

"Always celibate?"

He turned away. "I accepted the concept of detachment from worldly things at one time, and then I discarded it. I went from being a priest to an atheist in one whirlwind year."

"Any regrets?"

"My dear, never regrets. Life is one big adventure, and I've been a privileged player."

"Even in pain?"

"Especially in pain."

I shook my head. "I don't get that."

"Learn to love the questions," he said, "and someday you may live into the answers."

"I recognize that," I said, "but I don't really understand it."

He smiled. "Go catch another butterfly, my girl. We need a bunch to take with us."

"For bait?"

"No. For our party."

When I came back to proudly display my next catch, Theo had drifted off to a peaceful sleep. Gracie had brought him a midmorning fruit drink, and he nodded there in the wheelchair, with Sammy stretched out at his feet.

I hope he's dreaming of fishing, I thought, pleased that he seemed magically improved after the last few days of being so unresponsive.

I managed to fit the lovely creature I had bagged into the ventilated box we had rigged, which now housed six butterflies. We were ready for a celebration!

The first thing I noticed was Sammy, alternately licking and sniffing at Theo's hands, which rested in his lap. He went in search of Raul, who was occupied cleaning the van, and then returned to Theo and began his previous ministrations more energetically. Theo remained motionless, and a shiver of apprehension moved through me.

"Lynn," I called out in a less-than-steady voice, reluctant to approach the wheelchair, though I felt certain this was just my mind playing another game. Things don't happen like this. Theo didn't just die in his sleep.

Across the courtyard, I saw Lynn come out the kitchen door. She was dressed in a turquoise shirt, looking very festive. Her eyes met mine, questioningly.

"Can you check on Theo?"

"Let him rest. We won't be ready to leave for another thirty minutes."

"Please?" I called.

She took note of Sammy's strange behavior and moved toward me, quickening her step as she approached. I could see first concern, then incredulity cross her face. Just what I had experienced. When she reached Theo, she put her hand on his face in a familiar way and patted his cheek with enough force to get his attention.

"Wake up, my friend," she said softly, but there was no response.

We called the others. Kitty checked for a pulse as the rest of us watched, and then slowly shook her head.

"He did it," Totie whispered in a voice full of awe.

Raul crossed himself. Kitty reached out and took my hand; I reached for Lynn, who reached for Totie, who reached for Raul. Gracie had come from the kitchen and was standing at a respectful distance. Kitty motioned for her, and she approached hesitantly.

"Tell her this is exactly what he wanted," she said to Raul, "and we're going to celebrate."

Raul translated as Gracie shook her head and began to cry.

"No tears," Kitty commanded.

"*No lágrimas,*" Raul said firmly, and Gracie wiped her face with her apron.

After a few stunned minutes, Kitty said, "Let's go."

"And leave him here?" Lynn's voice was shaky, but determined.

"Of course not. We're taking him. Raul, can you get him in the van by yourself? If so, I'll bring the wheelchair. Gracie and Lynn, get the food. Yes, Gracie, you're coming also. Totie, be sure everything else is in the van—games, decorations, everything. And, Allie, you lock up."

She looked down at Sammy, who lay, belly to the ground, at Theo's feet, watching with eager eyes. "You too." She nodded, and he wiggled with excitement. He loved going in the van, but was seldom allowed.

Stunned, we all did as we were told. What in the world was she thinking?

When we left the driveway, Lynn asked her.

"Don't you think Theo would want us to continue?" Kitty asked her. "Didn't he always want to end up in the lake? This will be easy. We'll just slip him overboard. Totie, isn't that how you all did it with Vanessa?"

"Well, yes, but she died at sea, and we had no choice but to get rid of the body. How are you going to explain this?"

"I'll think of something," Kitty snapped.

A couple of miles down the road, Raul said, "Señora, I have an idea."

Bless Raul, always there when we needed him.

"The man at the boat dock is my friend and not too smart. I will tell him jokes while you ladies take the food and things from the van to the boat. Everyone will wear their hats, and don't look up. He won't count how many get on—just a bunch of gringas, I'll say, having a party. When we get off, one of you will ride in the chair. He won't count. Move around. Go back and back again. Look like you are more people."

We sat in silence as he spoke in Spanish to Gracie. It sounded like the same instructions, but my Spanish still wasn't good enough to follow it all, especially under stress.

I looked over at Gracie, whose face was impassive. "Does Gracie understand?" I asked Raul.

"Gracie is my cousin. She will do what I ask and not say nothing. She is a good girl, and she likes to work for you. She ask me about Mr. James, and where he went, and I tell her not to worry and not to say nothing and I will see that her boy goes to the private high school starting next year."

"We can take care of that," Kitty said.

My gracious, I thought. *What a tangled web we weave when first we practice to deceive.* So now we had expanded to include Gracie. What were we going to tell our friend Dr. Ferrano?

"We'll just tell Dr. F. the truth," Kitty said, as if reading my mind. "He won't like it. He's a stickler for rules, but he also has a soft heart and he'll know it's true that Theo would have wanted it this way."

"And it's better to ask forgiveness than permission," Totie added.

By the time we got to the boat, we had worked out most of the kinks. Raul drove up close to the dock where our party boat was waiting. Everyone put on their large straw hats and began unloading the car. Raul carried the heavy cooler with some of our food and drinks onto the boat, then came back, and while Kitty and I counted out cash to the man in the office, Raul and Lynn managed to get Theo into the wheelchair. Sammy moved back and forth between groups, his tail wagging wildly. Then we traded places and Raul began a conversation with the guy in the office while Lynn and I maneuvered the wheelchair across the planks that led to the boat. Lynn had buckled him into the chair, but his head kept lolling about, a grim fact that caused Totie to giggle, setting me off in a fit of nervous laughter.

"Get control of yourselves," Kitty barked. Still recovering from surgery, she wasn't up to handling the wheelchair, but she was still the boss.

Somehow, it all worked. Totie stretched decorations across the rails of the boat while Lynn and I made a few more trips between the boat and the van, trying to walk with varying attitudes. Gracie and Kitty poured champagne, and Raul, complete in a captain's hat, came aboard, with Sammy at his heels. Theo was positioned with his back to the dock, and we all lifted our glasses in his direction as we moved toward the center of Lake Chapala in search of deep, green waters.

The lake stretched for fifty miles along the border of the Mexican states of Jalisco and Michoacan and was approximately eight miles across. Kitty and I had taken a guided tour around the lake one long, touristy day, during which we made numerous stops in villages along the way. In each, a miracle had happened, and the people had commemorated the miracle with statues, murals, markers, and even a Jesus high, high in the air. Aside from the miracle, each village seemed indistinguishable, full of simple people at work, children at play, and posters announcing the next fiesta, soccer game, or traveling circus. The churches were more notable than the schools, decay more pervasive than growth. These were the twinkling lights we saw across the lake at night. Until that trip, I had imagined something more like the villages on the north side, something verdant and alive, drawing from the bountiful source of water, the rich growing season, the geological formations, and the human history, but the far side seemed yet untapped and showed few signs of modern development.

Cell phones abound, of course, as did aged autos and cheap labor. Year-round, on farmland that bordered the lake, Driscoll Farms raised tasty blueberries, strawberries, and raspberries beneath plastic tenting, and shipped them to remote markets. Despite Mexico's stabilizing economy, emerging middle class, rich resources, and pockets of polished excellence, it remained a land of paradox, contradictions, and superstition.

Lake Chapala was celebrated in story, ritual, murals, and folk art. Mythical in stature, she was the mother, source of life, giver of abundance. And as I glided across her smooth surface with three of my dearest friends, two trusted employees, a beloved dog, and a dead man, I was called back to the present. We had all been silent, calmed by the motion of the boat and the actuality of being suspended in this notable body of water that had seen more serious dramas than our small play of the day.

We are too old for this kind of excitement, I tell myself, *yet here we are.*

"As the person in charge of games," I announced, "I think it's time to study the sky and see what we might find among the clouds." We stared up into a haze. There was not a cloud to be seen.

"Sorry." I gulped, embarrassed that I hadn't checked that game out before I started it. "Okay. New game. We're going to play I Spy, and I spy something..." I looked around, and nothing stood out. There were brown mountains, gray-green water, and blackish birds. "Never mind."

"I'd like to talk about Theo," Lynn said.

"Me too," Totie said, and Kitty nodded.

"Okay. Let's each come up with a word we think best describes him," I said, determined to fulfill my role as game person.

"He was *inspiring* to me," Lynn said. "No one has ever made me think so deeply without trying to change me."

"That was my word." Totie pouted. "But give me a minute, and I'll come up with another." She thought a minute. "He was *timeless.*"

We all nodded.

"I didn't know or care how old he was, or even whether he was male or female."

"He was spirit," Kitty said quietly. "Pure spirit."

"Just pure," I said.

"You don't do *pure*," Kitty said.

"I know. That's why I said it. He was a step beyond."

"*Un hombre muy fuerte*," Raul said, clenching his fist and raising it to the sky, and we recognized he was speaking to his strength of character.

"*Misterioso*," Gracie whispered, and we all smiled that she would understand and join our remembrance of Theo.

We then ate the lovely food that had been planned and prepared with care. Strange, to be eating in the presence of a dead man, and yet it seemed like one long communion, if one were to do such things. We came together to bless the food and share the moment and remember and be awed by the majesty of life and death. Totie reached behind her, pressed a button on her iPod, and suddenly, we were engulfed in the lovely strains of "Claire de Lune." The music was perfect. When had she had time to hunt that up? I looked over at her with the question in my eyes.

"It's my fave," she said. "I had a whole menu of upbeat stuff, but it doesn't seem fit."

A few minutes later, we slipped his body into the waiting water. Raul said it was a good place, about as deep as the lake got, and he tied some weights to his legs, just to be sure. The fish would have a feast, perhaps. Or maybe he would meet up with the green goddess of the lake, the beautiful source of life and sustenance, the one depicted in the mural in the city hall of Chapala. Theo would have liked that. With *Ave Maria* playing softly, I released the six butterflies caught just hours before, one beautiful thought from each of us present. There were no tears, only quiet on the way home—quiet, and a sense of accomplishment.

Now all we had to do was get off the boat with one less than when we started and not attract anyone's attention. Lynn was elected to ride in the wheelchair because she was small and somewhat like Theo in general shape. Gracie and I were to move quickly back and forth from the boat to the van, creating diversions, calling attention to ourselves this time, making sure no one was counting as we disembarked. It went off without a hitch. At least, it seemed to. If anyone had asked, Raul was going to say we let one off on the other side. *No problema.*

"How many cousins do you have, Raul?" I asked on the way home.

"I'm not sure. I never counted. My mother was one of eight and my father one of twelve. All but three are alive and have many children."

"That could be over a hundred. Do they all live in town?"

"No, señora. Just most of them. I didn't know Gracie until we met at the house."

"But now she's family and you're going to help her get her son into private school?"

"I see what good work she does. I see how much she wants to rise above. We help each other."

"You're a complicated guy, Raul."

"Not at all, señora," he said, slipping into his subservient role.

"*Soy anciana, pero no soy estúpida,*" I said to him, the equivalent of "I may be old, but I'm not stupid."

He dipped his head in embarrassment. "I know, señora," he said, "but there are things better not for you to know."

XXV

Exhausted physically and emotionally by the previous day's activities, we were all in need of quiet time. Totie remained in her room; Kitty puttered in the garden, separating and repotting plants that were crowding her favorite beds; Lynn set up her easel in a far corner of the garden and began sketching a mountain, still brown, but majestic, encircled by clouds, a white cross halfway up. Void of color, it was a distinct departure from her usual work. I walked into the village and down along the lake's edge, stopping for coffee at my favorite place on the square.

When I returned, Kitty had posted a note on the refrigerator.

MEETING TONIGHT - 6:00 P.M. SURPRISE GUEST

Oh my, I thought. *I'm not ready for any more surprises.* Yet something in me did a small flip. Interesting, how energy works and what anticipation does for the body as well as the mind.

Gracie had cleaned Theo's room, and Lynn had moved her things there. She had been sharing with me, apologetically, since Totie returned, and though we were seasoned roommates, it was good to reclaim my space. As I bathed and dressed for the evening, I suddenly noticed how bony my arms and legs were looking. I liked being thin, but not frail. What was happening to my body? I seriously looked at it in the mirror. Bad. I needed to eat more and get back to the gym. I had been careless in the last few weeks. Had this just happened in the last few weeks? I wondered. Or was I just focusing in? I stood up, shoulders back. That was a little better. Now I just looked like a thin eighty-year-old, not a shriveled one.

What else did I need? Color in my cheeks. I pinched my cheeks
and jumped up and down a couple of times. I fluffed my thinning
hair, smiled at myself in the mirror. Not very convincing. And then
I thought about Theo. He had been just a wisp of a person, but the
warmth and energy he exuded left us all enriched, happier, and
permanently changed.

Is it possible that at some point of enlightenment appearances
melt away and one becomes pure spirit? Isn't that what Kitty had
said about him? Pure spirit. Is that like Nirvana? And then, poof,
the candle goes out, and we disappear into the ether. I thought
about Sammy, who doesn't care how we look, only how we smell and
if we have a kind word or touch for him. Babies are the same way—
tiny ones. Of course, after a while, they respond to beauty, and lack
thereof, in people. I guess we're programmed that way. Fortunately,
I neither wanted nor needed to attract people anymore. I had my
friends and my family, and they found me acceptable. As for myself,
and my self-image, I'd just have to get over it.

I chose my favorite caftan, a soft royal blue; put on a bundle of
Mexican silver bracelets I had bought at the market, along with sap-
phire studs in my ears; and proceeded to do the best I could with
my face and hair. Tonight, I decided, I would eat a little more than
usual, and tomorrow, I would get back to the gym.

Living well is hard work, I thought, and then laughed at myself.

In the mirror, I saw my eyes light up, and realized something I
had briefly forgotten. Few things are better than a sense of humor.

We gathered in the courtyard at 6:00. Everyone had dressed
with care, it seemed. Gracie was gone, and Kitty was serving
wine. An assortment of healthy food was spread appealingly on
the table: fresh boiled shrimp, deviled eggs, guacamole, salsa,
assorted cheeses, tortilla chips, fresh pineapple and strawberries,
and chocolate dipping sauce, all covered with transparent tops
in a defense against random insects. A pitcher of fresh gazpacho
beckoned.

"Mmm." I nodded approvingly. "I was just thinking about food."

"Good. You're looking too thin," Kitty said dispassionately.

"And how are you feeling, Doctor?" I asked, just a little sarcastically

"Surprisingly well," she said. "Wouldn't have imagined I could have come back so far, so fast. If I could only get rid of this thing"—she patted the bag beneath her long dress—"I'd be great."

"So what's the deal?" Totie wasn't too fond of small talk.

"Yes, Kitty, we're all wondering what's up that other sleeve of yours." Lynn looked cautious.

"As I told you, I've invited a guest, and I want you all to go with me on this."

"Well, tell us," Totie said, letting her impatience show.

"Sit down," she ordered, and we did as we were told. Then she raised her wine glass and looked us each in the eye. "I thought we needed a little more closure on what we've just been through, so Raul contacted a medicine woman for me and is bringing her here tonight for a healing ceremony."

"Oh really?" Lynn rolled her eyes. "I don't know if I'm up for this. You should have asked us."

"I think it might be interesting," I said.

Lynn remained reluctant. "What if she does stuff we don't want? What if she won't go home when we're ready for her to leave? I've seen medicine men all over the world, and they're mostly performers. They do it for money."

"Two hours, that's all I ask. Let's give her two hours, and then Raul will take her back to her village, somewhere east of here, and we'll talk about it then."

"I can do two hours if I get to eat first," Totie said.

"I want you all to eat. We may need our strength."

"What do you know that we don't know?" Lynn asked.

"Only that it promises to be a bit intense and we need sustenance."

"Intense?" Lynn asked.

"I think she just means we need to be relaxed and open to the moment, and that works better with some food and wine," I said, hoping to ease the situation. I'd been living with Kitty for three years now, and had grown to appreciate her approach to this new culture. She was open, accepting, and ready to learn. Sometimes, she was disappointed; sometimes, she was entertained; sometimes, she was enlightened. Lynn hadn't been down that road with her. Maybe she didn't want to go, but I thought she ought to give it a try. Totie, of course, wasn't intimidated by anything—the weirder, the better.

About 7:00, we heard the van pull up in the driveway, and waited with building curiosity to meet the medicine woman. Small, brown, round, and wizened, she followed Raul into the courtyard, carrying a large woven bag.

"Señoras, this is Amaranta," he introduced us.

"*Mucho gusto,*" I said, holding out my hand.

She smiled and nodded, but didn't set down the bag.

"She doesn't speak Spanish," Raul said. "Only an indigenous language—a form of Nahuatl."

"How do you speak to her?" I asked.

"Mostly signs." He smiled.

"Does she know why she's here?" Kitty asked.

"She's a medicine woman. She'll figure it out," he said.

"Okay." Kitty took a deep breath. "Leave her with us and come back in an hour and a half." I noticed she had shortened the time. She motioned the woman over to the sitting area and held out her hand to invite her to sit.

Our guest approached slowly, looking around, taking in her surroundings. She sat on the ground, just off the pavers, and folded her legs beneath her, a position I'd observed so often in Indian women on the street.

Kitty and I looked at each other. What next?

It was Lynn who eased the situation. She brought the woman a glass of water and pulled up a chair to sit where she could face her. The rest of us arranged our garden chairs accordingly, all facing this stranger who sat and stared back at us. She was of an indeterminate age and quite striking in features: piercing eyes, full mouth, flat nose, and a single gray braid that hung to her waist. She sat proudly. We waited, for perhaps five minutes. I knew if I looked over at Totie, she'd make some subtle facial expression to mark the moment. I willed myself not to look.

Finally, the woman smiled. We smiled back. She folded her hands in front of her, prayer-like. We did the same. She began rocking gently, from side to side. We did the same. There we sat, smiling, hands in supplication. Kitty got up and brought another chair to the circle, then sat back down and resumed her position. The woman nodded. We all looked at the chair, looked back at the woman, and saw her eyes light with understanding. Someone was missing. She nodded again. Then she reached into her woven bag and brought out two drumsticks.

"Let's get this show on the road," Totie whispered softly.

The medicine woman looked sharply at Totie and shook her stick.

"Sorry," Totie mumbled, and lowered her head, chastised.

The woman began to tap single beats on the pavers. We began to answer by clapping our hands. Soon we were all moving in motion, and the pattern became increasingly complex, but the beat remained constant. We swayed and clapped for a time, and then she let out the most eerie of wails. Totie responded in kind. The woman nodded affirmation and called again. This time we all responded in kind. Then a different call. We responded. Soon we were half chanting, half wailing into the deep-purple sky.

Is this how you summon up spirits? I wondered. It felt so good.

Even Lynn, who doesn't like to sing, was giving it her best. This wasn't about performance; it was a calling out to whatever gods may be, a deep connection with the world of spirit. I was entranced, and so, it seemed, were my friends.

It came to a sudden end. Silence of the drumsticks. Silence of the voices. We sat in the almost darkness, and I thought I could hear my heart beat. From her woven bag, the medicine woman took a coconut shell with a rope attached on either side. From a small packet, she took some powder and placed it in the shell. Then, with a long phosphorus-tipped match, she lit the powder, and it sparked up, without a flame. She blew on it gently until the powder began to give off a fragrant smoke. Then she stood and beckoned us to follow, which, of course, we did.

She walked around the garden, expertly holding both ends of the rope and swinging the shell, much like priests spread incense. That was exactly what she was doing, I decided, spreading the smoke throughout, blessing the area, perhaps, or cleansing it of bad spirits, or simply marking it, as an animal marks its territory. Why do humans do such things? I have no idea, but it felt right, and it smelled beautiful. Whatever was smoldering in that shell was rich, elegant, and earthy, a blend of fruit and spices. I remember wishing it would settle in my clothes, and I wouldn't wash them for a long time.

As she walked, and we followed, she hummed softly, and from time to time, I could hear soft words, which, of course, I couldn't interpret, but they seemed a blessing. Around the perimeter of the garden we went, and then through the courtyard. She stopped, looking at Lynn, who had made the first bond, and raised her eyebrows in question. Lynn took her to Theo's room, now her own, opened the door, and accompanied her as she walked through the room.

Mine too, I thought, and touched her shoulder, guiding her to my bedroom.

Kitty and Totie had her bless their rooms as well. Then she returned to her place, and we watched as she placed her things back in her bag. Kitty approached her, holding her hands to her heart, head cocked to one side, as if to say she had been deeply touched. The woman's response was to hold her hands up to Kitty, palms out, as if warning her to stay away. Kitty stood very still, and after a moment, the woman approached her and touched her eyelids to close them. Then she began moving her hands in a rapid circular motion around Kitty's body, up and down, about an inch away, never touching, just appearing to stir the air that encircled her.

"She's fluffing her aura," Totie whispered. "I've had that done before. It's wonderful."

When the woman was through with Kitty, Totie presented herself, eyes closed, for fluffing. Lynn and I took our turns as well. It was incredibly comforting and energizing.

I imagine it was tiring as well, for when she was through, the woman sat down, drank her glass of water, and closed her eyes. When Raul came a short time later, she was still sitting there, and we were all stretched out as well, enjoying the night, with some of Totie's Peruvian flute music playing softly in the background.

Kitty took Raul aside.

"I need to know what I owe her."

"She doesn't take money," he said.

"Doesn't take money?" Kitty repeated, caught unawares.

"No, señora. She lives by barter. You must pay her with things she can use to support herself."

"Why didn't you tell me this before?"

"I didn't think it would be a problem."

Kitty motioned us all over into a huddle.

"She doesn't take money," she said. "Each of you go and get something you think she can use in a barter economy."

I went to my room, as if on a scavenger hunt, and brought back a blanket, some beads, some chocolate bars I had been saving for a special occasion, and two blouses I no longer wore because they seemed too young. The others had similar gifts: pens, ink, and a pad of drawing paper from Lynn; blue jeans, eye shadow, and pillows from Totie; gallon-sized baggies, safety pins, a pair of scissors, a needle and thread, and a kitchen knife from Kitty. We placed our gifts in a colorful carryall and presented them to the medicine woman, who still sat resting in the garden. She accepted the package with a smile and didn't look inside. I felt we had been generous, but who's to know? She had given us a wonderful evening and we had tried, on short notice, to reciprocate. When she and Raul left, we didn't even clear the dishes from the table. We simply went to bed.

When I returned from walking Sammy the next morning, everyone was at the table drinking coffee.

"Allie." Totie waved. "Get yourself over here and tell us what you thought."

I poured myself a second cup and came to the table.

"Amazing," I said. "Did everyone sleep as well as I did?"

They nodded.

"She was just beautiful," Lynn said. "I wish I had gotten a picture of her, but I'm going to try and paint her from memory."

"Sure changed your tune," Totie said.

"I reserve that right," she answered.

"Lynn was the first to communicate," I pointed out, a little irritated that Totie always had to have the last word. Turning to Lynn, I said, "You do that so well."

"For a minute, I thought we were all going to stand and look at each other all night."

"But she caught on fast," Totie said.

"That's what she does," Kitty said. "Reads signs."

"She did more than just figure out how to please us," I said. "I've heard magic described as the ability to change consciousness at will. Didn't she change our mind-set, dispel the ghosts of Theo, if you will, make us all feel better physically and spiritually?"

"Spiritually? What do you mean by that?" Totie asked.

"It's just a word," I said. "I use it to talk about serious things I don't have language for."

"Bumbershoot," she said.

I reached over to pat her well-padded thigh. "Except, I'm not afraid of it. How did you sleep?"

"Really well."

"And how do you feel today?"

"Really well."

"And does Amaranta get the credit?"

"Perhaps. Partly, at least."

"Without touching you or giving you any medicine?"

"Right." She nodded.

"So, what was that?"

"Magic," she said.

"An experience of the spirit rather than just the body?"

She paused, thinking. "Do you have to use that word?"

"Of course not."

"I'm wondering," Kitty said, "what Theo would have thought about her magic."

I had already considered that question. I think Theo would have told us his work was just exploring the powers of the mind. Hers was real magic.

"I googled 'fluffing the aura' this morning," Kitty said. "It's a fairly common practice. Some people even use feather dusters instead of their hands. One blogger said it looks and feels kind of silly, but it was positive. It makes people feel good, like a belly laugh, increases energy levels, and has the benefit of touch, without the invasion."

"I had my aura fluffed one time at a pagan ceremony in Austin," Totie said. "There was this event called the Harmonic Conversion. Remember that, back in the eighties?"

I nodded. "Vaguely. I'm surprised you would go for that."

"I went to a couple of their meetings. Loved the idea of being a pagan, but it involved more than I wanted to do."

"Most things do," Kitty said.

Totie stuck out her tongue.

"I feel younger," Lynn said.

"Because of last night?"

"Partly. Because of everything going on. Life is so different here. I'm surrounded by beauty. I don't feel rushed. I have time to think and to feel. What we just went through with Theo was incredible— can't imagine anything like that at home—and I thank you all so much for what you did, for him and for me."

"You could have kept him in your house and called in hospice and sat with him while he died, but he wouldn't have enjoyed his final days nearly as much. I'm sure of that," Kitty said.

"And you could have had him cremated and then spread his ashes with a little ceremony," I said, "but he wanted to sleep with the fish."

"Just for the record," Totie said, "I don't want to burn or sleep with the fish. I want a traditional burial, with a beautiful headstone that says *awesome* on it, and I want my peeps to visit me on the Day of the Dead and spread out a blanket and set out my favorite foods and have a party with me, just like they do it here."

"Duly noted," Kitty said, "but I want to get back to Lynn."

Totie made a pouty face. "So, Lynn, if you like it so much, are you going to stay?" she asked.

"I'm still thinking," she said. "I'd like to stay on for a while and see how it goes."

I was thinking that, a couple of weeks ago, she had been ready to take in a child and stay for however long that required. I had been going through such shifts ever since I came to Mexico. Something about taking that first step, leaving one's home and stepping into another culture, was quite freeing, if not unnerving. It might have seemed that we were opting for comfort. There was much talk about the material side of living in Mexico—maids, gardeners, and all kinds of services at a fraction of the cost in the States. But the comfort we all had found in this place was much more about a way of life—a pace, if you will—than about cost-effectiveness.

Having taken the step of moving here, I felt emboldened to make other major changes at will. Age so often limited our choices, but we had multiplied ours. It appeared to me that Kitty was here for the long haul. She had made her decision and wasn't likely to change. That was fine for Kitty. Totie, of course, could—and would—change in the flick of an eye. She'd been doing that for most of her life, and it didn't frighten her. I fell somewhere in between. My family was gently pressuring me to come home. I was resisting. Every day seemed a gift, and I wanted it to stay that way, but I knew it would change, and it's my nature to want to be prepared. Perhaps the most important lesson of this place, which I so dearly loved, was that you couldn't be prepared. You never know what's coming, so you must treasure the moment. What will be, will be. I just wished for that potion.

XXVI

*A*s I have often observed, life in Mexico moves in currents. Maybe it does the same in the States, but perhaps because there are more distractions there, the shifts are less easily discerned. Shortly after Lynn moved in, our sense of safety began to change. It began with a shootout in the next village.

Our small community, along with sister villages that form a link of habitation along the north side of the lake, had been relatively free of the drug-fueled violence experienced in other parts of Mexico, especially at the border. From time to time, reports of an occasional kidnapping, carjacking, or shootout in the area would reach our attention, but we weren't tuned in to daily news reports. Sometimes it was a week before we became aware of a "happening," and for the most part, such things involved Mexicans, not foreigners. They happened to people who drove fancy cars, or otherwise flaunted their wealth, or those on the highway late at night, making themselves vulnerable. We were sensitive to security, and we had Raul, whose knowledge and presence was our comfort and our safety. Or so we thought.

Lynn, who hadn't been here as long as we, was more nervous about the recent news than the rest of us. She still held tightly to her purse and approached new surroundings with caution. We, who had learned to carry our wallets in our pockets, were more relaxed. We knew which shops and restaurants were established and safe. Then, a few weeks after Theo's departure, we passed a newly arranged shrine of plastic flowers and a cross in the median of the main road in nearby Chapala. When we asked Raul about it, he told us it was for the city official who had been gunned down the previous week, after having lunch at a familiar restaurant.

"Right there?" I asked, appalled. I had heard talk of it, but seeing the spot, in the midst of mothers and children, vendors and shoppers, dogs and horses, bankers and cabdrivers, it seemed so unlikely. Perhaps it would happen again. Today.

Raul nodded.

It could happen anywhere, anytime, I realized. That's probably just what the bad guys wanted everyone to think. And they were successful. From that moment, a seed of serious unrest had been planted.

Raul surprised us one morning with an invitation to the shooting range. He had promised long ago to teach us to use the gun Kitty had found, and maybe, he proposed, this was a good time. Where he took us wasn't really a shooting range. It was a field that belonged to a friend, or a cousin, or someone he knew. There was a deserted shack and, behind it, mountains, appropriate for stopping errant bullets. Raul circled the area first to be sure no cows were grazing, and then he had us get out. On the hood of the van, he set the gun and a box of shells, then proceeded to open the revolver and load it. He took the shells out and had each of us open, load, and empty it in turn.

"I want to shoot," Totie said.

"I want to be sure I can load and unload this thing first. Is there a safety?" I asked.

Raul pointed to a button on the side. It had been a long time since I prepared to shoot a gun, and I felt a twinge of excitement. Or was it anxiety? Once we had gone through the loading routine, Raul put in six shells and handed it to Totie, pointing to what looked like a thick wooden wheel suspended by a rope from a tree about forty feet away.

"*No problema.*" She snorted and pulled the trigger, but no sound of contact was forthcoming.

"That thing really has a kick," she complained, rubbing her right wrist with her left hand.

Raul grinned, stood behind her, and showed her how to rest her right hand on her left for better control.

"Yeah, this is how they do it in the movies," she said, getting off another shot, which also missed. "Hold on, I'm getting the hang of it now," she called out, and tried again.

Still no sound of contact.

Raul turned to me. "How do you say *presionar?*"

"Squeeze," I said.

"Squeeze, Señora Totie," he said.

"I only have one more left in me," she said as she took careful aim, squeezed the trigger, and hit the wheel. She squealed in pleasure and handed the gun back to Raul. "Wouldn't want to do that very often. It hurts."

We all took our turns and all agreed we were glad to have the lesson but didn't look forward to using the thing. Raul assured us that no one, face-to-face with that gun, was likely to come near.

"It will destroy anything within fifteen feet when I put in the shotgun shells."

"Then why did you bring us for target practice?" I asked.

"I wanted you to be ready," he said, "just in case."

"And why didn't we get to shoot shotgun shells?" Totie complained. "I would have rung the bell every time."

"Too easy," Raul told her.

Raul had also suggested that we keep the gun in the house in a place where we could get to it easily. When I asked if we should keep it loaded, he grinned and nodded. We needed to tell Gracie then, I thought. I wouldn't want her coming across it by surprise when she was cleaning. We agreed we'd keep it in the kitchen, a central part of the house. Sammy, of course, was our first line of defense. But I was troubled by Raul's new attitude and behavior. He didn't keep as regular hours as he had before. Sometimes he didn't come home at all. He seemed preoccupied and was keeping the glove compartment locked when we were in the car. I felt sure he had another gun in there.

⟨⟩

It was about this time I realized I was going deaf. Kitty had been after me for weeks to have my hearing checked. She complained that she had to repeat everything she said, and I told her she was always walking away from me when she spoke. If she would just look at me and speak clearly, I could hear.

"Just have it checked," she implored, and handed me the name of a clinic in Guadalajara.

On the way into the city, I had a chance to talk with Raul alone.

"Something seems very wrong," I told him.

He shook his head and said nothing.

"If you have a problem, Raul, we all have a problem. Better to tell now than later."

I could almost see him arguing with himself. He was young and strong and in charge, and the last thing he wanted to do was confide in a woman, especially one he worked for.

"I may have to quit," he said finally.

My insides flipped. What would we do without him? He was irreplaceable—a link in our chain of life. "*Por qué?*" I asked why.

The story he told me came out partly in Spanish and partly in English, and it came out rapidly. I didn't hear it all and my head was reeling as he spoke, but generally, he was being pressured to deal in drugs and guns for a group he used to be a part of long ago, back when he was a teenager. He had run into some guys when he was in Guadalajara looking for the drug we wanted. They remembered him and tried to recruit him, promising lots of money. He told them he had a family and a good job and wanted to stay clean, but they kept calling. They threatened his family. He had been staying nights with his ex-wife and showing up at our place early in the morning. He worried that they'd find the house, come after him—or us. He worried about his son and even his ex-wife, who was either mean enough or stupid enough to tell them where he worked.

"But if you don't work for us, where will you work? What will you do?"

"I drive my van, señora, just like before."

"How can we help?"

He looked at me. "Perhaps a loan? Maybe I will fly my family to the US for vacation and they will stay for a while."

"That might work. Would you come back?"

He shrugged.

That was the day I found out I had a 50 percent hearing loss in one ear and a 70 percent loss in the other. I guess I had gotten pretty good at lipreading. There was some irony in the fact that loss of hearing was one of my seven deadly events and I had hardly noticed when it left me. Not that I was purely deaf. Just almost. The doctor wanted me to come in for hearing aids, and I wasn't too excited about that. I've always felt uncomfortable looking at those pink globs in people's ears. He assured me there were a variety of styles. Great! I wanted to check out those styles about as much as I wanted to try out the adult diapers I saw for sale at the *farmacia*. I take that back. The diapers were worse. Please, please, if I wear hearing aids, could I be spared diapers? Foolish thought, as if some unseen wizard stood behind the curtain deciding who was going to struggle with what. I reluctantly took some hearing aids home with me to test.

At dinner that night, I talked with the others about Raul.

"Of course we can lend him money to go to the States," Kitty said. "What should I do about gifting him the house?"

"I think that should be put on hold," Totie said, without even a chuckle.

"This is making me very uncomfortable." Lynn's regular Botox shots rendered her incapable of a full frown, but her mouth was a tight line.

"Bad things happen everywhere," I said. "We just need to be more cautious." Which had become my new word of choice. "We'll beef up our security, set up a system to alert each other, get some pepper spray for our bedrooms, and find a good home for the gun."

"I decided when I came down here I wouldn't be afraid," Totie said.

"Worst case, we get robbed," I said.

"Our money's in the bank," Kitty said. "Worst case, we get killed."

"We're here to die, anyway," I said softly.

Totie giggled, but Kitty continued to frown.

"I want a plan," she said, "and I want a replacement for Raul."

No one could replace Raul. We all knew that.

In a small village between ours and Guadalajara lies an even smaller village by the lovely and almost unpronounceable Indian name of Ixtlahuacan. It lies across the mountain, and we have occasionally driven over for dinner. A sleepy little place, it always seemed—that is, until a couple of weeks after the shooting in Chapala, when a car with various body parts of approximately twelve Mexicans was found by the side of the road there. It was surely gang-related violence, but why there? Was the danger so close, in our backyard? American and Canadian expats made a loud and unified call for action, like a flock of sheep with a wolf at the gate. A town meeting was called. The police were questioned. What were they going to do about this? The press got into it. A curfew was put into place so that no one was to be on the streets after dark. An emergency phone number promised police attention within ten minutes of a call. An anonymous hotline was established, and locals, who had born the brunt of the violence, were both fearful and angry. Unused to spying on their neighbors or reporting suspicious activity to unreliable police, they were caught in a dilemma of modern Mexican society.

We had a meeting with Raul and asked if he thought he could stay until Kitty had her colostomy bag removed and whatever reversal of systems was required. She had tried to tell me about it, but I hadn't wanted to hear. Sometimes deafness is a blessing. This was going to require numerous trips to Guadalajara and perhaps a week's stay in the hospital, and she wanted him to be around. He said he would stay on but would be looking for a replacement. Maybe his cousin who drove us the first time from the airport, he said.

"See if he's available," I said, but I wasn't sure about taking in a stranger.

We could rely on taxis for travel and be on our own for everything else. And then I thought of all the things Raul did for us, from tending bar at parties to hiring and overseeing workmen, translating with professionals, and dumping bodies. There would certainly be no more of that!

Kitty was strong and in good condition, but surgery at any age is rife with dangers. No one knew that better than Kitty—our medic, planner, and super-attentive attendee to detail. She held a meeting the night before she went into the hospital.

"I may not come out of this," she said.

"Boooooo," Totie let out a Bronx cheer.

"Let her talk, Totie," Lynn chided.

"Here's the deal," Kitty continued. "If I die on the table, I want my body to go to the medical school for research."

"You know the students will give you a nickname like 'Gertie,' and they'll be cutting you up into little parts, poring over your organs, pulling on your ligaments and tendons, squeezing you places even you've never been squeezed."

"Hush, Totie," I said.

Kitty ignored her. "If I come through it, and I expect to, my recovery may not be as easy as it was last time. You never know. I may come home and decide it's time, and I want you to be up for that."

"We don't have a potion," I moaned.

"I talked with Dr. F. yesterday, and he agreed to hook me up to an IV here on the third day so I can come home early and still be able to get liquid food and antibiotics with just a local nurse.

So, Allie"—she focused on me—"you need to arrange to rent the equipment through the local clinic."

I nodded.

"And, Totie, you need to do your phenobarb plea at the doctor's again."

"All someone must do is pour the phenobarb into the line, and I'll slip away. I can probably talk you through it."

Tears were running down Lynn's face.

"None of that," Kitty said. "You'll be doing me a favor."

"It's still painful," Lynn said, "just contemplating the whole scene."

"Was it sad with Theo?"

"Not really."

"Because he wasn't sad. So do I look sad?"

"You look bossy," Totie said.

Kitty gave us a smile. "That's how you'll always remember me. So now get us some wine. I'm not going to be able to drink for a couple of weeks, if I'm lucky. Oh yeah, and I pulled out the old will, the one that leaves the house to my kids, and put today's date and my signature on the envelope so you'll know which one to use."

Kitty came through just fine. Lynn spent the entire time with her at the hospital, and as one who had once been a doctor's wife, she was satisfied, even surprised, at the level of competent and compassionate care she had received. On the third day, Raul brought them both home, and Dr. F. came to check on her and set up the IV. Afterward, he sat to enjoy a cool fruit drink in the garden.

"What ever happened to that fine gentleman who was visiting you?" he asked.

"Theo?" Lynn asked innocently. She lowered her eyes. "He died in his sleep."

"What a blessing," the doctor said, and my pulse quickened, fearing his next question.

"Doctor," Totie interrupted, "watch and tell me if I'm doing this right." She got up and started goose-stepping broadly around the pool in front of him.

Lynn and I laughed.

"They laugh whenever I do it," she complained.

Dr. F. got up, took her hand, and they goose-stepped together. "Maybe you're exaggerating it a bit much," he said. "You'll be sore if you do that for long."

"Like this, then?" She smiled and lessened her ferocity.

"More juice, Doctor?" I asked.

"No, thanks, I need to get back to the office. Keep up that pace," he called to Totie as he gathered his bag and Lynn and I walked him to the door.

When we returned to the pool, Totie, collapsed in a chair, gave us a thumbs-up.

When I thought about what Kitty had been through, I gained new respect for her. Starting with the original pain and discomfort, through the first operation, through three months of a bag into which her intestines drained (a bag that she had to manipulate, empty, and clean), followed by another operation of reconnection, and finally down to recovery and whatever trials lay in store as she came to deal with a shortened digestive tract, she had handled it all courageously. I didn't even like to think about it. I would have surely complained and been fearful and felt sorry for myself. I hoped that some of her practicality and self-containment had rubbed off on me. I made a decision right there to settle on a hearing aid and let go of my vanity. Hadn't I decided that second part before?

Since I didn't want my devices to be visible, the preferred style was the type that fit completely in the ear canal. I slipped the small but ugly apparatuses into my ears and picked up the mirror. While it's hard to look in your own ears, I figured if anyone were really checking, they could see them. I pulled some hair over my ears and wondered who would seriously be checking. My children, perhaps. So I was worried that my children, who lived in another country, would see my hearing aids? What was that all about? I didn't want them to see me as needy or disabled? That was a tall order.

I went into Kitty's room, where she was watching television, and stuck my head in front of her face.

"Can you see my hearing aids?" I asked her.

She beamed. "I'm glad you did that. It was about time."

"Can you see them?"

She lifted my hair from my ears. "Yes. They're really small. Do you like them?"

"I don't know. I just put them in."

"They're virtually invisible. Can you hear what they're saying on CNN?" she asked.

My back was to the TV, but I could hear. I nodded.

"What?"

"Is this a test?"

"Yes."

"They're saying that the stock market went down forty-five points yesterday and recovered nicely today," I said.

She lowered the sound with the remote. "Now can you hear it?"

"Something about Microsoft and an earnings report."

"Excellent," she said.

"Don't make a big thing of this, please," I begged. "I'll tell the others when I'm ready."

But I knew Kitty, and I knew she couldn't wait to spill the beans. She loved being the bearer of new information. I walked out of her room, resigned. I had broken the ice, which was probably what I had gone in there for.

After a week of wearing the blasted things, I took them out, put them in their sweet little container with roses on it, and swore I'd never put them in again. I had noticed that people never raved about their hearing aids. They often complained. There's feedback, sounds that are exacerbated in certain situations. There's buzzing. There's the constant changing of batteries. Some people turned theirs off; others failed to put theirs in. Some got lost. Mine felt like I had carrots in my ears. Think about it. If you filled the ear canal and put an amplifier in it, most certainly you could hear better, but your ears were stopped up. Could I get used to it? Probably. Was I willing to try? Absolutely not.

XXVII

There's something wonderful about the moment when a child tells you his or her first joke. It's a new level of communication. Whenever I understood a joke in Spanish, I felt very smug about it. And I remember clearly when my firstborn went to kindergarten and came home with a joke.

A woman got on a train, and a man with carrots in his ears came and sat beside her. She looked at him, then looked away. He said, "Hello." She said, "You have carrots in your ears." He said, "I'm sorry, I can't hear you. I have carrots in my ears."

When Raul translated "carrots in my ears" for me, it came out like this: *zanahorias en mis orejas.* The handsome young doctor, who certainly was unfamiliar with this term, burst out laughing. He quickly recovered, apologized for his loss of professionalism, and brought out another style. This one I had seen before. One piece slipped over the top of the ear, and another, attached by a monofilament line, tucked into the ear canal. It was small, not as intrusive as the previous one, and I could cover it with my hair. I agreed to try it. I even wore them home. When the sounds of the traffic made me a little uncomfortable, I knew I was indeed hearing more.

I asked Raul about his jewelry business and what he planned to do with it. He said he might turn it over to Lauren and her boyfriend. They were quite talented, he told me, and he thought they could make a good business of it, but he would sell the inventory and just let them pick up the lease. At this point, that was all they could afford.

"Why don't you bring us your inventory?" I suggested. "That might be a good way for you to raise money."

He brightened at the idea.

"Are things better with your situation?" I asked tentatively.

"Very quiet," he said. "Maybe good, maybe not."

We agreed that he'd check with Lauren and set up a meeting for an evening later in the week.

"Open up your pocketbooks, ladies. We're having a distress sale," I announced.

Kitty was up and dressed for the first time. She was feeling well, though experiencing various problems with gas and increased bowel activity, but kept it pretty much to herself. And we didn't ask. Raul, Lauren, and her boyfriend, Rick, showed up about 7:00 p.m. on a Tuesday evening, laden with boxes. The sun was just setting, and the evening had turned cool. We had finished our shrimp quesadillas and adjourned to the pool area, our favorite gathering spot. Lynn and I were enjoying an amaretto on the rocks. Stretched out there, the four of us and Sammy, rebozos across our shoulders and soft ballads playing in the background, the thought crossed my mind that it didn't get much better than this, even with potential danger and loss hovering in the wings.

The three worked quickly to set up a display. Lauren threw a rich velvety cloth across the table while Rick set up an array of molded hands and heads, to which he attached rings, necklaces, and bracelets. They were of silver, mostly, set with a variety of stones: tiger's eye, amber, tourmaline, garnet, turquoise, opal, and onyx. The pieces were varied, from simple to grand, but what caught my eye were the Aztec patterns and symbols, lending each a unique quality and substance not always present in Mexican jewelry. As we admired the pieces, Raul set out a couple of boxes, also lined in black, and arranged a plethora of unset stones. How they shimmered in the soft garden light!

"My," I heard myself say.

There are things in this world that please the eye and excite the imagination. Almost always, it is nature that draws me in: a red-wing blackbird flashing across a field, a waterfall cascading down a mountain, a sugar maple tree afire in the fall, a line of wild geese in a windswept sky. Never have I been much for jewelry. That being said, I was enchanted by the platter set before us.

"*Encantada*," I whispered.

"From the one who never liked diamonds or such," Totie remarked.

"I know," I said, fingering the stones. I felt like King Midas, wanting to fill my hand with them, let them slide through my fingers.

"Yes," Kitty said. She turned to Raul. "These appear to be high quality. What do you figure the whole collection is worth?"

"For you, señora, fifteen thousand US."

"We'd need to have it appraised for insurance purposes. You wouldn't object, would you?"

"Not at all, señora."

She hardly waited for his answer, having turned her attention to Lauren and Rick, who were helping Totie and Lynn with clasps on various necklaces that had caught their eye. Kitty had gone into business mode, grilling them on how and where they learned to make jewelry and how they were going to fund their operation without any inventory. Did they plan to stay in the area or branch out into the Guadalajara market? She had innumerable questions, some quite personal, and I was inwardly flinching at her forwardness.

Kitty's plan, which she shared with us when the others were gone, was to buy the inventory and then sell it back to Rick and Lauren, as they desired.

"If it's as good an investment as I think it is," she said, "we can make this a win-win. Raul gets his money, the kids get their inventory as needed, and we have a storehouse of solid commodities. Too bad there isn't more gold, but these items should hold their value. The stones are well cut, it seems to me. Assuming the appraiser agrees to their value, I'm in. Anybody else?"

"Oh, yes," I said, thinking how much fun it would be to go to the closet and choose something for gifts for my daughters and grandchildren. "But I guess we'll need a safe."

"Doesn't that make us more vulnerable?" Lynn asked.

"Everybody here has a safe," Totie announced. "I used to hear them talk about it at the theater. It's like a status symbol."

"Just what we need," I groaned.

"I think it's cool," she purred. "And maybe I'll rent a piece of jewelry from time to time."

"If you lose twenty pounds, I'll give you one," Kitty said.

"Where did that come from?" Totie shot back.

"The elephant in the room," Kitty said. "You're asking for trouble, my friend. I just want you to get back to healthy eating."

Totie stalked off to her room, then came back a few minutes later, as if nothing had happened.

"So what did you all think of Rick?" she asked.

"Seems a little soft around the edges to be Lauren's boyfriend," Lynn observed.

"They say he's a flamer on the dance floor," Totie said. "I think they have an arrangement. I understand he's from a good family here and Mexican gays aren't too well accepted, so he pretends she's his girlfriend and she goes along for the house and the business."

"An interesting arrangement," Lynn mused.

"Honey, there are lots of stories in this naked village. Some of them would singe your ears."

"Then I don't want to hear them," Lynn said.

"Well, I do," I told her.

"If you gain ten pounds, I'll tell you," Totie said, without cracking a smile.

Raul came into the courtyard the next evening with a smile so broad and relaxed I had forgotten how beautiful his face could be.

"Great news, señoras," he said, depositing a newspaper on the table. "The police located some safe houses here, and in one, they found some heads."

"Well, that's grisly," I said.

He frowned at the unfamiliar word but didn't hesitate to continue. "But, yes"—he pumped his fist—"they were heads of the men who were after me."

It took me a while to sort it out, but apparently these heads had belonged to the body parts found in Ixtlahuacan a few weeks before. Raul had heard nothing since the bodies were discovered, but had no suspicion that his tormentors had been among those found.

"So you're safe?" Kitty asked.

"For now." He dimpled. "Someone's looking out for me." He looked toward the sky and crossed himself.

XXVIII

We moved into a season of rest and joy. The rains had come yet again, and the land flourished. All was green and bursting with bloom. Kitty, too long restricted from tennis but craving exercise, walked with Sammy and me in the mornings. Our travels often extended past the neighborhood, along the *carretera* (road). So much to see, so little time. There were flame trees, jacaranda, bougainvillea, noche buena, hibiscus, thunbergia, amantilla—a rainbow of shades spread against the blue sky and silver lake, circled by verdant mountains. Lest I had forgotten, it reminded me once again that this was a paradise.

Raul was back with us and happy to be so. First, he had dodged a huge bullet from his checkered past. Second, he felt he could come back to the casita and put some distance between himself and the ex-wife. As long as he was generous with her, she would leave him alone. A final plus was that he was free of the shop. A friend, perhaps a cousin, had enticed him into the business. It had been fun at first. Selling ordinary jewelry to tourists could render a small profit if one paid attention. But when he had brought Lauren and Rick aboard, both the cost of materials and the sales had increased. He had put more money than he should into it and, under pressure, had found a way out. *Las ancianas.* He was grateful, and we were happy to have him back. He'd do whatever we needed.

"I don't want you looking for that drug anymore," Kitty told him.

"But, señora?" he made an appropriate willing response.

"Absolutely not. It got you in a lot of trouble last time."

We had talked about it among ourselves and decided that we'd go without a potion if that was necessary to keep Raul safe and happy. But we would all keep our eyes and ears open. All we needed was to befriend a veterinarian.

⌒

Having Kitty with me on the morning walk changed everything. Where I had been content to nod a pleasant hello to my neighbors, in their gardens or on the street, Kitty insisted on stopping to talk. I had been studying Spanish since we arrived, but she was a better communicator than I, and although many of our neighbors were Mexican, she managed to establish connections within a few weeks.

"Watch out, or you'll be recruited for the board of the home-owners' association," I warned her.

"Well, it might be interesting," she said. "Some of these roads need work, and there are vacant lots that have weeds waist high. The owners need to clear them, and the tennis court could use a resurfacing, too."

"You don't even play tennis anymore," I reminded her.

"A good tennis court speaks well of the neighborhood," she informed me. "I'm taking care of our investment."

So she can give it away, I thought.

It was not particularly surprising when Kitty announced that we should have a neighborhood party.

"We've lived here for more than four years," she said, "and hardly know our neighbors."

"The people next door don't speak English," Totie said. "I say *hola* to them and they say *hola* to me, and that's about as far as it goes."

"I'd like to invite them anyway," Kitty went on. "There are the Nixons on the other side, and a doctor down the block who I know speaks English, and this morning I met a gay couple with a poodle who've rented the house with mustard-colored trim on the corner, and there are two artists who live where the wall has that floral mural. I bet we could come up with thirty people or so. Wouldn't that be great? A neighborhood party?"

Having little choice in the matter, we threw ourselves into the event. I had acquaintances from Spanish classes and the gym whom I felt I could invite, and Lynn had artist friends. We had never been called to party with any of them, but it would liven things up. This was a season of bounty, and we were all feeling well. How many more of these would we have?

Upon overhearing a young woman at a table next to me talking about doing something for the next five years or so, I realized, with an acute stab of awareness, that planning five years ahead was beyond me. I was reluctant to plan one year ahead, which isn't to say I didn't expect to be here a year from now, but one can't avoid the odds. As my financial advisor had gently put it a few years back when I was looking for income-producing investments, "You've pretty well transcended the need for additional income. You're not spending what you bring in now. If I were you, I'd seek solid investments with a minimum of risk." At first, I felt slightly insulted, but it was good advice and very freeing. I could have all the parties I wanted—really nice parties.

We contacted our dear Caroline. Back safe and happy from her Ecuador trip, she was overseeing the remodel of a new restaurant. She jumped at the chance to cater for us and, in a remarkable piece of serendipity, offered that her gentleman friend was a classically trained guitarist. If we wanted him to entertain, she said, she'd ask him and felt certain he'd agree. Their romance was still in the discovery stage, and they enjoyed teaming up on projects.

Kitty was appointed to work with her on the menu. Totie quickly claimed her place as music director, which left decorations and entertainment up to Lynn and me.

"A party is like a fire," Lynn said with a hint of mystery. "It needs to be fed from time to time."

I wasn't sure what she meant, but she had traveled in urban social circles for years, so I was happy for her to take the lead. She wanted two or three food stations so people could wander and explore, and suggested that tents would be fun. Lights and piñatas could be strung overhead. Raul could have a tequila-tasting station. A young señorita, like the precious ones with long hair and short skirts who set up tables of free tequila shots in front of the liquor store every Saturday morning, could help him. And while we were talking young señoritas, one could wander around offering finger food, like stuffed mushrooms or cold shrimp.

She had other ideas as well. We would stagger the invitation time, with the neighbors coming at 6:00 and other invitees at 8:00. There would be food, music, and conversation—a chance for everyone to loosen up—and then, zoom, in would come the next wave, bringing fresh energy like a log on the fire. The guitarist would have his own playlist, but would also be ready with some favorite ballads for later in the evening. Totie could arrange in advance to have a couple of guests who would agree to sing, if called upon. By that stage of the party, Totie would surely take the microphone herself, but we decided not to ask her. She liked for things to be her idea.

"We need one more touch." Lynn sat, chewing her pencil. Then her face lit up. "How about a clown?"

"Hmmm," I said.

"There may be some children early on, and even if there aren't, everyone loves a clown."

"Lynn wants to have a clown at the party," I said to the others when she wasn't around.

"A *payaso* at our party?" Totie burst out laughing and started humming the tune "Seems Like Old Times."

Kitty ignored her and asked how I felt about it.

"It seems a bit weird, and I could have sworn we told her that story, but maybe she's forgotten. I thought I should check to see how you felt about it. You had more contact with him than I did."

She shot me a small dagger, then shrugged. "Make sure he's a happy clown—and young."

The party was a grand success. Not only did we meet our neighbors and some new friends from Totie's group, but we also entered into what seemed a new phase of life in Ajijic. When we were at a stoplight on the *carretera*, people knocked on our car window to exchange pleasantries or information. In the village or the market, I saw people I could call by name where previously they had mostly been familiar faces. Having experienced a special evening together, my acquaintances acted more like friends. They beamed when they saw me and were quick to ask about my housemates. I think four old women living together and throwing parties was fodder for talk around town. There were a lot of old men and women around, some who liked to party, but few who themselves entertained.

"I feel like a minor celebrity," I told the group.

"I know the feeling, and it may get old," Totie said. "You'll be the new darling of one group or another for a while, should you choose."

"I don't choose to be anybody's darling."

"Just watch out," she warned. "They'll be calling."

I did choose to join a book group, only one of a world of possibilities that had opened up. Totie had been recruited for a small part in another play and was gearing up for that. Kitty, who had agreed to work with the neighborhood association, was on the telephone so much we would have had to get another line, if not for that fact that we all had Mexican cell phones as well as some magic system that hooked up to our modem for calling the States. We took a tenuous pride in our familiarity with technology, until something or other went wrong. Then we called on Raul, our *mayordomo*, and if he couldn't fix it, he knew someone who could.

Lynn had the most interesting development to come from our event, but didn't divulge it until almost a week later.

"Do you all remember Alec from the party?" she asked.

"The guy from your art class, with the thick glasses?"

She nodded.

Totie took a sip of wine. “He’s pining for you. I could see it in his body language. He’s on his last legs and looking for comfort. I’d steer clear,” she said.

Lynn sighed deeply. “Now, can I finish?”

“Please.”

“He has a supply of pentobarbital.”

Kitty jerked to attention. “How do you know?”

“He told me. He got it for his wife a few years back when it was still available. She was suffering with something awful and terminal, and they went to the border and got some, but she died before they used it.”

“Glory hallelujah!” Kitty said. “Can we buy it?”

“This is touchy,” Lynn said. “He doesn’t want it for himself. Blind as he is, he’s still full of life and excited about art, and he does some very interesting pieces that reflect his limited vision. He did one that—”

“Can we get back to the point?” Kitty interruped. “Does he know you want it?”

“He knows I’m interested, but not for myself,” she said. “And he trusts me enough to give it to me.”

“And what does he want in return?” Totie drawled smugly.

“He wants us to paint together once a week—make a day of it.”

“Like a date?” Totie said. “Are you willing?”

“I’m thinking.”

“How much?” Kitty asked.

“I told you he doesn’t want to sell it.”

“I mean, what quantity does he have?”

“Three doses. He was going to take it when she did, and they got an extra for her sister in Canada, but she changed her mind and didn’t want it.”

“What if we all want to go at the same time?” I asked.

“I never thought about that,” Totie said.

I had thought about it a lot. If we had the potion and one of us said it was time, could I deliver it and then go on with my life? It seemed easy at first, considering that we’d all be going at different times, without a potion. But as I imagined delivering an ending and then picking up the pieces, I began to think it might be easier if we all went together.

"Are you in?" I asked Lynn.

"What do you mean?"

"Do you want to be a part of our final plans?"

"I want the option," she said.

"That's really all any of us want," Kitty said, "but I guess Allie's doing the numbers here, and if we all wanted to go at the same time, three doses wouldn't be enough."

"A group final exit is a ridiculous idea," Totie said. "Think about our kids, our friends, what people would say, how they'd remember us. It would be horrid."

"That's about the smartest thing I've ever heard you say, Totie." Lynn walked over and hugged her. "I agree completely."

A mental vision shot before me: the courtyard swimming with police, our four bodies stretched out lifeless, Raul in the background, a tearful Gracie at the kitchen door, Sammy sniffing us in turn, and headlines like SUICIDE PACT ACCOMPLISHED in the *Guadalajara Reporter*.

"I guess I hadn't thought that all the way through," I said. "We want dignity and privacy and a peaceful good-bye. If an event comes to pass, no one but the four of us should ever know."

"Raul will know," Totie said. "Or at least suspect."

"And Gracie," Lynn said. "She's no dummy."

"And Lynn's new friend, if he lasts that long," Totie added.

"No, no, no. We're down to the nitty-gritty here. No one has to know," Kitty broke in, emphasizing those words as if they were a chapter heading. "We won't have a final party until the 'hostess' is requesting it, at which point she'll be pretty far down the road. We give the medicine, with a good slug of her favorite tipple, and it looks like she's died in her sleep, which incidentally I think we should work on concomitantly."

"Where the hell did that word come from?" Totie asked.

"My vast storehouse of vocabulary." Kitty smiled. "It means—"

"I know what it means." Totie snapped, not letting her finish.

We're moving along, I wrote in my journal. It felt final to have the potion within our grasp. And finality was strangely unsettling. I tried to put into words what I was afraid of, but failed. The unknown, I suppose. I had often thought that the beauty of life lies in its impermanence.

If we all lived forever, if suddenly death were eliminated, people would be begging for a way out. As it is, we're handed a piece of time—a gift, if you will—and are driven by biology and culture to make the most of it. Genetically, we're impelled to reproduce. What we do after that is of questionable value, though we try to make it seem important. We spend time helping others, building community, supporting activities that appear to enrich life, nurturing our offspring or other promising members of the species, and we try to have some fun while nurturing ourselves. Old women in our village and throughout Mexico sweep the streets with straw brooms. It doesn't seem to matter if the streets are cobblestone, or paved, or even dirt. That's what they do. We all try to do something.

The end lurked around the corner, and we were prepared. Lynn had brought us a white plastic bag containing three vials of Nembutal—liquid death, her friend had called it. He had heard about it from his wife's sister, a Canadian living in Melbourne, Australia. For a brief while, its availability in Mexico was international gossip. They had driven to Matamoros to buy it at an over-the-counter veterinary shop. Alec was happy to get it out of his house, almost as much as he was to have struck a deal with Lynn.

She was truly fond of Alec and undoubtedly enjoyed the Wednesdays she spent painting with him. He was Canadian, large and well built, with good teeth and a headful of white hair. Except for his visual disability, he would have been quite a catch, with a good education, a fondness for sports and outdoor activities, and a willingness to try new things. He was moderate to conservative on most issues, except his art, and quite carefree with his money, unlike many of his countrymen we had met here. He said his wife's illness had scarred him, and Mexico had made him whole again. He had no plans to go home, though one wondered what he'd do when he completely lost his sight. That didn't seem to be on his mind at the present.

It was the art that brought them together. His pictures were alive with color and imaginary creatures: grinning lizards with children on their backs, bugs with faces peeping out from behind huge green leaves, organ-pipe cacti with wiggling hands, feet, and ears. It was totally different from Lynn's work, and she found it amusing and engaging. Watching her with him, I was reminded of how often she had been drawn to superior minds. Life continued to present us with new situations, and she was open to its offerings.

XXIX

I was having trouble with my hearing devices again. The second ones were much better than the first, but they gave me a headache. The doctor insisted they shouldn't, that he had never heard this complaint before, but they did. Whenever I put them in, my nose began to run, my sinuses felt congested, and my head ached.

"If you don't wear them all the time, you may lose the ability to understand what people are saying," he warned me. "The conductors in our inner ears that move sound along get lazy without sound. Soon the brain will lose its ability to translate sound into meaning."

Good grief. I could have gone a long time without hearing that. I wondered if it was similar to theories on drinking water after a massage so that the toxins released wouldn't settle back into the same muscles. It sounded about that far-fetched to me, but medical science is coming up with new stuff all the time. I went home and googled it. Brain atrophy, it is called, losing the ability to understand complex sentences, and there were MRI measurements that seemed to validate the theory. Subjects with untreated hearing loss showed loss of activity in the aural areas of the brain. Just thinking about it gave me a headache.

But I wasn't troubled for long because I received some wonderful news. My grandson, about to enter his final year of college, was looking ahead to possibilities in international medicine and wanted to brush up on his Spanish. He called to ask, shyly, if he might stay with me while taking a six-week course in the neighboring town of Chapala. He also wanted to check out the medical school in Guadalajara. I was overjoyed at the chance to share this time and place with him. Of course, I didn't know him very well, and though I loved my friends, I felt certain our lifestyle would be very tame for a twenty-two-year-old.

I tried to remember what I had been up to at twenty-two. I had been married a couple of years, was teaching school, and had a baby on the way. That was a far cry from his being single, with no prospects for a wife, as far as I knew. I didn't even know what he did for entertainment, what kind of music he liked, whether he was into the arts, or history, or geology, if he played or even watched soccer, if he liked beer or wine or fruit juice. This place was rich with possibilities, but if, like Kitty's granddaughters, he was expecting young adult excitement, he would be disappointed.

"Don't worry about it," Totie said. "He asked to come. He'll find something fun to do in his free time."

"And if he's doing a crash course, he won't have too much free time," Lynn added.

They were trying to calm me, and I needed it. The process of trying to remember being that young had taken me down a more serious path. At that age, and without realizing it, I had been sorting out confusing feelings about sex, morality, self-esteem, careers—you name it, I was trying to figure it out. Somewhere between the age of eighteen, when I had graduated from high school and felt prepared for the world ahead, and the age of twenty-two, life became much more complicated and difficult than I had been led to believe.

"Chop wood, carry water," the Zen master says, meaning attend to the business of life, and seek to make it a spiritual practice, a gift to the world, rather than drudgery. I've often thought that Buddhism is well suited for societies less affluent and with less class mobility than ours. We are programmed to always be seeking more—more money, more information, more stimulation. We educate our young to fill their minds rather than quiet them, and we challenge them to aspire to great things, and look down on menial tasks. We prize knowledge, not as the key to happiness, but rather, as the key to a better job, more money, and thus an easier life.

We may not actually have to chop wood and carry water, but metaphorically, it's hard to escape. I remembered back to my college days, feeling elevated by contact with outstanding minds and great ideas, and I thought I was learning about hard work and discipline by paying my bills, getting papers in on time, and coming up with fresh responses. Still, I was protected from the vision of getting up every morning for the rest of my life as a wife, mother, and employee, and doing whatever it was I had contracted to do.

There are those who take alternate approaches. They may never marry, never have children, never have jobs they fear losing, but even they, I've observed, must at some point deal with the angst of daily living, and their aloneness makes it more difficult. But surely my grandson hadn't come to this realization. He was still in the protective womb of school and self-determination, with resources to travel and no one to answer to but himself. I could only wish him well along his way and that he find worthy companions to share his journey. And I wanted to be one of those. It was important that we have some fun together.

Raul and I picked up Will at the airport. It was an easy flight from Houston, but he looked sleepy and disheveled coming off the plane.

"I slept the whole way," he said.

"Lots of people sleep on planes, I've noticed," I said, giving him a pass.

He laughed. "Not me. Usually. But I was up all night."

"Going away party?" I asked.

"No. This dog got run over and I found him in the street and took him to the emergency vet and they had to set his leg and I stayed to watch and it was really interesting. Expensive, though," he added. "They gave me a bill for three hundred and fifty dollars. If I'd have known that, I might not have taken him." He paused. "On second thought, I couldn't just leave him in the street. And, besides, I learned a lot. They said I could come back in the fall and help out."

"Sounds like quite an experience," I said, admiring his blue eyes and open manner."

"Yeah, and that was before I even started my trip. I'm pretty excited about this," he said with a smile.

"So am I."

He looked confused.

"Excited about showing you this place I love," I explained.

He laughed. "For a minute, I thought you were signed up for the language class."

"That would be a little intense—all day, every day."

"Well, to hear my mom talk, you take on a lot of challenges."

"I'm glad it seems that way. Actually, as you'll see, I've got it pretty easy."

⌐⟶

His real name was William, after his grandfather, but he had never been called anything but Will, and it seemed to fit. He was, as his mother had promised, easy to have around. He asked for very little and was happy to spend time alone. He picked up after himself and never intruded on conversations. If anything, he was too reticent. That first weekend, before his classes started, he slipped in and out of our vision like a ghost.

He swam early the first morning and then went to his room with a book. Later, he came out and played ball with Sammy and joined us for lunch, providing polite but brief answers to our questions: Are you comfortable in your room? Do you have any special food preferences? Did we tell you the water is purified? Do you want Raul to take you to class?

He wanted to ride the bus.

"I can't tell what he's thinking," I told my daughter on the phone.

"He's fine, Mom. That's just the way he is. If he needs something, he'll get it himself, or ask you."

I was still concerned, and knocked on his door that first Saturday night. "It's Saturday night. Would you like to go out?"

"Most definitely," he said.

I was then presented with the problem of where to go, and decided on a bar where I knew country and western music was played. Totie had agreed to come along, but when Raul pulled up, it didn't look like our kind of place. It was a sports bar, with a preseason US football game playing on various television sets. There was a lot of noise and beer, which wasn't what I wanted my grandson's initiation to Ajijic to be. I asked Raul to take us someplace quieter and more authentic, which he did. His cousin had a place up on a hill overlooking the lake, where we enjoyed excellent cream of poblano soup, followed by grilled dorado, fresh vegetables, and key lime pie. I had insisted that Raul join us.

The young men drank beer while Totie and I enjoyed a glass of red wine. The view was spectacular, looking down the lake for as far as the eye could see, lights dotting the shoreline. As an added bonus, we got special attention. Each time Raul's cousin came to the table, he had something pleasant to share, sometimes in English, sometimes in Spanish. Sometimes Raul translated; sometimes he let it go. I could see Will trying to follow the conversation, smiling on occasion.

"You speak some español?" Raul asked.

"*Un poquito*," Will said. "But I expect to get much better before I leave."

Raul nodded. "You want me to talk to you in español?"

Will nodded. "I may not always understand."

"That's the way I learned inglés, making mistakes, feeling dumb," Raul told him. "But if you want to get good fast, you have to be brave."

"I'll try." Will ducked his head.

"*Bravo, hombre.*" Raul extended a clenched fist to bump knuckles with Will, a male bonding sort of move that made us smile and my grandson blush. Dear Raul, he was a man for all seasons—and not considerably older than this dear boy at our table.

"Any place special you'd like to go tomorrow?" I asked, and was a bit dismayed when he asked to go to the church in Chapala.

"I read it was built in the mid-1500s," he said, "and I thought I ought to see it in operation."

"Are you a Catholic, Will?" Surely I should have known.

⟨⟩

I found out a lot about my grandson in the next six weeks. He shared some of my liberal positions on religion and politics, but was still forming a worldview, and I could see it would be much different from mine. The world was shifting rapidly, and he existed in the crucible. We discussed education, the environment, sustainable economies, democracy, the military, racism, private property, and taxes. I started to bring up euthanasia, but refrained. He commented on his good fortune.

"Just being born in the United States puts me way ahead of the game," he said. "Add to that being white and from professional parents with considerable assets—"

"And good genes," I broke in.

"I feel an obligation," he told me. "I want to make a difference."

"'To those to whom much is given, much is required,'" I quoted, and then felt silly being so stilted.

He laughed. "You sound like the Queen Mum."

Will went to class and studied during the week, and on the weekends, we explored. We walked in the village, took photographs, shopped in street markets, and ate assorted nuts and candies from street vendors. I cautioned him not to get any more daring than that, but I suspected he ate lunch regularly in Chapala at places I wouldn't have recommended. He was a grown man—almost—and I had to give my best advice and then let it go.

"Wash your hands regularly," I cautioned him. "I've found it's the best thing you can do to avoid *turista.*"

The aspiring medical student smiled indulgently at my grandmotherly advice.

He liked sitting on the square at my favorite restaurant and watching the hum of the town. And I had thought that would bore him. One night, we went to a drumming ceremony where people drummed and danced freely. We found a Thai restaurant run by a local family, offering tasty, healthy meals. We visited the clinic, where he got a feeling for how medicine was dispensed here. We went bird-watching along the lake and visited the hot mineral baths, and on the last Sunday, he surprised me with a kayak ride.

"I've never done that," I protested. "What if I tip us over and we drown? I'm not a good swimmer, and as much as I love this lake, I don't want a mouthful of it."

"Weren't you the one who told me you should do something every day that scares you a little?" he teased.

"*You* should do something every day that scares you. Not me. I'm an old lady."

He wouldn't accept it. "Don't you want me to remember you as a daring old lady?"

And I knew he had my number. We went kayaking and had a grand time. I was sore after, but it was well worth it. When I asked what he would remember most about Ajijic, he frowned, as if running the whole scene before his eyes.

"I was really fascinated by the old ladies sweeping the cobblestones. I'm sure they don't get paid, and if not, why do they do it?"

"I've wondered that myself," I said. "I used to think they wanted to keep the dust out of their houses, but I've seen them working far from any doorways."

Will was still thinking about my question. "But I also liked the village dogs," he said. "I never heard one bark or growl. And I never saw any poop."

"Maybe that's what the old ladies are sweeping," I said.

When we took Will to the airport, he sat up front with Raul, and the two talked in Spanish the entire trip. I could follow much of it, but some of it went past me. A serious student and a quick learner, he had gotten what he came after. And I was so grateful to have been a party to it.

"*Agradezco tu ayuda*, Dandy." He hugged me as he got out of the car and thanked me for my help. "And I'm glad to see you're wearing your hearing aids," he whispered. "Last time we were together, you had to ask me to repeat everything I said."

Embarrassed, I blushed and pulled my hair over my ears. "It's no big thing," I said.

"It helped me get to know you better. That's a really big thing. Thanks again." He kissed my cheek quickly and headed for the large glass doors. "I'll be in touch."

He looked back and waved.

XXX

Suddenly it was September and the children were going back to school. I saw them in the square in their white shirts and dark pants, the girls in pleated skirts, their hair in pigtails or held back neatly with barrettes or headbands. Men on ladders were decorating the bandstand for 16 de Septiembre, a celebration commemorating the day in 1810 that began Mexico's struggle to free itself from three centuries of Spanish rule.

It begins with the call to revolution by a liberal priest—in this case, Father Hidalgo. Each year, this shout, or *grito*, is reenacted from the balcony of the National Palace on the eve of September 15, but there appears to be no actual record of what was said. Much like our call to revolution from England, there is talk of tyranny, and tributes, and shameful taxation. There is an emotional fervor for freedom and homeland. Spain arrived in 1519, baptizing the Indians who lived here, dividing and claiming the land for themselves, and essentially making slaves of the native peoples who lived on the land. And so the Mexican call for revolution calls out against the crimes of slavery and mistreatment of the Indians.

I briefly pondered that we who revolted from English rule were also concerned with self-determination and taxation burdens. As for crimes of slavery and mistreatment of the Indians, we would become the perpetrators. When I found myself critical of the government of Mexico, I glimpsed back across the country's checkered history and reminded myself of all she had borne. She was a newcomer to democracy.

As I watched the workmen placing and attaching palm fronds, then stringing garlands and tricolor Mexican flags, my attention was drawn by a commotion in one of the busy streets that formed the boundaries of the square. Commotions in the street were common—accidents, traffic jams, advertisements shouted by loudspeaker from moving vehicles, impromptu performances of one variety or another—but this had a different air. It was a parade of sorts, one black limousine moving slowly toward the large cathedral at the far end of the square. Following the limo marched six men carrying a fine casket of a finely polished honey-colored wood. Beside the limo, mourners walked, some tearful, their hands touching the car, as if to offer support to those inside. Behind the men who carried the casket walked a large number of others, young and old, some families holding hands, a man carrying a young child, a woman carrying a baby, an old woman on a walker, young boys, an adolescent couple with arms intertwined, and random dogs. They were marching to the church, I supposed, but I had no idea from where they had come. Their path was certainly longer than the three blocks I could see. So much about the church makes me angry, especially in Mexico, but this scene was about devotion and communal support, and I couldn't watch without feeling reverent myself.

On the way home, Raul told me that Gracie's son would soon be starting school, and it was time to make the first payment. I almost asked what payment he was referring to. With all the things that had been going on, it had slipped my mind—our tacit agreement with Gracie that we would help her son go to private school if she would "keep our secret." Kitty, of course, hadn't forgotten and had a plan. She and I, having the most expendable income, would share his school expenses, with a payment every semester, provided the boy kept up his grades. We had met the boy a number of times when he came to the house with Gracie, but knew very little about him. He seemed polite and well behaved, but he was at a dangerous age. Gracie recognized this as well, which is why she wanted him to go to the private school.

We could have told her that private school didn't ensure that kids wouldn't get in trouble, but it was more likely that their minds could be engaged and their aspirations lifted with higher education. Feeding a child's spirit, however, was another challenge. Kitty had been thinking about that too. She thought we should have him come to the house once a week for English and art lessons.

"You're crazy," I told her. "We don't even know this kid."

"We need to. We're his sponsors, and as his sponsors, we need to take a personal interest in him. If he doesn't take to the art, we'll hire a music teacher. We'll teach him to cook fancy stuff, or play chess, or…" She trailed off. "So what do you think?"

"I think there's never a dull moment with you around," I said, and I meant it.

Totie came home with news of a sock hop. A local restaurant called The Blue Lagoon was planning a dance night, and Totie thought we should all go. There would be a disc jockey, music from every decade back to the '40s, good food, and some fabulous people-watching, she told us. We decided to give it a try, but I didn't have a thing to wear.

The first sock hop I ever attended was in seventh grade. It was an afternoon affair in the junior high gym, which is why it became known as a sock hop. We were required to take off our shoes because we couldn't have hard soles on the gym floor. The student council sponsored it, and I'm sure I must have gone with a girlfriend because I would have been too shy to go alone. I vividly recall standing against the wall, trying to look nonchalant, while alternately hoping that someone would come my way and ask me to dance and that no one would. I would have been content to watch had I not been so self-conscious. But there I was, at a dance, and no one was asking me to dance. I suddenly realized the meaning of the word *wallflower* and felt even more awkward. Then someone came.

He was a new student in school and generally thought of as a weirdo. Shorter than most of the girls and all of the boys, he had come from France. He seemed to understand English pretty well, but spoke with a strong accent, and common to that age, the other students either laughed at him or left him alone. But there he was, Pierre, standing before me, grinning, motioning for me to join him on the dance floor. This was before the days of rock and roll. We slow danced. And unless you knew someone really well, the boy put his left hand on the girl's waist, his elbow ever so slightly bent, and she put hers on his shoulder. You joined right hands and tried to move to the music, keeping a discreet distance. Some boys followed the beat better than others. Some even knew how to fox-trot or waltz. This shrimpy guy pulled my body to his and laid his head sideways on my shoulder so that I could feel his nose against my neck. He hardly moved to the music, just kind of swayed. His nose wasn't all I could feel. Down below, where he pressed his lower body against mine, I could feel something hard. He had an erection, right there in the gym. I didn't even know what it was called then, but it was mortifying and I didn't know what to do. We stayed in that position until the music was over, and then I quickly broke hold and walked away as fast as I could. People were smirking at me, as if to say they'd been watching and found it amusing. I remember that he wore thin trousers, not blue jeans like the other boys, and I stole a glance at what I had felt. It was a significant bulge, but it didn't seem to deter him. Smiling, he walked over and asked another girl to dance, while I beat it to the restroom and washed my hands, as if somehow to cleanse myself. How much I had to learn.

I didn't expect to dance at the Ajijic sock hop, much less encounter unwanted erections, though the idea brought a smile to my face. I looked forward to watching others dance and enjoying the music. We reserved a table for six and asked Raul to join us, as well as Lynn's friend Alec. I wore a long white cotton dress with a blue sweater and sandals. A few of the women came in bobby socks and loafers, circular skirts, and white shirts, with scarves around their necks. When the disc jockey asked who remembered the music of the '40s, there was a flurry of hands, and when the big band music started, I was amazed to see how many came forward to jitterbug.

Totie leaned over. "And you thought we were the oldest broads in town."

There were also younger folks—some in their fifties and sixties—who looked quite perky and ready to rock and roll. They did the twist, and the mashed potato, and the monkey. We ate dinner, shared wine, and reveled in the contagious good spirits, cool evening, and lovely open patio flanked with blossoming plants. Friends and acquaintances stopped by our table, happy to see us, urging us to come out more often. My heart felt full, receiving yet another gift of pleasant ambience and camaraderie.

When the music changed from Latin to country and western, Totie pulled Raul and me out to join in a line dance to the "Boot Scootin' Boogie." It was simple, and he caught on right away, dimpling at the two of us as we showed him how to hook his thumbs into his belt loops and boot-scoot across the floor. On the way home, Totie insisted on singing "Trailers for Sale or Rent," and Raul tried to recall his part.

"Don't have anything to smoke," he said, shaking his head. "That's not it."

"Ain't got…" Totie prompted.

"Nothing to smoke," he said.

"*No tengo nada cigarros*," she said.

"Ain't got no cigarettes," he boomed out, and then swerved to barely miss a boy on a bicycle with no taillight.

"Excuse me, señoras," he apologized quickly. "Better not to sing when I'm driving." He took his job quite seriously. I was sure it wasn't always easy to be in charge of us *ancianas*, though he tried to make it look as such.

Driving in Mexico was fraught with challenges, and I was ever appreciative of Raul's prowess, whether it was getting into a tight parking

227

spot in the village, or out of the lot at the local market, or maneu-vering the heavy traffic of Guadalajara. There was much to watch out for, despite the able assistance of street men who made it their daily business to direct parking lot traffic and solicit car washes.

There were pedestrians who darted in and out from between parked cars or between moving cars in stopped traffic. There were bicyclists who did the same. There were youngsters who rode through the streets on ATVs, sometimes three and four on a single vehicle, sometimes bouncing off if a bump was hit unexpectedly. There were motorcyclists whose main intention seemed to be pass-ing everything in their path. One moment, no one was behind you; the next, a searing flash of red zoomed by, leaving a trail of dust and sound. There were also dogs, hunkering on the side of the highway, waiting for a chance to scamper across without getting hit. There were people on horseback, sometimes tourists on joy rides, sometimes workers coming or going to the job.

Children often played in the street in the village, reluctantly moving back onto the sidewalk when a car passed. Sometimes someone stopped his car or truck in the middle of the road and engaged in conversation with someone else, whether that person was in another vehicle or on the roadside. Lots of business seemed to get done on the street. Raul did it himself from time to time.

In addition, cattle roamed freely across *ejidos*—unfenced land held in common by a peasant class. So one must be on the lookout for the occasional cow or bull. We saw one dead on the side of the road on the way to Guadalajara. Dusted with lime, it lay there, white and decaying, for weeks.

Parking was by guess and by gosh. Sometimes cars met each other on narrow streets, and one would have to back up because people had parked on both sides. Turn signals were often used on the highway to suggest to those in the car behind that they may pass safely. But it was only a best guess as to whether the driver was signaling a turn or safety to pass. The right-of-way was often deter-mined by assertiveness rather than rules or courtesy. Driving too slowly would get you in more trouble than driving too fast, except when it came to potholes and *topes*, the Mexican version of speed bumps.

Attention to safety was not one of Mexico's sterling qualities, and accidents involving both pedestrians and those in vehicles were one of the leading causes of death in the country. On the other hand, random acts of kindness abound. Green Angels, government-employed mechanics, patroled the highways around the clock and could be reached by cell phone to provide emergency help if your car broke down or you ran out of gas. We'd never had occasion to use them, but it was comforting to know they were there.

Driving with Raul had been, on the whole, a priceless experience. He kept the van in excellent condition and handled it with the ease of a professional. When people asked if I drove in Mexico, I smiled and told them I have a wonderful driver. It sounds so decadent, like a gardener and a full-time maid, but these helpers had become a necessity. So we were spoiled. That was part of the plan.

When we were in the early stages of thinking about the perfect retirement, we talked about regular massages, but after a few uncomfortable experiences with one practitioner who engaged in local gossip and another who failed to change the linens between customers, I grew less enchanted. Still, old bodies tend to creak and benefit from loosening up, and it just feels darn good to have warm hands working on you. Each of us scheduled a treatment from time to time.

I liked trigger point therapy with special attention to my neck and shoulders. Kitty had back issues and felt she benefitted from hot stones. Totie just liked to be rubbed—tickling, I called it. When we used to have sleepovers, she would flop her arm across me and insist that I tickle her by softly running my fingers up and down her arm. If I stopped too soon, she would pout. As long as I continued, she would tell stories that made me laugh. How long we have danced that dance!

Once, we visited a spa in a neighboring village. It advertised itself as a health spa and hotel, with a variety of services drawn from the wisdom of many cultures. When we arrived, we discovered they offered eight different types of massage, from ayurveda to indigenous, oriental, and classical, each approaching the goal of rejuvenation from a slightly different perspective. The clinicians were young and beautiful, with unlined faces, smiling mouths, and impenetrable eyes. Their prices were staggering, though not out of the ordinary for a top-of-the-line spa in the States. As they spoke of purification, holistic healing, stimulation of digestion and circulation, visualization techniques, and the regeneration of body and spirit, we exchanged amused glances and decided just to have lunch.

A light and flavorful seafood salad was served impeccably, with real silverware on white tablecloths, warm multigrain bread, and wine poured delicately into glasses that sparkled in the sunlight. Sonoran flute music played softly in the background. After lunch, we opted for pedicures, then went home and started looking seriously for a massage therapist who would come to the house. Though we appreciated the exclusive spa's attention to detail, we had transcended the need for such an exotic atmosphere.

"Who says Mexico doesn't know how to do classy?" Lynn murmured.

"You're the best judge of that," Totie said.

"Well, that place gets an A-plus, although it looked like a dump from the street. I almost stayed in the car with Raul."

"Until they opened the gates."

"And I saw that beautiful hotel, with the swimming pool and the gardens and the lake beyond."

"I love that about Mexico. You can never tell what's behind a wall or gate."

"Kind of like New Orleans."

We all agreed on that—a pleasant, though unusual occurrence.

The list of those who regularly came within our walls had grown over time. In addition to Gracie, there was the gardener Fernando and his grandson Federico. There was a plumber/electrician/handyman whom we called on regularly, as well as assorted technicians whom Raul brought in to oversee our electronics. Nevertheless, we decided we needed a massage therapist to come two evenings a week, which would allow for each of us to have at least one massage a week, at the end of the day, when we could then fall into bed, totally relaxed, if not purified.

We ended up with Consuela, a grandmother herself, though only fifty. She worked at a medical clinic during the day, doing what I imagined to be practical nursing, and gave massages at night. She had learned her skill from her own mother and had practiced it until she found regular work in nursing. Now she supplemented her income with night work. When we each had experienced the pleasure of her hands and had discovered that she was sensitive to our distinct tastes and could tailor her ministrations to our needs, we tried to make her an offer she couldn't refuse.

If she could come regularly, two nights a week, and give two massages a night, we would pay her $2,500 pesos a month. She agreed, though at the time I thought she might be wondering what we would require of her to pay so handsomely. It was about what a baker or a chambermaid would make for full-time employment. I figured it would increase her income by a third. Her face didn't show the enthusiasm I thought she might feel, but as I later learned, she was both a proud and a cautious woman.

Consuela was yet another good person who made our lives better in Mexico. She was attentive to what we wanted and was reliable to a fault. Sometimes she came straight from work, still dressed in uniform and white shoes.

"Are you tired?" we would ask, and she would shake her head no and begin to set up the table we had bought for this purpose.

One night, Kitty sent her home because she looked exhausted, and when it was time for her to be paid at the end of the month, she gave back some money, the rough equivalent of a night's pay. Only after some discussion would she accept pay for work not completed. Again and again, we came across individuals with a strong sense of honor, a kind of nobility about what they did and how they were compensated. This isn't to say there weren't others willing to take advantage. *Caveat emptor* is a universal warning.

Our housekeeper Gracie was another example of one who performed consistently and with a minimum of direction. After four years together, she was a member of the household, and her son Javier was about to be taken into the fold. A soft smile spread across her face when Kitty had broached the plan for the boy to spend time with us on a regular basis. Kitty did everything on a regular basis, usually once a week, and it was all scheduled on a chart on the refrigerator. After checking on the boy's school schedule, Javier was penned into the late-Friday-afternoon time frame, which meant we were all expected to be present on Friday afternoons for his cultural development.

Lynn thought this had the potential of blowing up in our faces.

"High school boys don't like to be told what to do, especially on Friday afternoons," she warned.

"This is just an extension of his education," Kitty insisted. "I told Raul to explain it to Gracie, and she is to explain it to him."

"Well, that makes it all work," Totie said.

"It will work," Kitty announced with authority.

The first Friday that Javier came, we sat with him in the courtyard and tried to talk.

"Tell us about your school," Kitty prompted.

He gave her a blank look.

"*Tu escuela?*" I asked.

"*Bien,*" he said in a bored voice.

"It's okay," I replied in English.

"That's what I said," he shot back.

Uh-oh, I thought.

"Do you like to paint?" I asked. Lynn had set up an easel.

He shrugged.

I got up and went into the kitchen, where Gracie had positioned herself to watch without being seen.

She gave me a worried look, and I patted her shoulder.

"Why don't you bring us some drinks and chips?" I suggested.

"He *nervioso*," she told me in an apologetic voice.

"I know. *Kids*," I said, and rolled my eyes, which made her smile.

In my room, I found some playdough I had bought to use for the arthritis in my hands. It hadn't worked as well as the soft rubber ball I now kneaded in the mornings while having my coffee. There were four small containers, which I took out to the table and set one in front of each of the four *ancianas*.

Javier watched suspiciously. The others looked dubious.

"When I say go," I said, "we each have three minutes to make a pig. Javier will tell us when the time is up and will be the judge of the best pig."

I checked to see if he understood. "*Entiendes?*" I asked.

"*Cochino?*" he verified "pig," nodding.

As we worked, he sipped on his drink and petted Sammy, close by as always, inspecting the newcomer. Javier appeared disinterested but stayed at the table dutifully, with an eye on the hourglass I had brought.

"*Alto,*" he called when the sand had ceased to fall, and we all stopped, placing our various pigs on the table for inspection.

"*Juez?*" I acknowledged his power as judge.

Totie made her pig dance, trying to enhance its appeal. Kitty's curly tail had fallen off, but her ears were good. Mine looked more like a fat dog.

Javier took his time, walking around and assessing each. He was getting into our game. Totie danced for him again, and he chose hers.

"Yah!" she shouted. "The best pig!"

The boy couldn't help but laugh, and before the mood changed, I had rolled my pig into a new ball and put it before him.

"Now I'll be the judge. Everyone start again, and this time make a rat. *Ratón*," I added, to be sure he got it.

"*Uno, dos, tres,*" I counted, then turned over the timer. "*Ahora!*"

Javier was quite good with the clay. He worked with nimble fingers and a sharp eye. He didn't just do a rat; he did the Disney character Ratatouille, complete with big eyes and snouty nose. We all clapped; there was no contest.

Kitty suggested that, as a prize, Totie should show Javier the sound system and our CD selection. She let him choose a favorite, which happened to be rock and roll, and instructed him how to use the components. Our friendship had begun.

In time, Javier came to know each of us as individuals, although we continued to work with him as a group, mostly because it was more fun that way. Our exquisite familiarity with each other allowed us to let one or the other take the lead as necessary. I found it interesting that, although we vied for attention when alone, we worked quite well together when on a mission. And Javier was a mission of sorts. We had set out to broaden his life, and of course, he had brought new energy to ours.

He wasn't interested in art and didn't want to learn an instrument, though he enjoyed our music system greatly. But Kitty had noticed he was good with numbers and kept toying with ways to explore that. It was Lynn who suggested we teach him to play bridge.

"Mexicans are excellent bridge players," she told us. "It's a status thing, I think. The ones I've seen at tournaments are usually well-dressed upper-class types. I think it's a game the wealthy indulge in."

"That would give him an edge, to be a good bridge player," Kitty said, always working the angles.

"Let's see if he has any card sense," I said, so we started with Hearts.

Javier had never played cards before, but he rose to the challenge. He learned quickly about taking tricks, holding back, remembering what had been played, and counting cards. But we were afraid that the intricacies of bridge would put him off. It was Kitty's idea to have him watch the four of us play for a while, and then he could sit in. This strategy didn't work too well. It's a complicated game and boring to watch unless you know, or care, what's going on. Then Kitty had another idea. She bought a laptop and said he could keep it if he would learn to play computer bridge against robots. He'd have to show us what he could do each week, and based on his progress, he could keep the laptop another week.

"You know, there's a lot of other things he can access on that laptop besides bridge," I told her.

"Duh," she said. "Don't you think he can do that other places, without this laptop?"

"Probably," I said, "but you're creating a temptation."

XXXI

*I*t was 4:44 a.m. by the green glow of the alarm clock when I heard a knock on my bedroom door. Before I could get my bearings, the door opened and Totie stumbled in and plopped herself on the side of the bed.

"Allie, something's wrong with me." She had her hand over her heart and seemed to be struggling for breath.

I woke up quickly and turned on the lamp. She looked haggard.

"Tell me what's going on," I said, taking her hand and trying to sound very calm.

"I woke up, like suddenly, and had this buzzing feeling all over me—like there was an Energizer Bunny inside and it was humming. I rolled over and tried to get comfortable, but my heart keeps missing beats, acting weird, and it won't calm down."

"Did you take your pills?" I wasn't sure what pills she took, but we all had a regimen.

She nodded.

"Anything strange you did or ate that might bring this on?"

She shook her head. It was strange to see her completely serious. I didn't know why I was trying to act like the doctor. I got up to go toward Kitty, but she grabbed my hand.

"I don't want to get her into this. Will you take me to the twenty-four-hour clinic."

"And not call Kitty?"

"What could she do, except get all bossy and upset?"

"She could listen with her stethoscope, take your blood pressure."

"I can bet it's off the chart. And now I'm feeling sick to my stomach."

"That could be nerves. Can you get dressed by yourself?"

"I'll go like this." She had on a long black T-shirt gown and solid slippers.

"Give me a minute."

I was nervous myself at this point. I seldom drove the car, but it wasn't far to the clinic. I willed myself to stay calm and keep Totie calm. She could work herself into a frenzy even if nothing was wrong, and it appeared we had a real problem on our hands. After I pulled on some clothes and located the keys, I grabbed an aspirin and told Totie to put it under her tongue. I had read that was what you were to do if you thought you were having a heart attack, to lessen the chance of stroke. I kept them in the drawer beside my bed, because if you wake in the middle of the night thinking you're having a heart attack, it might be hell trying to find the aspirin bottle. Opening it would be another challenge.

Fifteen minutes later, a young person at the clinic desk asked our problem and relayed it by phone to whoever was at the other end.

"A doctor will be here very soon," he told us in heavily accented English.

Not long after, a sleepy-looking young woman in her late twenties came downstairs, wearing the two-piece green scrubs so common to medical professionals. Hers were badly wrinkled, and she stifled a yawn as she took us from the lobby and into a small office. She recorded vital signs and then painstakingly proceeded to ask questions and fill in blanks on the sheet of paper she had taken from the desk drawer.

"Are you under stress?" she asked.

"No. Except for this, right now."

After many questions, she had Totie lie down and then hooked her up for an electrocardiogram. It was a quick and painless process that I felt should give us some immediate information. The machine spit out a chart, which the young doctor took to her desk and studied while I helped Totie get her gown back on.

"You have an arrhythmia," she said dispassionately. "You need to see a cardiologist." She had taken out a ruler and appeared to be measuring intervals between peaks or valleys. I couldn't tell what she was doing, but I wished she'd look up.

"Can you give me something to calm down?" Totie asked.

"You need to see a cardiologist," she repeated, still measuring. "He'll give you something." Finally, she raised her head to hand us the card of Dr. Ramon Vasquez-Hinojosa, cardiologist. "He'll be here at one p.m. today."

We paid her and left. Totie was still looking uncomfortable.

"Well, the price was right," she grumbled.

The doctor had charged us the equivalent of $40 US.

I looked over. "Good to keep your sense of humor."

"I didn't think heart problems just came on suddenly," she said. "I thought you got some warning."

"You did have a little stroke a while back," I reminded her, wondering if she had truly forgotten that.

She was silent.

"We're going to check it out and do whatever we have to do," I said, trying to sound encouraging.

She took a deep breath and let it out. "Well, this is most unnerving. Seems like my whole body is struggling. Like I'm Humpty-Dumpty and I've rolled over on my side and can't get straight and all my systems are short-circuited. 'Alert, alert,' it keeps saying, and I have to wait how long?"

"About five hours," I told her.

"Shit," she said.

When we got back to the house, the lights were on, and Kitty sat at the kitchen island, drinking coffee. Raul stood at the door.

"Where in the world have you all been?" Kitty greeted us.

With the arrangement of our carport adjacent to the front of the house, I didn't think anyone would have heard us leave, but I had forgotten about Sammy, who had apparently noticed and had awakened Raul, who had found the car gone and had awakened Kitty.

We told our story as Totie poured herself a cup of coffee.

"Don't put caffeine in your system if you're fibrillating," Kitty snapped at her.

She headed off to get her stethoscope and blood pressure cuff.

"I told you." Totie looked at me.

Kitty took her own measurements and agreed something was indeed amiss. She took the chart we had brought with us, found a small square of white paper, and started making marks on it. Then, just like the doctor we had seen, she began measuring that against the chart. It looked like mumbo jumbo to me, but she obviously knew what she was doing.

"There's something here," she said. "But I'm not a cardiologist."

"That's what the doctor said," Totie said, and inhaled deeply again.

"We need to call Dr. Ferrano," Kitty said.

"He's an internist," I said.

"We need his feedback. He's an excellent diagnostician," Kitty insisted.

At 8:00 a.m., she left a message at Dr. F.'s office. He wasn't due in until 9:00, but at 9:05, he called us back.

Kitty explained the situation. He asked a couple of questions, and Kitty asked if he knew this other doctor, Vasquez-Hinojosa.

"Don't you dare go to him," he told her. "I can't see you until late this afternoon, but I want you to bring Totie to me at five p.m."

Totie was anxious to get some answers and unhappy at the turn of things. While she liked Dr. F., she wanted to get on with the cardiologist, but Kitty insisted. She did go online and check about arrhythmia, only to find that it was sometimes caused by electrolyte imbalance, so she questioned Totie about what she had eaten the day before, not Totie's favorite subject to discuss with Kitty.

"Nothing," Totie said.

"Nothing?"

"Well, remember I was going out with the theater girls for a happy hour and I didn't want to overeat because I'm trying to lose ten pounds? So I had frosted flakes for breakfast and nothing for lunch, and a couple of margaritas for dinner, with some pineapple salsa and chips."

"Nothing else?"

"Well, I take a spoonful of honey with cinnamon every day about noon. It's supposed to be good for you, and it tastes delicious. When I'm skipping lunch, it keeps me from feeling hungry."

Kitty decided Totie's electrolytes might be out of balance, so she sent Raul to the drugstore for Pedialyte, the stuff you give babies when they have diarrhea. It's supposedly better than Gatorade but is rather thick and sweet, and when Totie tried to drink it, she said it made her nauseous. Kitty then gave her club soda with lime juice and salt, a concoction she had come up with by herself to replace electrolytes.

Totie was restless and unable to lie down or sit still for any length of time. She paced back and forth through the courtyard, holding her chest, trying to breathe deeply. It was unnatural seeing her this way. Usually, at this time of day, Totie lay stretched out on the chaise, feet up, watching cartoons or reruns of *The Mentalist*. We turned on her favorite shows, and she would stop and watch for a while, take a drink of one concoction or another, and then drag off on another round. We worried that she might fall, so Raul walked with her most of the time.

"I'm really tired," she'd say. "Is it time to go?"

At 4:30, Raul took us to Dr. F.'s office, and we didn't have to wait long.

"I couldn't let you see that man," he said. "He's been heard to say that foreigners are made of gold and it's his job to mine it. Too many of his patients have died because of his bad medicine, but the medical society is very protective, so we work around him as best we can. Now that you know where I stand, let's see if we can figure out what's going on with you."

He took Totie into his inner office, and she came out thirty minutes later with a relaxed but confused look on her face.

"Good news, bad news." She laughed. "It's not my heart. It's diabetes."

Dr. F. had asked if there was diabetes in her family, and she had told him yes. Her father and her father's mother had diabetes, but she'd never had a problem. She knew the symptoms—excessive thirst, frequent urination, extreme hunger, blurred vision, tingling in the hands and feet—and she had a lot of those, but she hadn't put them together. She thought she was too old to suddenly develop symptoms.

"But he just stuck my finger, took a drop of blood, and read a number on this meter, then told me I had diabetes. He's going to do some more checking, but he was pretty sure."

"You seem relieved," Kitty said.

"I guess I am. Somehow it seems easier to handle than a heart that doesn't know what to do with itself."

"Diabetes isn't easy to handle," Kitty said. "It has all kinds of side effects."

"Well, I'm in the early stages. He told me heart palpitations are a regularly overlooked symptom of the onset of diabetes. He's going to give me some medicine that will help all that."

"I hope so," Kitty said.

"Well, can't you be happy for me?"

"Of course," she said. "I'm embarrassed I didn't pick up on it when you told me about all the sugar you had yesterday. And then I gave you that super-dextrose drink. That was a big help. I could have put you over the top."

Totie laughed for the first time all day. "Another notch in your belt."

Kitty grimaced. "You must be feeling better. Seriously, if you'll let me work with you, we can plan out a regular diet that will help."

Totie tipped an imaginary cap. "Aye, aye, Captain."

XXXII

ynn had committed to being with Alec on the day of Totie's drama, so she had left the house early, during Totie's pacing phase. By the time she got home that evening, we were deep in discussion of the newest development.

"I worried about you all day," Lynn said. "Heart trouble is the worst in my mind. Well, strokes are the worst, but a weak heart can drain your life pleasures as well. I kept picturing you an invalid."

"Thanks a lot."

"I didn't want that picture. It just kept running around my brain—you, in a wheelchair, with portable oxygen."

"It's one of the seven deadly conditions," I said. "Immobility."

"Wouldn't be so bad, having someone push you around," Totie said. "Kind of like having Raul drive us around. I rather enjoyed it when I had my knee replacement. But I don't fancy oxygen tubes up my nose."

"You've got to be kidding," I said.

Totie shrugged. "Well, it's not a five for me. Maybe not a four."

"Be careful what you wish for," Kitty frowned. "Diabetes leads to neuropathy, which can also highly limit your mobility. There'd be no more 'Boot Scootin' Boogie.'"

"You're just a bundle of fun," Totie said.

"I got rid of my colostomy bag, and I don't want to see you reliant on medical devices."

"Then you won't. Can we stop talking about this? I've had a hard day, and I'm hoping to sleep tonight. Dr. F. did another electrocardiogram and said there was nothing wrong with my heart and that if I eat right tonight and drink this stuff"—she indicated the lime water in her glass—"I'd probably be able to sleep. He also said if I'd gone to that other doctor, he would have had me in the hospital by now, getting ready for a pacemaker."

We raised our glasses and drank to Dr. F., to our good luck, and to a restful night's sleep.

"Funny thing," Totie added, "after all that thinking about dying in your sleep, it was pretty scary. Even if that's what you're after, your body has a will of its own."

⌒

Lynn was spending more time with Alec, and he often joined us for wine and a light supper in the afternoons. He was pleasant company, and we were becoming fond of him, but that doesn't mean we thought she should move in with him. They had taken to volunteering at a local school for handicapped children. Lynn thought it was good for the students, who had a variety of serious limitations, to see that adults could have limitations as well and still find ways to be friendly and useful. He was good with the children, she told us in his presence, bragging about him in her inimitable style.

We could see her going down a dangerous path. He lived in town, and they walked through the village together to restaurants and other destinations. She had arranged his home so he could get around more easily, then instructed the cleaning lady not to change anything. She helped him mark his medicines and food containers and was always coming up with new ideas for his comfort and convenience. She decided he should have a Seeing Eye dog for when he was alone, and was trying to arrange to have one sent from the States. He was legally blind, but still able to function well, even paint. We wondered how long that would last.

"He's degenerating quite fast," she told us. "He wants me to move in and says I can name my own terms."

"And what do you want?" I asked.

She sighed heavily. "I really like him. And I know I make his life better. But if I take this route, I'll end up taking care of him until one or the other of us goes. And I don't know how he'll react when he goes completely blind. Maybe he'll be angry, or terribly depressed, or helpless, or frightened, or just uncomfortable to be around. And what if it falls to him to take care of me?"

"You don't know him well enough to take that on," Totie said, inserting her opinion.

"I think you're right, but what exactly does one companion owe another at this time of life?"

I had wondered that myself. Before we made the move, Kitty had escaped a relationship much like the one Lynn was contemplating, as her partner had developed a disability that changed their relationship. If you were married, it was different. You had made a vow to stick with each other in sickness and in health until death do you part, although that often became very demanding.

Kitty, Totie, and I had a commitment of sorts to stick it out to the end, but even with that, there was room to waffle. Especially now that we had the potion. I figured we owed one another good company, respect, and help in temporary setbacks. We were damn lucky to be functioning as well as we were, but it was almost certain that at some point we'd need extra help.

"I think we should think about nursing care," I said.

"Where did that come from?" Kitty asked.

"Thinking about Lynn's situation. If and when one of us can't function without help, then I don't think we should expect the others to provide that assistance."

"What exactly are you talking about?" Totie asked.

"Getting up, getting dressed, feeding yourself, taking care of personal hygiene—I could go on."

"Spare me," Totie moaned.

"The truth is, we thought we were old when we got here, and that was four years ago. We thought we'd go along until we wanted to die, and then we'd take the potion. But the closer I get to the end, still feeling good and interested in life, like Alec, I may not want the potion. I may want somebody to help me do some of the things I can't do alone."

"You want to hire a nurse?" Totie said.

"Not now. But I think we should be reevaluating our situation. Things keep creeping up on us. Like your event the other night."

"It was just a spell," Totie said.

"I never heard of a diabetes spell," Lynn said.

"Remember where you heard it first." Totie smiled at her.

"Feeling better now?" Lynn asked.

"Still a little weird, but I've put myself in Dr. Kitty's hands and I'm going to do whatever she says."

"It's only taken seventy years to convince you to take care of yourself," Kitty said.

"And I've held up about as well as the rest of you," Totie reminded her, an uncomfortable truth, considering how much time and attention the rest of us had given to staying fit.

And then we lapsed into something we seldom did anymore, which was to reminisce about our seventy years together. We talked about when we had surprised each other. Maybe *shocked* is a better word. I reminded Totie of the time we were riding in her high school sweetheart's truck, the three of us in the front seat. She had spread her left hand high on his thigh, then nudged me, as if urging me to watch, and moved it yet closer to his crotch.

"Well, Allie," she drawled, "you never surprised me."

"How about when she briefly left her family and ran away with that marine with the tattoos and the Vitalis hair?" Lynn said.

I shrugged, guilty as charged.

"Lynn, you surprised me with your art, and Kitty, with your book of wonderful poems your son illustrated and bound for you," I said.

"Oh, so I'm the only one who surprised you with sexy stuff?" Totie complained.

"How about when Kitty told us she had slept with so many men she'd lost count?" Lynn laughed.

"That set me back, especially since at the time I had only slept with one," I agreed.

"Totie, you surprised me that you loved being a grandmother," Kitty said.

Totie made her pouting face. "So sad. They don't adore you forever."

I reminded Lynn of the time we were just learning to play duplicate bridge and she dragged me into a tournament and we had no idea what we were doing.

She nodded, embarrassed now by our naïveté. "But we got to be pretty darn good."

"Totie surprised me by becoming a drug counselor," I said.

"Takes one to help one," she said.

"You were never addicted," I challenged.

"No, but I have an addictive personality and very little self-discipline, and I know where those people are coming from."

"Why'd you stop counseling?"

"It was too depressing."

"And Kitty surprised me by not becoming a doctor."

"She had too many other things going on," Lynn said.

We laughed then about the business card Kitty had handed out at one time, introducing herself as "MS in Microbiology, Marriage Counselor, and Realtor," along with three phone numbers.

"And how about punkin.pi for an e-mail address?"

"I wanted something that sounded down-to-earth, yet memorable," she defended herself.

"It's memorable and totally unique," Lynn said.

"I just don't picture you when I see it," I said.

"That's good. It's like my alter ego."

"Mine's Mary Lou Madness," Totie said.

"I can be Mexicali," I said.

"Lynn, you can be Miss Manners," Totie said.

"I don't need an alter ego," Lynn announced.

We recalled trips we had taken with one another. Totie and I had backpacked in New Mexico. My first trip to Europe was with Kitty for the christening of her granddaughter in Paris. Lynn and

I had traveled with husbands to Puerto Vallarta, Palm Springs, and Lake Tahoe. We had eaten, drunk, danced, swum, played tennis and golf, and attended book reviews, operas, movies, and art museums together. We had been through countless partners, celebrated the birth of babies, buried parents, and followed the fortunes and misfortunes of children and grandchildren.

"I never cease to marvel at what has kept us together," Lynn said.

"It was that damn pledge Kitty made us say," Totie teased.

"Pledge?"

"Don't you remember? At the sorority party where we had to promise to always support each other, and if we didn't, we'd go to hell."

"Allow our bodies to be burned and the ashes be scattered to the four winds," I said, "that our memories would be forever lost to our fellow man."

Totie snorted. "Only you would remember that."

Kitty smiled. "I remembered it."

"You should," I said. "It was pretty impressive."

I had become an old lady. People opened doors for me, held out hands to steady me when I got out of a car even though I didn't need it, and wanted to help me with my packages. I was perfectly capable, and it sometimes made me angry. Totie loved the attention. Kitty strode purposefully wherever she went, though her posture had deteriorated more than mine, and she seemed to have less offers of help. I was reminded daily that I was traveling down the far side of the hill of life. As Kitty liked to say, "A drop of sperm one minute, a handful of dust the next."

Kitty came to talk with me about nursing arrangements. She had been thinking about what I said and realized it made sense. We were further along than when we started, and better able to imagine what might follow.

"I don't want Raul being our nurse, even if he would agree to it," she said, "but maybe he can help us with this decision."

"Are you still planning to leave the house to him?"

She nodded. "I've put it in my Mexican will that all my possessions in this country go to him at my death, including my local bank account. My US will covers all my other possessions, and each will makes reference to the other."

"Would you like to buy me out?"

She raised an eyebrow.

"I'll make any deal with you that seems fair," I told her, "but I'd like to divest my holdings everywhere, get as liquid as I can, and start making regular distributions. My idea is to die broke, or as close to it as I can figure. I don't want it to be difficult for the girls to settle my estate."

"I don't mind if my kids struggle a little, after what they've put me through. They've regularly counted on me for personal and business loans, legal arrangements, and tax maneuverings. They'll need to figure out how to do it by themselves."

We came to an arrangement whereby she bought my half of the house. I bought her half of the jewelry, which, at some point, I intended to divide between my girls. I agreed to pay Kitty's third of the household overhead, in lieu of rent. But we had done nothing about nursing care. That would be an added expense, but personal services were relatively inexpensive in Mexico.

Raul was paid $1,000 US a month, plus probably another $1,000 equivalent in housing, utilities, gas, insurance, meals, and auto repair. That was about what an engineer or university professors here would make. He could only do better if he were an airline pilot, we had decided. For that sum, we could obviously afford good nursing care here, if only we could find it.

One of my Spanish teachers made a vivid point about sunrise and sunset in her beautiful language. She reminded us of the common myth wherein the sun makes a daily journey across the sky. *El sol sale* is how to say "the sun rises," although literally, it translates to "the sun leaves," or sets out on its journey. At the end of the day, *el sol se pone*, or "it puts itself down." She told us to think of it as compartmentalized, each day a journey.

When I awoke each day in Mexico, I summoned an image of the sun rising, intent on making a lovely arc through the sky, perhaps in a horse-drawn chariot. This was my day, which stretched out before me. What would it bring? And with that thought came a stunning awareness of just how discrete and countable my days had become. I was grateful for the freedom to enjoy them in this way. Few had this luxury. I must not let it slip through my fingers, this day and all it had to offer. I'd taken to talking to myself, as the old are want to do, announcing things I saw or wished to be attentive to.

"The birds are singing in the garden," I said aloud.

The mountains were a rich shade of green against the gray sky. It was cool and damp on this particular morning, and there was a wispy mist across the mountaintops. Orange was the color of August—the flame trees, the trumpet vine, and that other tree with all the tiny orange blossoms whose name I didn't know. I could smell the coffee now. I would walk with Kitty and Sammy and perhaps see some neighbors. I was going to market today to look for *jícama* and *epizote* for a new recipe I wanted Gracie to try. I would stop by the jewelry store to visit with Lauren and Rick and deliver the pieces they had requested. I would have an afternoon fruit drink in the square—watermelon, I thought. Perhaps I'd take the book I was reading for book club. Maybe I'd have my nails done. Tonight I'd have a massage and a dip in the hot tub before going to bed. I'd try to think in Spanish, and if I was stuck for a word, I might or might not go to my dictionary. And what else?

There was always the unexpected.

XXXIII

*J*avier missed his regular visit two times in a row. The first time, Gracie told us he had said he was busy at school and wouldn't be able to come. When he didn't show up the next week, we asked where he was, and she began to cry. He was coming home late every afternoon and wouldn't tell her where he had been. The teacher had called about his homework. He got angry when she tried to talk to him. She was worried it was drugs. She went through his pockets and found nothing but tickets to the movie theater.

Javier had a girlfriend—a different sort of drug. Yesterday, Gracie had seen them holding hands and kissing on the street as she rode by on the bus. He was only sixteen. Relieved in a way, she now worried he would get the girl in trouble and not finish school. She had seen too many times what happened with the young, and she wanted more for Javier.

"He needs condoms," Kitty said, but Gracie didn't understand.

I looked it up in my dictionary.

"*Condon*," I said, surprised that she hadn't gotten the idea, considering how similar it sounded.

Gracie hid her face.

Kitty took her hands away. "Gracie, *es importante*."

"*No puedo*," she said.

"Well, I can," Kitty said. "I've given the sex talk many times."

I could tell Gracie was unsure. "Let's let Raul do it," I suggested.

Of all the things we've discussed in detail with Raul, sex hadn't been one. It was awkward to broach the subject, but when he finally understood what we wanted him to do, he grinned.

"It will be practice for when I do this for my own son," he told us.

He later reported that Javier had been resistant. This was his first girlfriend and she was a nice girl and he didn't want or need a condom. Raul had said just to take it and save it, so if he ever needed it, it would be handy. Kitty wanted to force a conference with the boy, but I begged her not to. It wasn't our business, I told her, and after all, he was just sixteen. It was that moment of his life to begin noticing girls. We didn't have to spoil it by jumping in, expecting the worst.

"You know how boys are," she told me. "They're hardwired for sex. We have some influence over him, but none over her. Maybe she's a tramp. Maybe she wants a baby, or to get out of her house. Maybe she doesn't even know where babies come from."

"It's Gracie's job to meet the girl, make an assessment, and talk with her son if she thinks there's a problem," I said.

"You try telling her that," Kitty snapped, putting it on me.

I did go to Gracie, and using my Spanish, I asked if she knew the girl, then suggested she try to get to know her. I realized how little I knew of Mexican family life, even among those individuals I considered my friends. We had said enough, and I was ready to let it go.

Then she shared something even more distressing with me.

Gracie had more serious family problems than a son coming of age. She had a younger brother who was in big trouble. He was thirty and still lived at home with his parents. Her father couldn't control him. He killed dogs for fun. He talked to himself. He said he was Jesus, and he talked to God. He set fire to things. He watched the girl next door, tried to climb in her window three times. Her father put bars on it, but still, he stood and watched.

Everyone in the neighborhood was afraid of him. When he drank beer or tequila, he was even worse. He had no money and couldn't keep a job. He tied red-soaked bandages around his head, faking injury, and stood in the street at stoplights to beg for money. His mother quit her job to stay home and watch him, but according to him, God said he might have to kill her if she didn't leave him alone.

Gracie thought he was possessed by the devil, so she talked to the priest, but he was no help. The police were no help. "We can't lock up every loco around," they told her. Gracie thought we could help her find a way to get rid of him.

"Good grief," Kitty said. "This is touchy. What do you think she wants?"

"She knows we have some way to get rid of men, and she has a man she wants to get rid of," Totie summed it up.

"You can't seriously consider this," Lynn said.

"We helped you," Totie said.

"That was different," Lynn said. "Theo was ready to die. That was—or would have been—an act of compassion. This is like murder."

"More like the electric chair," I said.

"First we have to learn more about the situation," Kitty said.

We called in Raul for a conference. Gracie had told him her story, and he had gone to see the family. The father was his mother's brother and a very good man, but the boy had been strange a long time. He was smart enough, but hadn't finished school. He had worked at many jobs but kept losing them because he either didn't show up or did something to make the boss angry. He lived at home, which was normal for Mexican families, and no one thought much of it. Only recently had he turned mean. He ate a lot and had gotten really big so that no one could manage him.

"I tried to talk with him," Raul told us. "He wasn't friendly at all—kept turning away to watch the wrestling on the television. I asked why he would be mean to his mother, and he told me to leave him alone or he'd show me just how mean he could be. He's a bad hombre."

"He needs psychiatric help," Kitty said. "Has he seen a doctor?"

"Won't go. They tried."

"Is there someone we can call who will intervene?"

Raul shrugged. "Gracie wants him dead—before something happens to her mother."

"We gathered that."

"If you will let us have the drug, I will help her. You wouldn't have to be involved."

At Kitty's direction, we were all to sleep on it and come together in the morning with our ideas. Lynn said she didn't think she should participate, but Kitty wouldn't let her off the hook. She was a party to all of this through Theo and the drugs, and she must give her input.

"I don't *have* to do anything," she had reminded Kitty, but she showed up at the breakfast table and listened as we shared ideas and concerns.

I pointed out that Raul and Gracie were almost family to us. Though we paid them for their services, they went out of their way every day and were loyal to a fault. They had helped us when we needed it and never asked questions or balked. I couldn't imagine a situation where they would divulge our secrets. Perhaps we had "bought" their loyalty, but we owed them a lot.

Totie wondered what their state of mind would be if we refused. "I don't think she'd quit or anything, and we are still taking care of Javier's school, but I don't think she'd be a happy camper."

"What about Raul?" I asked.

"He's just trying to help Gracie, but family ties are strong around here," Lynn said.

"Raul doesn't seem to have many qualms about life and death," I mused.

"Raul's a realist," Totie nodded. "If this guy is crazy and headed for bigger and better trouble, he's willing to take him out."

"Would you, if you were Raul?" I asked her.

"If I were Raul," Totie said, "I'd be chasing señoritas instead of dealing with old ladies and dead bodies."

Kitty had been silent so far, but we knew she had thoughts on the subject.

"My major reluctance is giving away the drugs."

"You want to sell it?" Totie was often uncomfortable with Kitty's capitalistic instincts.

"Of course not," Kitty shot back. "I just don't like having only two doses left."

"I thought about that," I said, "and I think two is enough."

"What if we use one? Are we going to arm-wrestle for the other?" Totie asked.

"Lynn isn't sure. You're not sure. And I'm wavering," I said. "I'm trying to figure the odds on how many we're likely to use. It seems selfish to deny them access to a simple and humane method of solving their problem."

"Are we deciding it's okay to kill him?" Lynn chimed in.

"We're acting like his jury, and we haven't even verified the charges against him," Kitty said, "or looked into getting him out of there and into a mental hospital."

"Then I guess we better get to work," I said.

Kitty and I were elected; Totie and Lynn opted out. The next evening, Raul drove us to Gracie's parents' house, where we sat in the small living room and tried to appear both natural and calm. To call the house modest would be a stretch. It looked pieced together, which is exactly what it was, Raul later told me. Poor people in Mexico couldn't get loans to buy houses. If they were lucky enough to acquire some land, they built a place to live by adding on a little at a time. Off the open area that served as both kitchen and sitting room were two small rooms—bedrooms, I supposed. There were some niceties of furnishing: curtains on the windows, a kitchen table and chairs, an old recliner, an end table with a lamp, and a television set. There was also indoor plumbing, a mark of sophistication in poor housing. The father had worked long in construction and knew how to do a lot of things. Outside were a small vegetable garden and an old car in the open shed that served as a garage. A rooster crowed somewhere nearby. A dog barked in the backyard. I could smell the neighbor's dinner.

Gracie introduced us as Red Cross nurses who had come to check on the boy to see if we could help the situation. We asked to speak to him. They called to him, but there was no response. The mother looked at the father nervously. The father went to the door of his room and spoke softly in Spanish.

"Ask if his behavior has changed dramatically recently," Kitty advised Raul, who spoke to his aunt in Spanish, received an answer, and turned to translate to us.

"She says in the last six months, since he got so fat."

"There may be a hormone imbalance that's setting this off," Kitty thought out loud, then turned to Raul. "Tell her we think we can get some medicine that will help."

"He refuses to take medicine," Raul said, after an exchange. "Says it's poison."

About that time, we heard a struggle ensuing in the bedroom. When Raul got up to check on his uncle, the boy came out, sweating and wild-eyed. Raul grabbed him and spoke softly as the boy rocked back and forth. Then he broke free and went over and slapped his mother, calling her *Malinche*. He turned to Gracie and kicked her, and then he started for Kitty. She stood up, as tall as she could, extended her arms in a U, looked him right in the eye, and growled at him. I had never heard such a sound coming from anyone, much less an eighty-three-year-old woman. The boy fled to his room. The father came out, wiping blood from his mouth. And Raul hurried us out to the car.

"You were wonderful," I told Kitty when my heart had stopped pounding. "What made you think to do that?"

"It was pure instinct," she said coolly. "I saw someone do it with a bear once on a hiking trip in Colorado." She then had Raul go back in and take the container of pepper spray she kept in her purse to his aunt. "Tell her, if he gets that way again, to spray him. But stay back because it'll get her too if she's too close."

Back at the house, the other two were anxiously awaiting our return. Over a glass of wine, we told our story, and when we got to

Kitty's part, I acted it out. I'm sure I didn't do it as well as she had, but they got the idea.

"It's really very sad," Lynn said, wiping her eyes from the laughter.

"And frightening, for those who can't make a quick getaway like we did," I said.

"He needs an immediate intervention and medical care," Kitty said with authority.

"How do we do that?" I asked.

"We'll check it out tomorrow."

"Tomorrow's a holiday. And then the weekend," Totie said.

If there were emergency services, we couldn't locate them, even with Raul's resourceful help. We called doctor's offices, the city government, and even a judge who could sign some papers. No one knew exactly how such things worked, and everyone suggested we talk with someone else. Many people, including our own Dr. F., weren't available until Monday.

"Even if you find someone on Monday, it will be weeks before we can get him out of the house," Raul said. "Things like that work very slowly here."

We believed him. We had observed it ourselves in the immigration office, the courthouse, the tax office, and the police station. That left us with the option of turning over a deadly dose to our trusted friend Raul.

"How will you get him to take it?"

"Tequila," he said.

Gracie and Raul accomplished their mission on Sunday night. Gracie went to the house to take her parents to church, and though they were reluctant to leave their son alone, they were also relieved to have an opportunity to get out. And maybe their prayers at church would be more successful than their prayers at home. That's what Gracie told them, at least.

Shortly after they had left the house, Raul showed up. He found the boy at the kitchen table, drawing on a piece of building tile. The picture featured Jesus on the cross, and large spiders with fangs were drinking his blood. Even Raul was horrified, he later told us.

He sat and thumped a bottle of tequila on the table.

"Have a drink with me," he offered.

The boy looked suspicious.

"We can go out in the car where no one can see us," Raul suggested, but the boy went on with his drawing and ignored him.

Raul took a chance then and left. He sat in the car and waited maybe ten minutes before the boy came out, squinting into the darkness. He came to the driver's window, and Raul raised a glass to entice him. He walked around to the other side and got in.

"It's powerful stuff," Raul reported. "He never seemed to feel nothing. Just drank it and dropped off." Raul closed his eyes and relaxed his body, acting out the final scene.

"But how did you get rid of the body?" I asked.

"I dropped him on a dark road, going down a hill, not far from the house," Raul said. "The first truck or car that comes will hit him, and maybe someone will put up a cross and plastic flowers where he died."

I had a hard time sleeping that night, although each time I examined my conscience, I reached the same conclusion that it was best for everyone. It would be hard for Gracie's family, coming home to find him gone, identifying the body at the police station, or wherever such things are done, dealing with their relief and sorrow. But it seemed to me that any scenario I could imagine for that young man was a bad one, and this way he never knew what hit him.

Kitty called a meeting after the funeral. It was the four of us, plus Raul and Gracie.

"We know a lot about each other," she said, pausing for Raul to translate, "and we need to make a promise that what we know, what we've seen and done, will forever remain a secret. We will never speak of it again among ourselves or to anyone else, and we will…" She stopped as if there should be something more to say, but she couldn't think of it.

"Kill anyone who does," Totie whispered to me.

XXXIV

We moved into a quieter season. For the first time in more than a year, Kitty went to Texas, where she tied up some legal and business affairs. When she returned, she announced she didn't want to go back to the States again. Everything there was rushed and worrisome. All people cared to talk about seemed to be politics and possessions—their stuff.

"No sense of beauty," she said. "No pleasure. No appreciation of the moment. No conversation, just talking. And when I say I live in Mexico, all they can ask is if I feel safe or when I'm moving back. They're not interested to know if I'm happy here. No one asks what I like about it so much, though some voice the opinion that it's probably a lot cheaper to live in Mexico." She shook her head. "They are so sure theirs is the best of all possible worlds."

I was surprised to hear her speak so vehemently on the subject. It seemed to me Kitty had exhibited some of those same traits once upon a time—a connection to possessions, an interest in politics, a sense of living in Mexico as a good investment.

Had Mexico changed us, or had we simply reached a different part of our journey? Age did offer perspective. It came in small flashes at first, often when watching young people make the same kinds of mistakes we'd made. At some point, you began to see everything through the telescope of time. All those mysterious predictions of the end of the world? I'd heard them many times before. The justification of war as a solution to political differences? I'd heard that too, in a variety of languages. Today, environmental problems threatened our very existence on the planet. Yet, life went on. Beauty existed. New ideas abound. Hope could be kindled. People could change.

Fear was the enemy, and fear was a source of power to those who promoted it. Movers and shakers seldom listened to those with the most perspective. It would, perhaps, be counterproductive because elders didn't move very fast, even when they approved of an idea. If age were to teach us anything, it should be how to deal with fear and accommodate change.

I had the opportunity to see how I felt about going back when one of my granddaughters suddenly announced she was getting married and that I must come. As grandmother of the bride, I was treated royally. My daughter had kept, unbeknownst to me, my mother-of-the-bride dress, a short navy chiffon number dotted with pink rosebuds. I had always remembered the dress fondly but had no idea where it had gone. She pulled it out, suggesting what a treat it would be if I wore it again. Plus, I didn't have to go shopping, except for shoes. There were numerous parties and lots of opportunities to reestablish relations with my granddaughters, who had slipped from me in their teen and early adult years. They were quick to ask what my life was like in Mexico, and the one who wasn't planning an imminent wedding promised she'd visit in the summer.

"Promises, promises," I said.

"What we all really want, Dandy, is for you to come back here so we can hear all your stories."

"While there's still time?" I smiled, thinking she wasn't going to hear all of them.

She looked embarrassed, and I reached over and patted her hand.

"I don't mind thinking about the end of my life. It's been very rich, and I wouldn't have done anything different, but I'm prepared to transition."

"Transition?"

"Well, that's a comfortable word for all of us, I think."

"It implies you'll become something else."

"Yes, a memory."

She smiled.

So my trip to the States was much more satisfying than Kitty's. Totie had given up going back completely. Traveling was too much of a hassle. Her daughter came down twice a year, regaled us with stories of life as a corporate lawyer, fed us tidbits about the rich and famous, and insisted on taking us out for exotic meals and irresistible liqueurs. We all looked forward to it and struggled to pace ourselves. Totie's granddaughter, adventurous and fun-loving as well, dropped in from time to time. Fortunately, neither overstayed her welcome.

But back to my family, who had been so receptive and sweet. They showed me a place they thought I would like, close to one of them and adjacent to a park, with lovely apartments and graduated care. They reiterated how nice it would be to see me regularly. And I knew they meant it, but I also knew that visiting elderly relatives was never first on anyone's list, no matter how nice the surroundings.

When I returned to the casa, there was big news as always. Lynn had agreed to move in with Alec for a limited time, until she could help him sell his house and get established in a casita on the lake that offered assisted living or a house that would accommodate a live-in nurse. She wouldn't commit to him in the long term, but she'd help him line up something. We were all happy about that.

"Don't waver," Totie warned her.

"The months float into years down here."

"I've set a six-month limit," she said. "And hope I last that long."

"You're feeling okay, aren't you?"

"Just high blood pressure. Okay as long as I take my meds."

"Men give you high blood pressure," Totie said.

"And kids," Kitty added.

There was more news. Gracie and Raul had come up with a plan. Raul had found a new business he was looking into. He had a friend who had bought a gym and was doing quite well with locals and expats dedicated to staying fit. He was already familiar with the machines, and there was a crash course in Guadalajara—six weeks to personal trainer. He would always be here to look out for us, but he needed to plan for his future as well. Even if he inherited the house, what would he do with his life? He wanted to have something of his own, and he knew we wanted something good for him as well.

Well, of course we did, Kitty had told him, but we needed him there, at our beck and call, day and night. He had smiled then, anticipating her response.

"Gracie and I have it worked out," he said, "and all we ask is that you give it a try for the six weeks I'm in Guadalajara."

Their so-called plan was for Gracie's parents to move into the casita that Raul had inhabited for so long. As he spoke, with Gracie smiling and nodding, I felt like a parent again, being sold on a program my kids had cooked up. Gracie's father had worked in construction, they reminded us, and was very good at fixing things. He also had been a gardener and a driver. He was an honorable man, and her mother had been trained as a nurse. They would take care of everything; they would help Gracie and Fernando, the regular gardener who was getting old and wanted to retire. (*Jubilado*, the Spanish word for "retired," always makes me smile.) Gracie's parents were in their early sixties and still healthy and strong. They could work for us as long as we wanted. We agreed to give it a try.

I was dumbfounded. Could our lives have gone any better if we were making it up?

"What did we do to deserve all this bounty," I asked when the three of us were alone.

"Maybe we shouldn't go there," Totie said.

December was a festive month in Mexico. Around Lake Chapala, Americans and Canadians had added their particular mix of activities to the native recognition of the closing of the wheel of seasons and the Catholic celebration of the nativity. There were shopping trips to Guadalajara, chorales, parties, and *las posadas*, where children with candles walked door-to-door, reenacting Mary and Joseph's search for a place for the Christ child to be born. There were fireworks, an abundance of traditional foods (*tamales, atole,* and *menudo*), and even a tour of homes.

December could also be a chilly month. It was a particularly cold and windy morning when I broke my leg while walking Sammy. It happened something like this. I hadn't slept well the night before and therefore was up early, still in slippers and robe, when Sammy asked to be walked. Normally, I dress for the occasion because I'm likely to see neighbors and also because I want to be sure-footed on the cobblestones. But we all get careless. It was early dawn and I could hardly see, but knew from experience that in ten minutes or so the sun's angle would have climbed the mountain to light our way. Until then, there were streetlights, and I was quite familiar with the path. What I didn't count on was the furry creature investigating a garbage container about a block down the way. Sammy bounded after the intruder and I, who had stopped to pick up a piece of trash in the street (like *ancianas* do) was jerked unsuspectingly and fell against the curb.

I'd never broken a bone, but for everything, there was a season. It wasn't a compound fracture, so I wasn't even certain it was broken until I tried to stand. Despite the coolness of the morning, beads of sweat formed along my upper lip. I lifted myself, crablike, both hands behind me on the ground, and scooted up to the sidewalk. There, I found a grassy place where I could concentrate on a plan. Sammy was still chasing a furry tail, but I knew he'd return shortly, and hoped he'd go home if I told him to. I knew he recognized the word in both Spanish and English.

"Home, Sammy," I said to him in my command voice when he returned a few minutes later. "*A casa,*" I repeated, wondering if that would lend clarity or confusion.

He wanted to stay with me, but after a while, with repeated commands and what I believed was awareness that something was amiss, he took off, looking back from time to time. I was reminded of the old Lassie movies where Timmy falls in the well and Lassie runs miles to report, in an agitated series of barks, the incident. We used to laugh about that, and now I was expecting it from my companion. We also laughed about the woman on television who has fallen and can't get up, a great sales pitch for home monitors for the elderly. She sounds so damn pitiful. Didn't she know someday she was going to fall and not be able to get up? Well, here I was in the same situation, and I hadn't brought my cell phone with me.

Be careful what you laugh about, I thought.

It was still quite early for activity in the neighborhood, and I was just as happy to wait for one of my own to find me. It would be embarrassing to be discovered sitting there, injured, in my robe and slippers, hair awry, in some measurable pain, anxiety oozing from my pores. I had begun to shake. That was when I remembered my own principle about the way to face fear—invite Mara to tea.

So here you are, my friend, I thought. *Sit down and let's talk.* And in my imagination I talked with him, God of Chaos, about my concerns, both immediate and long-term. An immediate concern was that I needed to use the bathroom. He said I might soil myself, so be prepared. Great!

I tried to move past that thought to the bigger picture. If my leg was indeed broken, and I was pretty certain it was, how long would it take to heal? I couldn't even remember being around anyone with a broken leg, though surely I had. Six weeks, maybe? The idea of not walking for six weeks made my heart sink. How would I maintain some muscle tone? Interestingly, Mara suggested weights and yoga stretches and seated machines at the gym. Could I learn to use crutches, or would I have to be pushed around in a wheelchair? He said that was up to me. Should I tell my children or keep it to myself? He seemed disinterested.

I was pondering the last question when I saw Kitty moving purposefully down the street toward me, still in her own robe, a worried look on her face. She looked gray and serious like my grandmother had seventy years ago when I came home very late one afternoon with a bloody knee and a torn dress. I waved, trying to look reassuring.

"What's wrong?" she snapped.

"Fell on the cobblestones. Can't seem to put any weight on it."

She knelt to examine my leg, asking if I could lift it, then turn it.

"Broken," she declared.

"Can you get me home to a bathroom?" I pleaded.

"Just lift your gown and do it in the grass," she commanded.

"No," I insisted.

"I'll look the other way and stand in front in case a car comes by," she offered a little more gently.

"I need paper."

She handed me a tissue from her pocket.

Not since I went deer hunting at age thirty and had to go potty in the woods had I experienced such an ordeal. That was nothing compared to this. I managed somehow. Then Kitty helped me distance myself from the telltale spot and covered my leavings with pine needles. She called the Red Cross on her cell phone after we decided that would be more appropriate than Gracie's father, Juan. If Raul had been there, I would have gladly trusted him to carry me to the car and into the clinic, but we weren't at that comfort point as yet with Juan. Hopefully it would develop. My leg hurt like hell.

Dr. Ferrano shook his finger at me. "I warned you years ago about the cobblestones and wearing sensible shoes."

I smiled apologetically.

"It could have been much worse," he told me. "You were lucky, but old bones get brittle. I want you to double up on your calcium and put on some weight. Next time, it might be a hip."

"You're no fun," I told him as he patted my shoulder affectionately.

"You have a lot of life left in you," he said, "and I don't want to see you slide downhill from forced inactivity."

"I won't be goose-stepping," I said.

"I'll send a therapist around," he promised, "and we'll keep you moving."

I was in a dilemma about what to tell my family. I had been planning a trip home for Christmas and knew if I told them the truth that it would open a much-too-serious conversation about me coming home for good—a conversation I wasn't ready to repeat. So I rearranged the facts and told them Totie had broken her leg and needed my help. All the "girls" rallied around and helped me set up systems for accomplishing life's daily tasks, including some social events, although a wheelchair was not my favorite form of transportation. It did help me get closer to our new helper, Juan, and I came to appreciate his quiet, competent manner. Raul, he wasn't. But Raul brought me his new skills. We let go the physical therapist Dr. F. had sent, and Raul devised a program that covered all the basic muscle groups while I was healing.

In early January, after the decorations came down and our household had returned to a more measured pace, Lynn returned. Alec had made a sudden decision to enter assisted living, and she had helped him with his final move. They both were satisfied with the new place, a family-style setting that offered friendly, compassionate round-the-clock attention. It wasn't his first choice, but it was near the lake and in the center of town. He could hear the birds and the sounds of children at play. He could sit on the porch, feel the soft breezes, and hear waves lapping the shore. He could hear the music of a nearby café and smell the fragrant spices of street vendors' offerings. There were other guests there with bright minds and less-than-perfect bodies with whom he could share life stories and explore ideas. In Ajijic, one regularly found people who were still delighted to have landed in this inviting spot.

It was Lynn who brought me a flyer on the writer's conference to be held at the nearby hotel.

"Juan could take you there every morning, and we could meet you for lunch," she said, excitement dancing in her eyes. "You've always loved writing."

Writing was indeed something I had always wanted to do, but it was getting a little late to acquire a new skill. I studied the flyer, which promised seminars on how to get started, how to write poetry, novels, memoirs, and screenplays. I recognized some of the names. There were even agents attending, so if you had something developing, it could be run by someone with authority. One might even get published. In truth, I had often thought of checking out this annual conference, but always shied away.

There was a writer's group that met in town weekly, headed by an American writer of note who had chosen Ajijic as a home in his maturity. But I had never made an attempt to join them either. I had been content to think about writing someday rather than get down to the awkward, demanding, sensitive, and sometimes embarrassing nitty-gritty of making private thoughts public.

Our lakeside community had long been a retreat for writers, as well as other artists. In the 1940s, before electricity had come to the village, back when ice came on a truck from Guadalajara, Dane Chandos wrote two books about living and building a house here. D. H. Lawrence lived here for a spell, during which time he wrote *The Plumed Serpent*. And there was a woman writer, Neill James, who came here to live and became very committed to the Mexican community. Her ideas had set a standard that remained in Ajijic, a bond between the locals and the expatriates in that they both knew their lives were better when they offered a measure of respect and mutual responsibility.

Lynn reminded me that Neill James had come to Ajijic to recuperate after breaking a leg.

"I bet she didn't fall on the cobblestones," I grumbled.

"She had been climbing Popocatapetl," Lynn said. "But stop feeling sorry for yourself, and think about doing something positive while you recuperate."

So I signed up for the conference. On the first day, I listened to experienced speakers who offered advice to aspiring writers. I had heard it all before over the years. Then, in the afternoon, I sat in on a class on memoir. Write about what you know, they said. Let it come out in a rush. Write with passion. Don't edit yourself. You can always rewrite. Speak in a natural voice. Be authentic. Don't procrastinate. Start. Right now.

I opened my laptop and began.
We once were girls.

Author's Note

This work of fiction takes an intentionally playful look at the serious subjects of aging and death. Increasing numbers of us write our own obits, plan our own funerals, and prepay coffins or cremation. But the choices for that gray area between self-sufficiency and the grave are more difficult to address and easier to postpone. Being prepared is good advice, even though, as my characters discovered, the best laid plans often go awry.

End-of-life decisions have religious, social, and political implications. The attitudes expressed herein are in no way meant to further a particular point-of-view, but rather, to encourage conversation and broaden perspectives on a sensitive subject. I believe this is one of the things fiction does best—opens our ability to see life as a myriad of possibilities.

Like all fiction writers, I've drawn from observations of life around me; on occasion, I've lapsed into memoir. It becomes difficult to separate the two, and I've made few efforts to do so. The Foolish Hearts do exist—a group of friends who have been together and supported each other since their junior high school days. Many are still around; a few have allowed me to display their unique charms and lifestyles to liven up my story.

Made in the USA
San Bernardino, CA
17 August 2014